FREEING
LINHURST

FREEING
LINHURST

Al Cassidy

For Sean
and everyone who dared
to venture into Pennhurst.

Contents

Introduction

The Inspiration to Freeing Linhurst

The story of Jack and Celia racing through Linhurst is meant to be fun, suspenseful and a bit spooky. But make no mistake...

Places like this really do exist.

In the 19th century, societal attitudes about the care of people with mental illness were undergoing significant shifts in the United States and other western industrialized nations. The thinking at the time was that the most effective and humane way to provide for those struggling with mental illness was institutionalization. In this model, a person struggling with mental illness is removed from the home and community, separated from the rest of society, and placed in an institution specializing in the care of such individuals.

In the United States, a massive push to construct state run institutions took hold in the mid-1800's, and by 1890, every state had at least one publicly supported facility. These places went by various names: insane asylums, lunatic asylums, psychiatric hospitals, state hospitals, and mental hospitals. They were founded on principles of moral treatment, and the desire to provide an alternative to the horrors of imprisonment, hospitalization, and other inappropriate and inhumane options. Over time, overcrowding and underfunding at these facilities (along with misguided approaches to treatment) led to abuse, neglect, and terrible suffering for those who called these places home.

The setting for *Freeing Linhust* is based on one such institution—Pennhurst State School and Hospital located in Spring City, Pennsylvania. Though it's purpose originally claimed to focus on education as those deemed to be "defectives," Pennhurst's history isn't far from other asylums now closed. In 1908, Pennhurst opened its doors to Patient Number 1 and roughly 10,000 residents followed until it was closed in 1987 following legal action based on allegations of overcrowding, lack of care and patient abuse.

I was barely in middle school when Pennhurst first appeared on my radar. Though my father's job required us to move quite often, Southeastern PA was home base, and you can't live in the Royersford/Spring City area without hearing about the infamous old property. Many of Pennhurst's former residents were fixtures in the community. By the time we finally settled in the area for good, I was in high school, and had nearly forgotten about Pennhurst. One day after school, a friend invited me to go exploring, and after a moment of hesitation, I agreed.

I will never forget that adventure (the first of many). It was a rite of passage of sorts—a badge of courage—for local teens. We reveled in the thrill of recounting new discoveries to our friends; retelling and perhaps embellishing the legends about what had happened in the dentist chair (where staff pulled the teeth of biting residents) or the padded rooms (where some residents were locked up for days on end). As teenagers, our thoughts didn't wander beyond the feeling of fear Pennhurst's abandoned buildings conjured up. It was like stepping into a horror movie—we savored the adrenaline rush, but failed to consider what it all meant or why a place like Pennhurst ever existed.

After leaving the area for college in Philadelphia and starting a career, then doing what adults do (buying a car and a house and starting a family and so on), I found myself returning once more to Pennhurst. This time, I went with my brother. He too had taken his turn at exploring its buildings as a teenager, finding hidden corners of the property my friends and I had never discovered (until he showed me, I never knew a there was a movie theater on campus until that day)!

By then, 15 years since my last visit, plant life had taken hold and the landscape was quickly reverting to forest around the crumbling buildings. Every structure was boarded and sealed up more tightly than he and I could remember. Eventually, we climbed and shimmied our way in, but once inside, found it hard to recapture the exhilarating rush we'd savored as teens. In its place was an eerie sense of discomfort and urgency. We made it through a few buildings before finding ourselves at the entrance to the tunnels. Without flashlights, we agreed it would be foolish to venture inside (though I suspect nerves played a part in the decision as well, whether we had light or not).

As I reflected on that trip, I was struck with the thought that while the horrors of Pennhurst are numerous and real, the reality of what occurred there is often overshadowed by the varying interests of those who visit it today, or make plans for the property's future. For the teenagers, it's a proving ground, for the elders, it's a bad memory that should be ignored, for the ghost hunters it's a platform for fame, for the middle-aged it's standing in the way of something new.

As Tommy Lee Jones said it in Men in Black:

> "A person is smart. *People* are dumb, panicky dangerous animals and you know it. Fifteen hundred years ago everybody knew the Earth was the center of the universe. Five hundred years ago, everybody knew the Earth was flat, and fifteen minutes ago, you knew that humans were alone on this planet. Imagine what you'll know tomorrow."

While Freeing Linhurst doesn't intend to come close to touching on the daily horror that was Pennhurst, it is meant to do at least these few things:

1. Recall how it felt as a teenager growing up in a small town that ignored a prominent facility where people were once imprisoned and kept from normal society.
2. Bring to light the ideas of what power and greed can do to people.
3. Touch on the idea of how we are all connected as one through an energy that travels through all things living and not.

If you would like to learn more about Pennhurst and the people that once lived and worked there, Pennhurst Memorial and Preservation Alliance was established to protect and preserve the Pennhurst property in order to "promote an understanding of the struggle for dignity and full civil rights for persons with disabilities." Their goal is through education to assure that we never repeat such atrocities.

The alliance wishes to create a world-class museum in honor and memory of the ongoing civil and human rights struggle of Americans with disabilities at a location of international significance. I encourage you to check them out.

I hope you enjoy Freeing Linhurst.

Prologue

Mom's Story

"The entire Linhurst campus is off limits," Jack's mom said, her voice thin and strained.

"How did they get in without anyone seeing them?" Jack asked nervously.

"It's easy to get inside Linhurst," his mom replied. "The warning signs are the only things stopping people from going in. The front gate isn't locked—you can just walk right through the stone towers as long as you wait until no one's around."

Jack was a string bean of a fifth grader with thick brown curls that were especially wild after several months without a haircut. He was glued to his mom's bedside, perched on the edge of the old wooden rocker. She had been in and out of sleep since morning, tired and worn from her long battle with chronic illness. Since she'd become confined to the bed, they'd started a tradition of reading the local paper together each morning. Jack was filled with questions about the cover story, written by local reporter Aurora Lux, his mom's protégé. The story was about a group of high schoolers who had been arrested for trespassing on the abandoned campus of the old Linhurst State School and Hospital.

"It said the kids were petrified when the police found them—why?" Jack asked.

"People say Linhurst is haunted," his mom replied quietly.

Jack swallowed the large lump that formed in his throat at the thought. "Haunted?" he asked, failing to squelch the nervousness in his voice. He was picturing the hulking old buildings hidden behind the overgrown forest just blocks from his house.

"After all the awful things that happened there, they say that unhappy spirits with unfinished business linger there, roaming the halls of the old buildings."

"Do you believe in ghosts, Mom?"

"That's a good question. How do I feel about ghosts?" She paused to think. "I think we carry an undeniable energy with us here on earth… I believe that some of that energy stays behind when we pass on."

Jack swallowed hard again. He hadn't thought much about death until his mom became sick. Now it seemed like it was all he ever thought about.

"What do you know about Linhurst?"

She paused for a breath—low and hollow—and winced in pain for a moment.

Jack tugged anxiously at a loose thread on the hem of his shirt, wishing there was more he could do. He wanted to forget his reality for the moment. Rain pounding on the roof overtook the uncomfortable silence in the room, and streams trickled down the bedroom window behind him.

"I never thought about Linhurst when I was young," she finally continued. "Even though I passed it at least twice a day—on the way to school and on the way home. And you couldn't ask about it either. Just the mention was enough to get an earful from Mom. And your grandfather worked there, but he wouldn't talk about it. Not a word…"

She put on a mean face and lowered her voice. "'Keep your focus on your schoolwork and your mind out of Linhurst, do you understand me, Amanda?'" she said, imitating Jack's grandfather.

Jack smiled. The impression of his grandfather was good—too good. The illness had aged her beyond her years, and the recent change in her features made her resemblance to his grandfather heartbreakingly striking.

"I first noticed Linhurst when I was young," she began again. "I was in middle school like you. I remember how nobody talked about it, even though it was right there—right in the middle of town. One day, on the way home from school—my friends and I always walked home together—we realized our friend Barbara wasn't with us. We looked back to see she'd stopped in her tracks right at the entrance. She was just staring down the winding road."

"What was she looking at?" Jack asked.

"We didn't see anything but the trees and the road," Amanda said. "But Barbara was frozen—lost in another world, almost. It was so strange… When I put my hand on her shoulder, she almost jumped out of her skin. I asked her what she was looking at—she seemed frightened at first, then suddenly very focused. She said, 'We have to go in there and see what's going on.'"

"Go into Linhurst?" Jack was enthralled, hanging on the edge of his seat. "Did you go?"

"No, Jackie, I honestly had no interest in going in there. What was there to see? A bunch of old buildings no one ever talked about? I never understood what Barbara saw that day, but she said she felt like something—or someone—was calling her to come inside."

Jack shivered. His mom paused, trying to give him time to collect himself, but he pushed for more information.

"Well…?" Jack asked impatiently, hanging to the edge of his seat. "Did she go in there?"

"A few days later… yes… she went inside."

"Alone?" Jack squeaked.

"All by herself," his mom confirmed. "My mom got a call from Barbara's parents that evening. A Linhurst administrator called Captain Hadaway and said that he'd found her on the property… petrified like the kids in the article today. Barbara hadn't even made it beyond the first building—the generating station with the tower. Apparently, she told her parents and Captain Hadaway that she saw a man with a burly mustache and a bald head threatening a man twice his size with a thick leather strap.

She even claimed to have seen some kind of white flash of light inside a window… like a ghost, she said."

"Barbara saw a ghost?!" Jack exclaimed.

"I'm sure she was only seeing things," his mom said, lowering her voice, attempting to calm Jack. "Captain Hadaway warned Barbara and her parents that she was never to go in there again under any circumstances. Linhurst was private property; no trespassing. After that phone call, I got a stern warning from Mom and Dad never to think about doing what Barbara did. And you didn't fool around with your grandpa's rules—so I just tried to forget about it."

Jack looked on as his mom paused to look out at the pouring rain. His mind was suddenly flooded with so many questions about Linhurst he didn't know where to begin. The thought of the place being haunted had captured his imagination.

"But there was something about Barbara's visit to Linhurst," his mom mused, staring out the window through half-closed eyes. "She was different after that."

"Different?" Jack asked. "Different how?"

"Those rumors that it's haunted? I believe them. After that night, Barbara kept to herself—at school, she sat quietly at her desk, ate alone during lunch. She went straight home at the last bell and never spoke to any of us again. Barbara and her parents eventually moved away and I haven't seen her since, but I often wonder what she saw when she went into that place before it closed."

Suddenly, his mom winced in agony. She held tightly to her stomach, pulling hard on the blankets.

"Mom?!" Jack cried out.

She took a few deep breaths then rested her arms back by her sides. Her face eased into a more restful expression. She opened her eyes and looked at Jack with the best smile she could muster—Jack thought it looked completely fake.

"I'm okay," she lied, her voice hoarse.

"Have you ever written about it?" Jack asked, wanting her to continue rather than fall back to sleep again.

"After college, I started writing for the Spring Dale Herald. I had been there a couple of years when I felt it was time to do something bigger and more interesting than the mundane day-to-day news stories. That's when I considered Linhurst, which had recently closed. I did some initial research and realized you can't find much of anything about it anywhere. That's when I really decided to do some digging and write an entire series about it."

She paused, closed her eyes, and took a few breaths.

"My editor liked the idea," she continued, her voice strained, "until we ran into road blocks everywhere. The town officials were tight-lipped, the state had deemed the property unsafe to explore, and the town librarian was anything but helpful. I asked around and started talking to some of the older residents in town, but most were unwilling to even mention the name. It was so frustrating. How could so many people in Spring Dale not know about or want to talk about the place? They were just turning a blind eye to all that happened there."

Recalling all this got her worked up, and she winced and began to take deep breaths. Jack rubbed her arm to calm her. After several minutes, her breathing calmed again and she turned back to Jack and opened her eyes.

"After hitting so many dead ends, we felt it would be too difficult to get anyone to talk and figured the story just wouldn't get any interest. I tried to convince my editor otherwise, but he told me to drop it. That's when I started to focus on other social injustices—like the loss of jobs, cuts in educational programs in our schools, and of course—the nuclear power plant. I wrote an entire series about the plant before it was constructed. We tried our best to stop it from coming here, Jackie. You know, your dad and I—along with a lot of other Spring Dalers—protested its construction."

"What was so bad about it?" Jack asked.

"It came at a time when we had safer alternatives to power our future. Nuclear is not what people wanted here in Spring Dale, but those people come with a lot of money and sway, and it was too easy to get our local officials on board with it."

She paused and looked out at the rain that continued to run down her bedroom window.

"I lost interest in Linhurst over the years. If no one wants to discuss it and it's so hard to motivate people to care, it's really an uphill battle. But you're right, Jackie—maybe I shouldn't have let it go. It is so hard to ignore. What is the truth behind those walls?"

He nodded furiously in agreement.

"How could a hundred-year-old campus remain such a mystery?" she continued with sudden passion. "There are over thirty buildings on that property. Hundreds of patients and staff lived there over the years. And why did it close suddenly and remain closed all these years? I feel like there must be more to the story than we know."

"We should try to find out!" Jack agreed excitedly.

His mom gave a hearty chuckle, humored by his intense enthusiasm, which immediately strained her. She pulled her hand away from his and clenched her stomach, pain showing on her face—though she tried to hide it.

"Mom!" Jack jumped to his feet and put a hand on her shoulder, the other over her hand. She took a deep breath, exhaled, then relaxed again.

"I'm okay," she tried to assure him.

He didn't believe her anymore when she said she was "okay," but he pretended like he wasn't aching with nerves at the idea that she might never get better. She looked up at him, eyes half opened, her energy drained.

"I would love nothing more than to slip into Linhurst with you," she said, her voice quivering. "We'll be the first in the history of Spring Dale to successfully explore beyond the gates and discover what really went on there. We'll tell the world!"

Jack smiled half-heartedly.

"When my energy returns, Jack, we'll do it together. I promise."

She rubbed his hand gently. He felt comfortable and encouraged. Within minutes, she was fast asleep; her breathing was low and shallow.

Jack watched her white comforter rhythmically rise up and drop down along with her breathing. The storm outside continued to pelt the house with rain. His eyelids grew heavy, and he leaned back in the rocker, fading off to sleep.

"Jackie?" his mom whispered softly, her voice gruff.

Jack awoke and rubbed his eyes. The room had grown darker. Rain was still coming down—a tropical storm, according to the paper that morning. His mom smiled at him weakly from the bed.

She leaned up from her pillow and, with all the strength she could muster, reached her hands behind her head to undo her necklace. She pulled it off and held the pendant out to him.

"Open your hand, Jack," she whispered.

He opened his palm and she placed the amulet inside, then closed his fingers around it and squeezed firmly.

He opened his hand to see the round silver amulet with a sun and peace symbol that she had worn for as long as he could remember. She closed her eyes and inhaled deeply, then breathed out twice as long.

"Your necklace?" Jack asked, bewildered.

"Your dad gave it to me as an anniversary gift before you were born—said he felt it belonged to me. I never fully understood his excitement for it, but I always did like the artwork. It's peaceful."

"Why are you giving it to me?" he asked, his voice rising.

"It will help you find strength and energy," she said softly.

Jack held the amulet in his palm, feeling the weight of the cool metal in his hand as he pondered the meaning in his mom's words.

She reached a hand up and gently caressed his face, looking into his eyes. "I wish I could be with you always…"

"I'm home!" his dad, Henry, called from downstairs, interrupting his mom's words. Jack heard him drop a few shopping bags in the kitchen then run up the stairs to the bedroom. He poked his head in slowly, not wanting to interrupt. Jack glanced up at the clock above the doorway— it was 8:30 in the evening.

"Anyone hungry?" Dad asked Jack.

"Jack has been a fabulous host, bringing me food and drinks all day, but I still haven't found an appetite," Mom told his dad softly.

Jack frowned as his dad's gaze traveled to the pills lying by a full glass of water and a cold bowl of broth on her bedside table. His father's face fell. The doctors had said she didn't need to keep taking the medicine if she wasn't up to it, and there they sat.

"How about you, Jack? Chicken noodle soup? Spaghetti? Mac and cheese?"

"I'm not hungry, Dad."

Dad understood. He entered the room slowly and sat at the end of the bed. Like Jack's mom, he looked tired and worn from the long days and nights. The rain outside began to pelt the window audibly as the storm grew and the wind howled. Jack's mom fell asleep and soon his dad laid across his mom's lap and dozed off.

Jack tried to keep his eyes open. He wanted to be ready when his mom woke up so they could keep talking. He ran his fingers along the raised artwork of the sun and peace symbol cast in relief on the pendant his mom had given him.

He opened his palm and looked down at the amulet. Rather than continuing to hold it in his hand, he decided to put it on. He latched the chain around the back of his neck, adjusted the amulet on his chest and ran his fingers over the surface of the design one more time, feeling the smooth metal symbols.

As the sun set, what little light had been finding its way through the broiling clouds all day faded entirely. A lone bedside lamp cast a faint glow in the otherwise darkened room. Jack fell fast asleep in the chair.

For the next several days, Jack stayed home from school. He was too nauseous and exhausted to sit in a classroom or keep up with homework. His dad took time from work to be with his mom as much as possible. On their final night together, Jack found himself sitting in the rocker as usual. His father was lying in bed, holding his mom's hand. Her breathing was fast and shallow. She hadn't spoken in over a day.

Jack's eyes were nearly closed when suddenly, a flash of green light illuminated the entire room—a blinding explosion that crashed against the walls and ceiling, then disappeared in an instant. Jack's eyes shot open and he looked around for several minutes trying to determine where it had come from. The room was completely dark but for the bedside lamp.

I must be tired, Jack finally admitted to himself. He felt the amulet one last time then looked to his parents lying softly on the bed.

Within minutes, he was fast asleep in the rocker.

Chapter 1

Renewing the Promise

Four Years Later

As Jack trudged up Main Street, headed for the town library in the historical section, a nearby police siren howled.

That's odd. Not so much that there was a police siren in Spring Dale but that it was coming from a road nobody ever used—the winding drive leading into Linhurst State School and Hospital.

Jack's languid stroll turned into a sprint as he raced toward the property's entrance. His mind raced briefly to the thoughts of the buildings that laid well beyond, covered in vines and brush. He had seen them only briefly when he strayed off his trail in the woods one day. He stopped dead at the intersection as Captain Hadaway's car rolled to a stop just inches in front of him.

"Careful, son!" Captain Hadaway hollered from the open window. A friendly giant of a man, Hadaway had been at the helm of the Spring Dale police department for over 35 years. The citizens of Spring Dale knew him as compassionate and friendly, but also no-nonsense when it came to matters of the law. Follow the rules and he was on your side; cross him and he was on your case until you straightened out.

The captain narrowed his eyes, scanning Jack's wiry frame, curly brown mop of hair, and blue-and-green striped hoodie. He paused at the amulet around Jack's neck, zeroing in.

"Are you Henry and Amanda Alexander's boy?" he asked suddenly.

Jack swallowed. "Y-yes," he stammered. He'd never been interrogated by a police officer before.

"Your mom was a delightful woman," the captain said with a bright smile.

Jack touched the amulet nervously as he stared at the captain. "Thank you," he muttered to the captain, who returned a short smile.

"Now, would you care to step back so I can pull out to the road?"

Jack looked down to see that he was practically leaning against the captain's cruiser. He immediately jumped back, feeling heat rise up his neck and into his face.

Suddenly, out of the corner of his eye, Jack caught a flash of green light. He turned his head and looked along the road into Linhurst—it seemed to have come from inside, near the massive smokestack peeking out above the tree line.

"Something the matter?" Captain Hadaway interrupted Jack's gawking.

"Did you see that?" Jack replied clumsily.

"See what, son?"

"That flash of light?"

Captain Hadaway adjusted his rearview mirror and glared sharply into it, trying to see what Jack was seeing. Then he popped his head back out the window.

"Be safe—be good," the captain said as he pulled out onto Main Street. That's when Jack saw Captain Hadaway's passenger—twelfth-grader Xavier Daniels, the toughest linebacker on Spring Dale High School's varsity football team, was huddled in the backseat of the car... looking shell-shocked. Jack locked eyes with Xavier for an instant, and the two boys looked away from each other just as fast. Jack watched as the car disappeared around a curve onto Second Avenue, headed toward the police station.

What is Xavier doing in the back of Captain Hadaway's car? Was he in Linhurst? Jack's thoughts raced as he stood squarely at the entrance to the old property.

Jack's cell phone buzzed and he pulled it from his hoodie pocket to see a text from his friend Celia: *I waited for you outside the school but you didn't show up.*

Jack started to text a reply but paused as his mind was once again drawn to Xavier in the back of the car. Was he inside Linhurst?

Jack couldn't resist looking back up the winding road into the abandoned property. All was still as the sun blazed down, illuminating the weeds pushing up through the crumbling blacktop. Vine-covered trees and brush stood like a veritable jungle to the very edges of the pavement.

Jack's gaze lingered on the curve that disappeared into the woods ahead, and he wondered what lay beyond the foreboding entrance.

As Jack stood staring, the leaves covering the road began to stir—very slowly at first, then steadily. A small vortex of wind formed, intensifying until it had managed to lift a great mass of lifeless autumn litter off the ground. Leaves, small twigs, and dry grass swirled into the air.

Suddenly, the airborne detritus shifted and rushed toward him. He lifted his arms in front of his face instinctively, peering out with one eye. In the midst of the broiling, leafy river of orange and red, Jack swore he saw a human figure. Before he could process his astonishment, the leaf-mass twisted into a new shape that looked for all the world like a large hand. As soon as it had formed, the fingers of the hand curled back toward the palm in an unmistakable gesture… as though it was beckoning him in. Jack felt the blood drain from his face as pure terror pulsed through his veins. He wanted to turn and run, but his legs refused to obey. Before he could manage to gather himself, Jack was met by a face full of dry, scratchy flying plant matter.

Then, all was still.

He lowered his arms and looked around to see the leaves harmlessly littering the road leading into Linhurst.

Then he saw a green flash of light again.

What could that be? All was quiet until a passing bike snapped him back to reality.

"Move it, nerd!" yelled the cyclist, who nearly ran him over.

Jack shook his head, completely unnerved.

He looked back to see Danny Slater—Spring Dale High School's number one bully—riding off.

"I'll run you over next time, twerp!" Danny hollered as he pedaled up Main Street with bully number two—his best friend Tommy Thomson.

Jack jumped when his phone buzzed again to remind him of the unanswered text from Celia. He sent a quick reply.

Sorry I didn't tell you. Going to the library.

Jack took a final look into Linhurst and sucked in a deep breath of air. The fallen leaves lay undisturbed on the ground. He blinked a couple of times to see if they would move again. Nothing. He shook his head and turned up the street for the library.

*   *   *

"Jack!" Celia hollered as she approached him a half hour later.

A loud shush came from nearby. Celia gave a quick, apologetic wave.

Jack was standing inside the town's spacious new public library, which had opened at the end of summer to great fanfare—even he and his dad showed up for the grand opening. And like so many of the historical places in Spring Dale, the town's previous 125-year-old library was one of the latest casualties to meet with a wrecking ball in an attempt to bring the town back to life. The old diner had been taken over by a national chain, the flag factory had been converted to new senior living condos, and the fire hall was getting a fresh makeover. It was part of a revival Spring Dale had been awaiting for over three decades in hopes of attracting new businesses and tourism, the efforts evident by the posters hanging throughout the library with the headline *"Make Spring Dale Great Again!"* displayed in large red font.

Jack was holding an open book, his backpack on the floor behind him. A sign reading *Historical Archives* hung overhead.

"Why didn't you wait for me?" Celia asked in a loud voice.

Another loud shush came from a few feet away. There, behind a massive, finely crafted wooden desk, sat Ms. Hilda Beck, the town librarian infamous for her cranky demeanor. Her beady eyes were barely visible behind her large glasses. She was peering at them disapprovingly from above the shining marble top of the desk.

"Sorry!" Celia whispered.

Celia had moved to Spring Dale from the city in sixth grade when her parents found jobs nearby. She lived just up the street from Jack, and the two became quick friends after Celia—who was shy and eccentric—immediately found herself at ease with Jack's open and accepting nature.

It was clear Celia liked to keep things simple—every day she wore a tattered sweater, usually with stripes, and a pair of faded jeans. No earrings, no necklaces, no makeup. She kept her curly hair tied back with a plain black hair tie. Her most distinguishing feature was a mole on her right cheek she had grown to like even though it earned her the nickname Milk Dud in elementary school.

"Why didn't you wait for me at the last bell?" she whispered. "I think today is the first time we didn't walk home together in months!"

"I've been working on Ms. Shields' writing assignment," he replied as he pulled yet another book off the shelf, this one titled *Most Noted and Historical Places*. He flipped through all the pages and the table of contents to inspect the tome for any sprinklings of information for his project.

Celia dug a stack of papers out of her bag. "I'm almost finished with my assignment," she announced proudly. "You better hurry, Jack—it's due Friday!"

Jack slumped a bit at the fact that his friend being so far along. He felt like he hadn't even started.

"I guess I never thought about it before, but it is hard to find anything remotely interesting about this town," Jack said glumly.

Their ninth grade creative writing assignment tasked the class with weaving a colorful tale based on factual information, and Jack's topic was *"An Adventure Through Spring Dale."*

At first, Jack thought the assignment would be a breeze—he was, after all, consistently on the honor roll in his grade. He soon learned that finding something interesting about his hometown was anything but simple. In book after book, website after useless website, and more newspaper clippings than he could count, he could only find history about the most humdrum places and events—sewing factories that hosted bake-offs, laundromats and car washes teaming up for local charity events, an iron foundry that supplied lamp posts for the major cities on the eastern seaboard.

How was he going to write something creative based on this? To make things worse, Ms. Shields expected 10,000 words or more. What should have been a simple project suddenly felt like an overwhelming task.

"What exactly are you looking for?" asked Celia.

"Anything about Linhurst," Jack replied.

"Linhurst?" Celia questioned. "The old buildings down the street?"

Jack nodded.

"Why not look for something online instead of in these old books? That's what I did for my assignment."

"I can't find anything more than a few brief descriptions no matter where I go," Jack grumbled. "It's like Linhurst never existed. I figured the historical archives are my last hope."

"Why not interview an adult?" Celia suggested.

"I've thought about it, but I already know most people won't talk about Linhurst."

"Okay… well, maybe I can help look," Celia interjected, pulling a book off the shelf.

"Good luck!" said Jack. "I've been looking for over an hour today alone."

"Let me help... it's what best friends are for!" Celia replied, trying to be helpful as usual.

Celia flipped through the large volume in her hand as Jack reached up for another book on a higher shelf. They pored through musty old tomes, flipping through what felt like an endless number of pages, searching madly without a hint about the old abandoned property. Nothing in the chapter guides, nothing in the footnotes. She was beginning to believe Jack was right.

Celia reached up and slid another book off the shelf, this one titled *Oddities of Pennsylvania*. As she opened it, a folded sheet of paper slipped out and floated right into Jack's arms.

"Good catch!" Celia said.

She snatched the paper and unfolded it to find what appeared to be an old map. Jack leaned over her shoulder and grabbed one side of the crumpled sheet. It showed a drawing of the town, with the words *Spring Dale 1984* written in the lower right corner.

"Whoa... this is kinda cool!" Celia called out.

"Shhh!" Another loud shush came from Ms. Beck working at her desk, this time a bit louder and unmistakably more agitated.

"Sorry!" Celia whispered. She turned back to Jack and leaned in over the paper. "Do you think this could help?"

"It's the best thing I've seen yet," Jack said, squinting to read the small writing on the map.

Jack saw the old train station, an iron foundry, a horse racing track, and the spring factory—all the usual humdrum stuff. But he also spotted something unexpectedly useful.

"Yes, this is very good," said Jack, pointing to an array of buildings stretched out across a massive area labeled *Linhurst State School and Hospital*.

"Take a picture with your phone," Celia said.

"Good idea," Jack replied. "Can you hold it up for me?"

Celia nodded and held the map up in front of her face. Jack pulled his phone from his pocket and snapped a photo. Suddenly, the map dropped and Celia was staring back at him with a surprised look on her face.

"What is it?" Jack exclaimed.

Celia flipped the map over for Jack, revealing what looked like an old newspaper clipping taped to the opposite side. The headline read *Linhurst Closes*.

"Could you hold it up so I can get a photo?" Jack asked.

Celia nodded as she held the paper up in front of her face, and Jack snapped another photo.

All of a sudden, the paper lowered again, only this time it wasn't Celia staring back at Jack—it was the grumpy librarian peering over Celia's shoulder, looking quite peeved.

"Where did you get this?" Ms. Beck demanded, her finger shaking as she pointed at the old paper. Her eyebrows were twitching just above her thick-rimmed glasses, looking like they were trying to settle on an expression. The thick lenses of her glasses made her eyes look unnaturally large. Her upper lip was wrinkled, probably from so many years of pursing her lips at students.

"It fell out of this old book," Jack explained nervously.

"What exactly are the two of you looking for?" Ms. Beck questioned as she snatched the paper from Celia's hands and held it close to get a better look.

"Hey!" Celia yelped. "Jack needs that for school!"

"I'll be holding onto this." Ms. Beck folded the paper and stuffed it under her arm. She leaned in closely to Jack, nearly nose to nose with him. "I suggest you mind your own business and forget Linhurst ever existed," Ms. Beck said in a raspy, hushed tone, her voice full of seething anger.

She stood up tall, her tattered brown cardigan swinging loosely around her waist, oversized pockets stuffed with note cards and markers. She snorted a breath of air at the two.

"Terrible awful things happened there that are best forgotten," Ms. Beck grumbled at them. "Our town is moving on to better times. You will do best to consider that chapter closed, especially as demolition of the entire property begins this Saturday and there will be nothing left to see."

Jack turned his face up at the comment, then suddenly felt the urge to explain himself. "I'm just looking for something interesting about Spring Dale for my class writing assignment, and it's the only thing worth researching. If I could just—"

"Forget about it before you get yourself into any more trouble," Ms. Beck interrupted harshly. "Now move along!"

Jack and Celia hurried away, putting several rows of books between themselves and Ms. Beck's wrath—which was of unusual proportions, even for her. Sharing a befuddled look with Celia, Jack crept to the end of a row closer to the librarian's desk, removing several volumes and motioning Celia to join him. Through the stacks, they had a clear view of Ms. Beck, who was now staring at the paper she'd confiscated. It was spread out before her, and as they watched, she flipped it to the other side. Her face paled visibly. She picked up her phone, dialed a number and began an urgent conversation in a hushed voice.

"I don't know how it got here!" she yelped frantically, before spying Celia and Jack's wide-eyed faces peering at her from between the books. As they locked eyes, her panicked expression transformed into a menacing glare and the teens hustled away.

"I will bring it tomorrow morning," they heard her say as they slipped out the door.

Chapter 2
Living Among Us

Jack pushed his way out the library doors into the crisp October air with Celia right on his heels. The fading sun cast an orange hue over the hundred-year-old brick row homes and large sycamore trees lining the streets. A cloth ghost, with suspiciously gleeful black eyes and a wicked smile to match, swung merrily from the stone-framed sign proudly reading *Spring Dale Public Library*. At the foot of the sign was a bale of hay and some pumpkins that reminded them that Halloween was the very next day.

"What was that about?" Jack questioned as the pair headed home.

"I don't know, Jack," Celia replied. "But I think you should forget about Linhurst."

Jack disregarded the suggestion—he was thrilled that he'd gotten a photo of the map and article before old Ms. Beck snagged it.

"All I know is that Linhurst was a home for the mentally disabled," Jack began. "They closed one day and basically released the patients out onto the streets of Spring Dale, and now those buildings just sit there unused. Aren't you curious what happened there?"

"I guess it is kinda weird," Celia replied cautiously. "But the assignment says that you can be creative. You don't need to know everything about your topic—just use your imagination and come up with something fun!"

Celia was onto something. She was even slightly convincing. Jack wasn't sure he was ready to stop looking yet. After all, he had a promise to keep.

As they made their way up Main Street, they passed by Bill Williams. Everyone knew Bill was a former Linhurst resident. It got Jack thinking about all the people who were once residents of Linhurst. Some referred to them as "the mentals." Some of the older people in town just called them retarded. Most ignored them—like they were ghosts. Linhurst residents were often neglected roamers who lived their lives on the fringes, mostly hiding among the living, unseen and unwanted—while their spirits were alive and well.

Bill Williams was no exception. A lively soul, he dressed head to toe in mismatched, tattered winter attire… no matter the season. He would wander in and out of the stores along Main Street all day, usually engaged in a very pleasant conversation—usually with himself. He would poke his head in the laundromat to see if he recognized any familiar faces; or he would pop into Harry's Music Store and ask about the banjos and harmonicas—though he couldn't play an instrument, he just loved to tap his feet to the musicians playing in the store. Most of the time, he could be found chatting up a storm outside the fire station, whether there was anyone outside or not. Every once in a while, he would randomly shout a few nonsensical words and curses at people walking by.

As they passed Bill, Jack gave a friendly hello just as Celia's backpack brushed up against him.

Bill snapped, "Watch where you walk, young lady!"

Celia apologized and scooted along a little faster. "Scary!" she yelped under her breath.

"I'm going to get a soda and chips... do you want anything?" asked Jack as they approached Collin's Stop & Shop.

"Sure, I'll come!" Celia chirped delightfully. "I could go for some gummy bears."

They pushed their way through the door past the window display decorated eclectically for Halloween—a large, hand-painted black and orange banner reading *For All Your Halloween Needs!* hung loosely over a patch of fake pumpkins and a trio of mannequins costumed as a werewolf, witch, and zombie.

Inside, Collin's was filled with the usual daily group of high schoolers looking for a sugary treat after a long day in class.

"Hey, Jack!" called Pete Sawyer, the school's star golfer, who was heading up to the register with an armful of drinks and snacks. A lanky ninth grader, Pete was obsessed with improving his golf game through a pre-practice regimen of caffeine and sugar. "Nice job at the science fair, Jack."

"Thanks, Pete," Jack replied as he continued on toward the cold boxes.

Jack was still enjoying the accolades from the week prior when he took home the high school science fair's first place prize in the solar power category by building and testing fuel cells. Science had been a passion of his since he was in first grade when his mom and dad helped him build a motorized solar system—he was the youngest to have ever done so at Vincent Elementary School.

Jack could see Celia dismiss the attention he was getting. Psychology was more her thing anyway. It wasn't that she had something against science—she knew he absolutely loved it. Over the years since they'd been friends, Jack had convinced Celia to help him with numerous science experiments: freezing water on demand, making glass disappear, creating a rocket with pasta noodles and countless others. Her least favorite experiment was the one that involved pouring a packet of mints into a soda bottle and making it explode all over them. Celia felt a little warning would have sufficed, then maybe being covered in sticky soda in the middle of a hot July day might have been somewhat funny rather than annoying.

While Jack had a framed photo in his room of Albert Einstein with his tongue hanging out, Celia had a poster with Sigmund Freud and a quote that read *Flowers are restful to look at because they have neither emotions nor conflicts.*

It made her happy to read it each day, remembering how delightfully complex people were beneath the surface.

Jack admired Celia for how she paid close attention to people and their feelings. He noticed early on how she was readily available to lend an ear to a friend who was upset or guide a tense situation when two people weren't seeing eye to eye.

As he and Celia pored through the huge selection of drinks in Collins' coolers, Jack heard Lisa Lexington's unmistakable voice come up from behind them—its lovely cadence was like the flutter of a hundred butterflies, and he was instantly transfixed. The topic being discussed was inconsequential. In fact, he didn't even process the words. Lisa could be talking about going to the mall with friends or running down an opponent on the lacrosse field and he would become engulfed in a dreamy state either way.

"Jack... Jack..." Celia was calling him back to earth. "Hello? Jack?!"

"W-what?" he replied, his voice sounding dreamy and distant.

"Are you going to pick something?"

"Oh... yeah... sorry," he fumbled.

Celia turned to look up at Jack in confusion. At the same moment, the cooler door was smashed against her face, her nose pressed firmly to the glass.

"Oh, my goodness—I am so clumsy!" said Lisa, closing the door quickly.

Jack looked up suddenly to see her standing right next to him. Her profile was even more radiant to him than her voice.

Celia pushed off the cooler window and shot a nasty look at Lisa.

"Oh, no worries, Lisa," Jack hurried to assure her.

"Oh, hey, Jack," Lisa said pleasantly.

Celia snarled under her breath. Celia knew, but wouldn't acknowledge the fact, that Jack had had a crush on Lisa since sixth grade. Celia thought of Lisa Lexington as just another stuck up rich girl from Cloverville.

"H-hey, Lisa," Jack stammered. He couldn't believe Lisa had said hello to him.

"Can I get an orange soda?" Lisa asked kindly, cutting in front of him.

"Yes, of course!" Jack gushed and immediately opened the glass cooler door for her. He watched her lean in slowly and reach for the bottle of orange soda. The light filtering through the soda bottle from the fluorescent lights cast her already glowing face in a new and hauntingly beautiful hue. Her dirty blond curls softly brushed along her shoulder as she pulled the bottle off the shelf and turned to Jack with a big smile.

"Thanks!" she said delightfully, then rejoined her friend Marcy Higgins to pay for their things.

"*Thanks!*" Celia mocked Lisa under her breath.

Jack snapped back to reality, ignoring Celia. He reached for an orange soda and pulled it off the shelf, reading the label.

"I love this kind," he announced confidently. "Haven't had it in years!"

Celia rolled her eyes and pretended to puke.

Jack shook his head and walked away—he knew Lisa wasn't Celia's favorite person, but she would just have to get over it.

Celia grunted and pulled a Dr. Pepper off the shelf.

They each grabbed a bag of chips on their way up to the front of the store to pay. Jack watched as Lisa and Marcy made their way out the front of the store into the fading sunlight, Lisa's curls bouncing merrily.

"Next!" hollered Mr. Collin, the store's owner, who seemed to never leave his post behind the cash register. An older man with thick dark eyebrows and a thin nest of dark graying hair on his head, he wore a short-sleeved faded blue button down with a number of pens in his front breast pocket. He was an imposing figure with a gruff but welcoming voice and always had the radio playing the local news station on the AM dial. Celia and Jack never paid it much mind—just background noise—until that moment.

"*The power plant at Linhurst will be a good deal... something we've been looking for.*" The town mayor was speaking, muffled and tiny through the static.

"Good afternoon, Lawrence," Mr. Collin told the man standing in line in front of Celia and Jack.

"Yes, hi, yes." An elderly man with no teeth, Lawrence stopped in at Collin's every day about the same time school let out. He, too, was a former resident at Linhurst. He lived just down the street from Collin's Stop & Shop, and the only time he left his apartment on the second floor above Lemon Furniture was for a trip to Collin's for a few packets of instant oatmeal and a half gallon of chocolate milk.

Lawrence placed his items on the counter, and Mr. Collin began to scan the barcodes.

"Will this be it today, Lawrence?" Mr. Collin asked.

Lawrence nodded as usual to the only two things he ever purchased. He began to dig inside his baggy navy sweatpants pockets to retrieve a bit of loose change and crumpled bills. Jack felt he'd heard the same encounter a thousand times—every time he went to Collin's and lined up behind Lawrence.

Suddenly, Mr. Collin paused, holding a packet of oatmeal in one hand and reaching out with the other to turn up the volume on the radio.

"*We begin demolition this Saturday, which will allow easier access for the project,*" Mayor Helowski said, sounding proud and resolute.

"*This seems to be the first time we are hearing such clear detail about the future of the Linhurst property, Mayor Helowski,*" said the radio host. "*After years of dormancy, why haven't you published the incredible scope of this project until today?*"

"*W-well.*" The mayor hesitated, sounding slightly perturbed. "*We felt it was in the town's best interest that we not rehash the history of the property. Folks feel better not talking about Linhurst and are more productive without it being in the spotlight. It's finally time to move on from this blemish on our town's past.*"

"*But certainly, an undertaking of this nature will have unprecedented historical and economic ramifications,*" the radio host pressed. "*Isn't it in the town's best interest to be involved?*"

"*We held town meetings and called a vote,*" the mayor declared. "*Granted, the attendance was low, but people in Spring Dale live busy lives—they don't have time to come out and talk about the demolition of Linhurst to make way for improved power at the nuclear plant. Our town has been through a lot in recent decades, and with energy prices so high and our resources limited, a new plant will bring a fresh start.*"

"What are they talking about, Fred?" asked a customer nearby. Jack turned to see the owner of Spring Dale Florist listening closely to the radio interview. She was holding a loaf of bread and a few bags of Halloween candy in her arms.

"The mayor is talking about demolition and construction at Linhurst," replied Mr. Collin. "Something about the nuclear power plant. I'm not entirely sure."

The woman moved closer to the counter to hear the radio better, standing just feet from Lawrence, who was fidgeting nervously, rocking side to side very impatiently.

"*People have been reporting recent activity on the Linhurst property,*" the radio host continued. "*Some claim to see strange flashes of lights at night. Have you already begun work?*"

"*I have not heard any reports of nighttime activity, and I can assure you that we haven't begun the work.*"

"*How would you explain the activity? There have been numerous reports. Are vandals or protestors trespassing on the property? Surely it can't be safe for people to be going in there.*"

"*Let me be clear here, the nuclear power plant has been there for a number of years and could benefit from these improvements,*" Mayor Helowski changed subjects. "*We need to provide a safe place to create energy, and the new reactor will be a significant improvement, bringing jobs to the town and certainly creating more revenue to improve the area overall. People will be very happy with this deal, and we will finally have a greater source of revenue with those old buildings gone—they haven't been used in years and nobody wants anything to do them anyway... too many bad memories!"*

The mayor sounded frustrated.

"It's about time!" said the florist with resolution. "Linhurst should have been demolished long ago!"

"Agreed!" replied Mr. Collin, swinging the oatmeal packet in his hand. He looked down to suddenly notice Lawrence looking terribly anxious. Sweat was beading up on his wrinkled brow below his old filthy Phillies ball cap. "My apologies, Lawrence! Let me turn this radio down again... all this talk about Linhurst... nothing you want to be hearing!"

Mr. Collin scanned the remaining packets of oatmeal and gallon of chocolate milk. "That will be $3.75 as usual, Lawrence."

Lawrence reached out his closed fist full of crushed one dollar bills and loose change—he was shaking awfully.

Mr. Collin put his hand on Lawrence's shoulder very gently. "So sorry, my friend—let's get you on your way." Mr. Collin bagged the items and reached the bag out to Lawrence. "No charge today, Lawrence," he said calmly.

Lawrence glared at Mr. Collin like a lost dog, a distant look in his eyes. He grabbed the bag with his free hand, stuffed the bills and change back into his sweatpants, then made his way to the door.

"Have a good day!" Mr. Collin called after him.

"Yes, good... good day... yes…" Lawrence muttered as he rushed out of the store.

Jack and Celia stepped up to pay for their items. As Mr. Collin scanned their things, Jack continued to listen to the radio in the background. Suddenly, he felt the urge to ask Mr. Collin a question.

"What exactly happened at Linhurst?" Jack asked in a quiet voice, unsure of his courage.

Mr. Collin dropped Celia's bag of Skittles and the bag burst open on the counter. Colored candy dots rolled everywhere. Mr. Collin stood frozen for a moment, then his hands began to shake.

"Awful things not worth talking about!" the florist interrupted.

Mr. Collin nodded nervously. "She's right," he replied. "Nothing you want to be learning about—you're just kids, and you don't want to go thinking about Linhurst."

Mr. Collin shook his head disapprovingly. The florist was standing in shock at the exchange.

"I was just curious," Jack mumbled under his breath.

"Get another bag of Skittles, young lady," Mr. Collin said hastily to Celia.

"It's okay," she replied nervously. "I didn't really want them." She chuckled awkwardly.

Mr. Collin hurriedly rang up their items, took their money, returned their change—then brusquely sent them on their way. Jack was beside himself. It was just a simple question. Why would they react that way? He hated the way some adults treated kids.

When they left the store, Bill Williams was standing on the sidewalk, watching the cars go by.

"Good night, Bill!" Jack called out, but Bill had no reply.

When Celia and Jack arrived at his front porch, he recalled the first time he really took notice of the former residents of Linhurst—and it was because of Bill Williams that he had a personal connection to their story.

Five years earlier—when Jack's mom first became sick—she was visited every day by the town's family physician Dr. Royer, who had been around Spring Dale a long time. He arrived to each visit wearing one of his quirky sweaters and carrying a classic black leather physician's bag that appeared to be a century old.

On one visit, Bill Williams tagged along with the doctor all the way to the front porch of Jack's house, where Jack awaited his arrival on the front swing. Bill was talking up a storm to Dr. Royer. Yes. Uh-huh. Is that right? Jack could hear Dr. Royer politely replying while Bill told the doctor about his favorite television shows. Jack hopped up from the porch swing and ran to the door to welcome Dr. Royer inside. Just as he turned to say hello to Dr. Royer, who was marching up the front concrete steps, Jack gave a nervous look at Bill, who was standing at the foot of the steps staring coldly at Jack.

"This is Bill Williams," said Dr. Royer, setting a hand on Jack's shoulder, carefully attempting to ease his nerves. "Bill is an old friend of mine." Dr. Royer turned back to Bill. "Would you say hello to Jack then?"

Bill had nothing to say. Instead, he also grew nervous, running the tip of his sneaker over the sidewalk before turning on a heel and heading back down the street.

Jack waited in the living room for Dr. Royer to finish his visit. As he sat on the sofa, he pulled at a loose thread on his sweatshirt, all the while picturing the doctor hovering over his mom, checking her temperature, wrapping that thing around her arm, telling her to drink plenty of liquids. The usual.

"How is she?" Jack asked anxiously as Dr. Royer came down the stairs. He leaped to his feet to meet the kindly physician and see him out the door.

Dr. Royer stopped and turned to Jack.

"You know, Jack, it's hard to tell," Dr. Royer began, placing a gentle hand on Jack's shoulder for a moment. "One week she seems to be responding well to the medication, then she is exhausted and struggling. Today she is showing signs of the latter. Let's hope by next week she has some of her old energy back. You know... I really miss her wonderful stories in the Herald... so much passion and energy she has for some of the more important things going on around here."

Dr. Royer turned and opened the front door to leave.

"Will she be okay?" Jack asked.

Dr. Royer turned again, holding the door to his back. "I am not in the habit of discussing life and death with young men such as yourself—you have far greater things to be focused on. You're in fourth grade now?"

Jack nodded, but he was growing agitated with the doctor's tone toward him. He had a right to know what was going on with his mom.

"Your mom is strong, and she's fighting hard. I've been keeping in touch with your father on a regular basis, and he understands what we're up against. You focus on keeping your grades up and participating in sports or other hobbies, and we'll make sure she keeps improving. How does that sound?"

Before Jack could respond, he caught a glimpse of the porch swing moving out of the corner of his eye. He popped his head around the door frame to see Bill Williams swinging happily, which made Jack very nervous.

"Are we ready for another walk, Bill?" Dr. Royer called to him, noticing Jack's nervousness once again.

Bill nodded and clumsily left the swing and made his way across the porch then down the stairs onto the sidewalk. He stopped and turned, folded his hands behind his back, then patiently waited for Dr. Royer.

"Bill is harmless," Dr. Royer whispered. "More bark than bite, really. When Linhurst closed just down the street, he was given the okay to live on his own here in Spring Dale. Not sure it was the wisest decision, which is why I took him under my wing and voluntarily keep up with him."

Jack nodded, staring blankly at Bill, still not sure what to make of him.

"Most folks in this town don't want to talk about Linhurst, Jack," Dr. Royer continued. "The simple truth is that it was just a big mistake not worth going over and over again. Basic human rights and all that—we've learned our lessons." Dr. Royer pat Jack on the arm. "Take care of yourself, son. I'll see you next week."

He trotted down the steps and joined Bill, giving him a little pat on the back. "Tell me more about this show that you love to watch."

Dr. Royer had helped Jack understand that the people who once lived at Linhurst were people with some form of mental illness or disability—autism, epilepsy, a low IQ—but they were harmless. He grew an appreciation for them as citizens of Spring Dale just like anyone else.

He also began to realize most of them were delightful and quirky, each one special in their own way. Thanks to the chance encounter with Bill and Dr. Royer, Jack felt comfortable with Bill and the others, even while everyone else completely ignored them. Which was why he always sent Bill a friendly hello in passing—even though Bill never paid him any mind.

LINHURST CLOSES

After over eighty years in operation, abuse and neglect shutter asylum for the mentally ill. The Linhurst State School and Hospital was opened in 1908 as an institution for people who suffered from mental and physical disabilities, and whose

Chapter 3

Secrets of the Map

"I'm going to download the photos of the map and newspaper clipping," said Jack as he and Celia headed up the front steps to his house.

He finished off the last of his orange soda and tossed it into the recycling bin at the base of the porch. The steps groaned beneath their feet as they climbed up toward the front door with the broken pane of glass in the storm door. The floorboards and rails of the porch were in serious need of cleaning and fresh paint—like so many other things that were unattended to in recent years.

"Want to come in and take a look at the pics with me?" Jack asked.

Celia hesitated, finishing her Dr. Pepper and tossing it in the bin as well.

"I don't know, Jack," she hesitated, tugging at the straps of her backpack and looking up at the porch ceiling, obviously uncomfortable. "I should get home."

Jack sighed—he could practically see the tug-of-war going in her head. Celia worked hard to maintain a low profile in life. If she followed the rules, colored inside the lines, and stayed away from sticky subjects and situations, most people didn't pay her any attention, and things remained easy and peaceful. But Jack knew Celia was also intensely curious.

"What are you worried about?" He held open the front door. "Come on, Celia, it's just an old map and a newspaper clipping. Let's check it out."

"I don't understand why Ms. Beck was acting so weird," Celia said, still struggling, eyebrows furrowed. "Everyone knows she's grumpy, but she actually seemed really angry today. Everyone gets strange when Linhurst comes up—Mr. Collin... the florist... Can't you just choose something else for your paper? Seriously, it's just a bunch of old buildings..."

"I've been looking for something significant about Linhurst for days now," Jack pleaded. "Then you show up and the first thing you pull off the shelf, this stuff practically falls in our laps! Do you think it's just a coincidence?"

"I mean—I guess it doesn't hurt to take a closer look," Celia replied cautiously, a slight smile catching at the corners of her mouth as she gave in to Jack's persuasive enthusiasm. "I guess I've always kind of wondered about it myself."

"Yes!" said Jack triumphantly, and he dashed inside while Celia trudged after him.

They dropped their bags by the door and entered the living room. It was a comfortable space with a simple beige sofa and coffee table, and family photos on the wall surrounding a painting of the countryside. In the far corner by the dining room doorway sat an overstuffed armchair where Jack's dad fell asleep every night after watching a few shows on an outdated television perched atop his mother's old sewing table.

Jack connected his phone to the laptop on the coffee table where he had been trying to write his story for what felt like months. He was growing more excited by the second and hoped a closer look at the map and an opportunity to read the article would shed new light on the mystery of Linhurst. He downloaded the files from his phone then opened the photo of the town map. It filled the screen of the laptop and the pair huddled closely together, getting their first good look at the old drawing.

"It looks like Spring Dale has changed a lot since then," said Celia.

Jack nodded in agreement, noting the multitude of thriving businesses and factories neatly labeled on the map. Most were now abandoned.

"I guess this is Linhurst," Jack said, pointing to a massive property taking up a good portion of the page. "It looks like a whole town of its own."

As he looked at the layout of the old institution, Jack mentally placed himself at the entrance. He had looked down the long, winding road more times than he could count in the past few days. The only part of the compound visible from the entrance was the same slim brick smokestack poking up above the tree line that Jack had noticed earlier that day. Beyond the boundaries of Linhurst, on a higher ridge in the distance, two massive concrete cooling towers stood shoulder to shoulder, looming over the town, spewing white steam clouds from their open throats day and night.

As Jack pictured the entrance in his mind, he remembered the only time he'd actually seen Linhurst's buildings.

"The closest I ever got to Linhurst was when I got lost in the woods behind the house," he began.

"You were inside before?" Celia asked, incredulous.

"A few years ago, I was coming back home from the river, and I took a wrong turn on the path and found myself staring at the old buildings. I just remember how the outside was covered in ivy and there were dead trees everywhere. The windows were huge with broken glass. I got closer... tried to look in the windows. I couldn't believe how dark it was inside—even with the sun out," Jack said quietly. "I was terrified but also really wanted to see better... I don't know..."

"Then what happened?" Celia interrupted his thoughts.

"I was looking at one of the open windows. There was a piece of a curtain blowing a little in the breeze." Jack paused, forming his words carefully. "I saw something... I thought I saw something move past the window."

Celia snorted skeptically, but her eyes were wide. "What was it?"

"It was so fast; I didn't really get a good look. It could have been an animal or the sun reflecting off something metal or shiny inside."

"Yeah, that's probably it," Celia said, nodding unconvincingly. A shiver danced up her spine.

Jack continued. "I kept standing there staring… like, I couldn't get myself to move."

Celia chuckled nervously.

"Then a crow landed on a fence near me and started crowing nonstop. Like it was screaming right at me. I ran."

Celia was silent, a puzzling mix of emotions playing across her face. Jack looked away from her and back to the computer.

Since that day, Jack had always wondered what he'd seen inside the building beyond the curtain in the window. *Was it the same thing my mother's friend Barbara had seen? Was it a ghost?*

"These buildings are supposedly where all the residents lived, but there were also working buildings, just like in town," Jack said, coming back to the map.

Jack and Celia squinted to read the labels on the property. Jack zoomed in as close as he could, but it was still a little blurry.

"What if we try to use online maps to get a closer view of the property?" Celia suggested.

Jack looked at her, raising an eyebrow. After all, hadn't she just encouraged him to stop exploring?

He grinned. "Good idea!" he replied. But when he brought up the map and zoomed in to Linhurst, the satellite image was pixelated.

"I guess they don't have quality images of Spring Dale yet," said Jack.

He zoomed out a bit and was surprised to see that the map blurring only affected the Linhurst property. Other streets, homes, and properties in the town were crisp and clear.

"That's really strange..." said Jack, an uneasy feeling washing over him. "Let's go back to the photo."

"See all the different buildings on the Linhurst property?" Celia, pointing at the map ran her finger over the labeled buildings and read aloud, "Auditorium, butcher, nursery, water tower, dairy barn, and generating station."

There were residence buildings labeled with letters and a main administration building sat in the center of the property. More than thirty structures appeared to be on the grounds of the abandoned property, which was nearly half the size of the entire town of Spring Dale. In a distant corner of the map almost off the edge was a depiction of the town's nuclear power plant.

"Look at this," said Jack, pointing to a red line on the map. It went from the administration building to the generating station with an ohm Ω symbol and the words *The Best Route* written along it. Jack put his finger on the bottom part of the red line, starting at the generating station, and ran his finger along the line going northwest, cutting through residential buildings all along the way. When he stopped at the administration building, he screwed his face up in bewilderment.

"I wonder what this means?" Celia pondered.

"Dunno."

They both shrugged and continued reviewing the map for another minute.

"Let's see what the article says," Jack said as he closed the map and opened the photo of the article. He read aloud:

LINHURST CLOSES

After over eighty years in operation, abuse and neglect shutter asylum for the mentally ill.

The Linhurst State School and Hospital was opened in 1908 as an institution for people who suffered from mental and physical disabilities, and whose families found it difficult to care for them at home.

In recent years, reports of patient abuse, overcrowding, and overall poor quality of life brought increasing public scrutiny to the management of the decades-old institution. In 1955, a landmark federal ruling calling for the deinstitutionalization of the mentally ill nationwide was the first nail in the coffin for the disgraced institution and precipitated the release of the remaining Linhurst residents to community living arrangements in the surrounding town of Spring Dale decades later.

When asked what he most hoped for himself and other residents at the hospital just prior to release, one resident replied, "To get out of Linhurst." This particular resident had been admitted as a child and suffered from an intellectual disability. He has no memory of any home other than Linhurst.

Following the complete closure, an investigation is ongoing into claims that Linhurst was home to many long-term residents who weren't in need of institutionalized care. Reports exist of parents dropping children at the facility for misbehaving at home or simply abandoning them outright. Some residents are reported to have had learning disabilities as curable as illiteracy or the need for proper eyewear.

Many residents were given massive quantities of psychotropic drugs as sedatives to stabilize nominally problematic behavior. Others were frequently restrained using straitjackets or held in padded rooms, abused or neglected in part or in whole.

Former staff have reported that living conditions at Linhurst had declined to deplorable levels in recent years, with residents fighting over food and space on a regular basis. Many have come forward to protest the inhumane conditions, including low numbers of staff unable to keep up with the rising demand and number of patients.

When reached for further comment, leaders at the hospital were unwilling to discuss the matters of the hospital's closure pending further investigations and potential legal action.

Jack continued to read aloud through some of the saddest cases, including stories about patients being left alone in their beds without food or water, and others who appeared to have no learning disabilities or mental health issues being put to work on the grounds without pay.

"It says it was closed when eventually word got out about the awful conditions," said Jack. "Some of the residents were abused... and some died in there."

Celia frowned, her eyes downcast. "Terrible."

"Now I understand why it shut down," Jack said, trying to process all that he'd just read.

"Jack, this is pretty heavy," Celia said, her voice quiet and serious. "I can't believe people were treated this way, and that it just went on for years. I'm not saying I want to ignore it, or cover it up and stop thinking about it, but I don't know if I can handle reading more about Linhurst tonight—do you have enough to finish your assignment for now?"

"Not quite," Jack replied. "There has to be more to this."

Celia grimaced as Jack quietly read the caption for the article's photograph. The photo depicted a man wearing a lab coat and holding a clipboard in his hand. He was standing with a few other men and women at the head of a wrought iron bed occupied by a little girl in a white gown. She had long blond hair, and her expression was sad and worn. The photo was taken in a large room with tall windows, a high ceiling, and large pillars. Many other beds sat closely together in the background, occupied by people of varying ages, mostly children, looking gaunt and weary. People in wheelchairs and nursing staff were in the background.

"It says that doctors were trying to treat the patients but that the treatments they suggested were not being approved by the administrators," Jack said.

"What? That seems crazy!" Celia sputtered. "Isn't the point of a hospital to take care of people who are sick?"

"I guess at Linhurst it was more like they just locked them up and didn't bother with them," Jack said. Then he noticed another thin red line. This time it underlined a sentence in the article that read:

The hospital's aging infrastructure experienced many problems, including major power outages, constant electrical shorts, and issues with heating systems. The lights were only turned on when necessary, and the heat ran at a minimal in the winter months.

As they reached the end of the article, Jack's dad came through the front door, startling the pair. They noticed the sun had gone down, the night sky settling in outside. The living room had grown very dark in the time they looked over the map and article, and the faint blue glow of the laptop was now the only light in the room.

"Would you like some light in here?" Jack's dad flipped on a floor lamp and dropped his things onto the bench by the front door.

He came over to Jack and Celia with a warm smile. He was a tall, thin man, with a five o'clock shadow and ash-gray hair. He had a kind face, but tiredness showed in his eyes.

"Working on homework?" he asked, giving them both a little pat on the shoulder.

"Doing some reading for a project," Jack replied.

"Hi, Mr. Alexander, it's nice to see you," Celia said politely.

"You, too, Celia," Jack's dad replied. "But please, Celia, as I've said before, you can call me Henry—Mr. Alexander was my dad!" He turned to Jack, "Are you ready to eat, son?"

"What time is it?!" Celia panicked.

Jack looked at the laptop. "It's 5:30."

"I have to get home for dinner!" Celia exclaimed, then quickly grabbed her bag and was out the door.

"Good night, Celia," Jack and his dad called after her.

"Funny girl," his dad said.

Jack smiled.

Dad leaned a little closer over Jack's shoulder and began to survey the article on the screen. Jack attempted to close the laptop quickly but was too late.

"What are you reading about?" Dad asked.

Jack reopened the laptop. "I found it at the library when I was looking for books about Spring Dale."

His dad gave it a quick scan, then sighed. "I'm not sure you should be getting into this, bud."

Jack didn't answer, but closed the image and opened the photo of the map. His dad leaned in for a closer look, immediately curious. "That's an old map of Spring Dale. What is that red line through the middle?"

"No clue," Jack replied. "What do you know about Linhurst?"

"The most I could tell you is that it was built over one hundred years ago to house people with mental disabilities," his dad began. "Things just got out of hand for the people running it and they had to shut it down."

"How did things get so bad?" Jack asked, and his dad leaned in closer.

"This was drawn in 1984," Dad said. "The same year the nuclear power plant was finished."

"Why do we even have a power plant?" Jack asked. "I feel like Spring Dale is a pretty small town."

"It does supply our power, but believe it or not, the plant mostly supports the energy needs of the city. They built it out here because they had people here who were friendly to its construction. Most people don't want a nuclear power plant in their backyards. In fact, your mom and I protested its construction."

"Because of radiation problems?"

"The nuclear power plant was supposed to be the safest way to generate electricity, but nuclear power creates radioactive waste and threatens our town if an accident were to occur. You know those evacuation drills you've been doing in school since you were little? The monthly siren test? A meltdown would have deadly consequences for miles around." Dad paused, then his face turned to surprise... he had an idea. "That's it, Jack—you could write your story about the power plant. Your mom wrote a series about it, and you could easily find her research to get you started."

Jack groaned. "Seriously, Dad? A creative writing assignment about a nuclear power plant?"

"Why not? You can write about the toxic ooze escaping into the river and giving the fish three sets of eyes!"

"Dad!" Jack laughed. He was half tempted to use his dad's idea, though.

"Why Linhurst, son?" Dad inquired nervously.

"I don't know—I just really want to know more about it," Jack confessed. "Haven't you ever wondered what the full story is? Why it closed?"

"It seems pretty cut and dry to me, Jack. It was a huge site full of deteriorating old buildings designed for a time when people didn't understand mental health and disabilities very well. It just doesn't translate to the way we do things today. In the end, the place was falling apart, they couldn't afford repairs, it was being poorly managed, and residents were suffering. It's for the best that it's closed now."

"I don't believe it's as simple as that," Jack said resolutely. "I think something really bad happened in there. I wouldn't be surprised if someone even lost their life over it."

Dad pulled back in surprise. "That's quite a conclusion to make after reading one article!"

"I just remember hearing that it's haunted," Jack said.

"Where did you hear that?" his dad asked incredulously.

Jack swallowed hard. His mom had told him Linhurst might be haunted. But even now, it was still hard to talk about her without getting choked up. And he could already hear his father's reaction to the story about Barbara's encounter, or his own strange experience just hours earlier—he would laugh it off as Jack's overactive imagination.

His dad leaned in closely. "Jack... listen..." his tone was calm and comforting, "Linhurst is off limits. People have been caught sneaking in there over the years and escorted out by police for trespassing and vandalizing. I don't mind you reading about this, but promise me you won't go in there."

Jack remembered seeing Xavier Daniels in the back of Captain Hadaway's car that afternoon. *Why did he want to go inside Linhurst?* He thought about the day he had gotten lost in the woods—he pictured himself staring at the open window where the white thing had floated past. He remembered the promise he had made to his mother the night she died. He knew he could get in there without getting caught.

"Jack?" His father's voice called him back to reality. "Promise me?"

Jack huffed. "If they're so worried about people trespassing, why have they waited this long to tear down the buildings? Or at least do something with them? I mean… they could demolish everything and make it a park or something. Why would they just leave everything sitting there dead in the middle of town, off limits and useless for so long?"

His dad closed the laptop and knelt close to Jack, placing a hand gently on his shoulder. "You are asking a lot of very good questions that I just don't have answers for."

"Do you know anything about the people who used to live at Linhurst?" Jack asked.

"Linhurst closed quite some time ago, maybe about—"

"More than twenty years ago!" Jack interrupted.

"That sounds right," Dad agreed, then sighed and continued. "Listen, son, it sounds like you are very passionate about Linhurst, but I would prefer you finish up this assignment by focusing on something else. Think about my power plant idea, maybe? I'm sure that whatever you come up with will be well done!"

Jack let out a deep, deflated breath, then looked up slowly.

"You could write about the spring factory that opened in the 1800s," Dad suggested with a huge sarcastic smile, pointing to the drawing of the factory on the map. "Or tell the story of the horse racing track." He laughed out loud, pointing to the track on the map. Then he stood up and tousled Jack's hair. "Or the old iron foundry—wouldn't that be a fun and creative tale, a story about a man who makes decorative iron streetlamps!"

Jack knew his dad was trying to cheer him up, but he felt derailed—and his dad could tell. He gave Jack a reassuring smile.

"Keep looking," Dad said. "I'm sure whatever happened to bring an end to operations at Linhurst is pretty straightforward and mundane—nothing more than politics as usual. The buildings and the overgrown property are likely the way they are because nobody can agree on what to do with them today."

Dad gave Jack a serious look and put a hand on his shoulder once more. "Whatever you decide to do, please be smart about it like always." He gave him another big smile. "Come on... let's go make dinner," Dad said merrily. "I'm hungry!"

Jack nodded.

*   *   *

"We'll do spaghetti and meatballs tonight," Dad said. "Would you run downstairs and grab a jar of sauce?"

"Downstairs?" Jack asked.

"Yes!" Dad chuckled. "You know where we keep the sauce."

Jack swallowed hard. He despised the dark, creepy basement under their old house.

"I can start the spaghetti," Jack replied. "That way you could pick out whatever sauce you want!"

"Your choice, Jack!"

Dad headed out to the kitchen, leaving Jack to stew in his frustration there on the sofa.

Jack pushed himself off the sofa then lumbered into the dining room and pulled open the old wooden door to the cellar. He poked his head inside the stairwell leading down into the dark musty cavern; home to canned goods, holiday decorations, antiques, and the thirty-three-year-old boiler that whistled and clanked in the middle of the night.

I hate this basement. He tried not to look at the pitch-black rectangle at the bottom of the creaky, rotted wooden planks posing as steps. As a small child, he was absolutely terrified of it—and mostly because it was off limits to kids.

One time, when Jack was five, his older cousin Doug tossed his favorite ball down the steps into the eerie cavern, daring him to try and retrieve it. Just as he'd willed himself to put one foot down onto the first step, Jack's dad had intervened. "Stay out of the cellar. It's not safe for children!" He still remembered his father's voice, uncharacteristically stern.

As a teenager, his fear of the subterranean space was more nuanced but no less powerful. Whenever he was down there, he made quick work of whatever task he'd been given, keeping a watchful eye on the dark corners, where various and sundry insects might be hanging out with any number of supernatural entities.

Jack reached up for the pull chain to the single bulb at the top of the steps and gave it a tug. The bulb snapped on—then popped off after a flash of orange. Ugh, blown. Thankfully a set of bulbs was close at hand—just above him on one of the shelves lining the wall of the stairwell.

Jack pulled the replacement off the shelf with great haste. His hands were shaking as he unscrewed the dead bulb from the socket and twisted the new one into place. It didn't work. The darkness seemed to ooze out of the corners and ebb around the base of the stairs as he pulled the chain again and again. *Why isn't this thing turning on? It has to be brand new!*

"Why can't Dad get CFLs?" Jack snarled.

"What's up, Jack?" Dad called from the kitchen.

"Nothing!" Jack called back.

As he reached up to pull another bulb off the shelf, he paused when he heard a small hum coming from the pit of the cellar. Is that the boiler? No..., not the boiler. Jack knew those sounds like the voice of an old friend.

Suddenly, a flash of faint green light illuminated the stairwell. Jack rubbed his eyes. What was that? He reached up to unscrew the blown bulb. To his surprise, just before his fingers made contact with the glass, the light burst back to life in a brilliant flash, filling his eyes with stars. He blinked, shook his head, and shrugged, placing the other bulb back on the shelf.

He stepped carefully onto the first step. It gave a mournful creak. He paused to look for any movement below—any more flashes of light.

Jack made his way to the bottom of the stairs, looking all around him as he went, one step at a time. He looked back every so often to be sure the cellar door above him remained open—just in case he needed to make a quick exit. It hadn't moved.

He stepped onto the dirt floor and began to look around for the source of the green light—his sauce-fetching mission momentarily forgotten.

Where could it have come from?

He wandered around the cellar, peeking behind the boiler that clanked and grumbled as his dad ran the hot water upstairs.

Nothing.

He searched around a stack of old cardboard boxes filled with family photos, crocheted blankets, and some of his mom's china dolls.

The cheap aluminum ladder casting a reflection? Off what, though?

Dad's toolbox—maybe it has a wonky headlamp inside it. Nope. He left it upstairs to fix the drain in the bathroom.

Maybe it came from one of my old toys. That must be it.

As Jack found himself growing each year—recently surpassing his father's shoulders in height and aiming to outgrow him by senior year—he discovered that logic crept into his thinking more often. Besides, what else could have caused the light?

It had to have been an old toy. He spotted the big cardboard box with all his old toys but it was covered in dust and dirt and taped shut.

No way a flash of light came out of the box.

I must have imagined it. He let out a huge sigh of relief and shook his head at the thought of his imagination running wild as usual.

As he made his way back toward the staircase for the spaghetti sauce, a slight breeze moved across his neck, causing him to pause for a second. He turned and found himself facing the old charcoal portrait of his mother in the antique mahogany frame, propped up neatly on the upper lip of the concrete wall.

She was smiling gently, her face pale and angelic. Her curly hair flowed down along her shoulders luxuriously. He could remember the drawing so clearly as a child—she would stop to frown at the massive portrait hanging on the wall in the living room, insisting it looked nothing like her. She had asked Dad to throw it on a fire on more than one occasion. Eventually, she'd pulled it off the wall, replacing it with a newly printed photo of the three of them together in the park, and retired the old charcoal image to the cellar.

Jack gazed longingly at the drawing, which—despite his mother's protests otherwise—looked very much like her for sure. He had seen this drawing hundreds of times, but somehow it struck him differently tonight. His eyes lingered on the amulet around her neck.

Jack pulled the same amulet out from under his shirt and ran his fingers over the contours of the artwork as he'd done thousands of times since she'd given it to him. He looked back up at the drawing to compare it to the one his mother was wearing, and noticed his reflection showing dimly in the glass of the frame, overlaid on the drawing, a comfortably haunting effect.

Just then, the amulet in the drawing seemed to glow a calm green light. Or was it his amulet in the reflection? Jack rubbed his eyes. He swore he was imagining things again. Maybe he had been staring at the drawing too long and it was playing tricks on his eyes.

The light atop the staircase popped a brilliant flash of bright white and the cellar was suddenly pitch black—aside from the necklace glowing around his neck that softly lit his face in unison with his mother's angelic portrait. The combination unnerved him and sent a flurry of chills down his spine.

He took one last look at his mother smiling at him, then raced up the steps as fast as he could.

He pulled the first jar of sauce off the shelf he could get a hand around, pulled the light chain, and was out the door in seconds, slamming it shut behind him. He leaned against the cellar door, breathless, and looked down at the amulet. It was no longer glowing. *I must have imagined that!*

* * *

"Eternal life," said Dad as they sat down to their spaghetti and meatballs. "Or infinite energy. I forget what she said the symbol on her necklace meant. Either way, Mom was really attached it… she wore it 24/7!"

"How did she know what the symbol stood for?" asked Jack.

"It's entirely possible that the person who designed the necklace had a specific meaning in mind, but we may never know. I think your mom just decided that's what it meant to her."

Dad's voice wavered as he spoke of his wife. He quickly stuffed a twist of noodles into his mouth, using the pasta to wall up the sadness inside.

Jack picked up a meatball and shoved it into his mouth whole, giving it a thoughtful chew as he touched the silver amulet hanging outside his sweatshirt.

That night, Jack went to his room thinking of all that had happened that day. Most curious to him was the flash of light he had seen in the cellar.

There must be something electronic inside that makes it light up.

He dashed to his desk in the corner by the window and slid out the old wooden chair. He sat down, opened the top drawer, and pulled out a small flashlight and a mini screwdriver used for fixing eyeglasses. Then, Jack lifted the necklace off and set it down gently on the desk. He flipped on the lamp and pulled it over top of the necklace, then flipped the metal amulet over on its face, looking for seams or screws.

After only a few minutes of investigation—screwdriver in one hand, flashlight in the other, and desk lamp lighting the scene—he was thoroughly puzzled. The amulet was clearly one solid piece of metal.

He was stumped.

He put away the tools, flicked off the desk lamp, then put the amulet back around his neck.

He changed into his flannel pajamas and crawled into bed. A galaxy of glowing star stickers was carefully and accurately placed across the ceiling, a project Jack and his mother had undertaken when he was much younger. He followed the circumpolar constellations of the Northern Hemisphere across the ceiling—The Big Dipper, The Little Dipper, Cassiopeia, Cepheus, and Draco—trying to calm his racing mind. A rotating model solar system—the one he made with his parents in first grade that had won first prize—hung from the center of the room, spinning melodically while his thoughts spun chaotically around his head.

He couldn't stop thinking of the traumatized residents of Linhurst. He wondered how bad it had been. He thought about Bill Williams and what it must have been like for him. He wondered who the little girl was in the photo with the doctor and where she ended up. And after all these years of the buildings just sitting there empty, an impassable forest growing up all around them, why did it seem like nobody wanted to know the truth about Linhurst?

He'd almost forgotten that the next day was Halloween. Costumes and parties were far from Jack's mind. It was times like this he wished his mom was around to give him a hand or even just a hug. As he nodded off to sleep, he remembered her face, her voice in difficult times, and he could almost hear her whisper softly, "Everything will be all right, Jackie."

All night, Jack tossed and turned in his bed. He dreamt of sneaking into Linhurst at night when no one was awake. He pictured himself finding people trapped inside trying to get out... trying to escape from doctors and nurses. He saw people in long gowns roaming the property aimlessly. He pictured himself trapped in a dark room and a ghostly figure appearing out of nowhere to warn him, "They are coming—hurry now before it's too late!"

In an instant, the dream scenery shifted and he was surrounded by all the adults in town, crushing in on him. They were reaching out, pulling at his clothing, tugging on his hair.

"None of your business."

"No trespassing, little boy!"

"Stay out of Linhurst!"

"Leave, Jack!"

He was suddenly swallowed by a vortex flying leaves trying to throw him down the road. Outside the twister, the people continued to holler; they seethed in anger at him. "Stay away! Turn back now!"

A firm warm hand took hold of his own. Peace and warmth overwhelmed his senses, and the voices and clawing hands faded away.

"Come with me... we'll uncover the truth together!" said the sweet soft voice of his mother.

Jack awoke suddenly and sat up, covered in sweat. His mother's voice echoed in his head.

He'd made a promise... and he was going to keep it.

He was going to get into Linhurst and discover the truth—and he would have to go tomorrow before the demolition began.

Chapter 4

Aunt Edna's Warning

October can sometimes show hints of winter, and that Halloween morning was no exception. Dreary gray skies hung low overhead, and a cold, metallic bite was in the air. Overnight, frost had settled over the town of Spring Dale, glazing windows, lawns, and the tops of cars parked along the sycamore-lined Main Street.

"How did you sleep last night?" Celia asked, jogging up to meet Jack at his front porch steps.

"Not well," Jack groaned as he slumped down the concrete steps onto the sidewalk.

"Same here," Celia replied drearily.

She was bundled up in a fluffy purple winter coat while Jack stuck with his favorite hoodie as always—he was certain it would warm up later.

"I told my parents about the map and article we found," Celia said.

"You told them?!" Jack yelped, alarmed.

"Yeah, it's fine. They don't care—not like Ms. Beck! They said they don't know anything about Linhurst. Of course, we haven't lived here for very long either."

"My dad saw what we were looking at," said Jack.

"What did he say?" asked Celia.

"He was nervous about it, but basically asked me to be careful."

Celia didn't offer an opinion, though her eyes clearly told him how she felt. She was going along with it for now, but Jack was sure she was probably nervous about what he might have in mind.

As they made their way to school, they passed Mam and Pap Saunders. The pair were a Spring Dale fixture, another casualty of Linhurst, Jack thought as they shuffled by. The two were brother and sister—old enough to be Jack and Celia's grandparents. Mam and Pap walked up and down Main Street three times a day, marching along a line five feet apart, engaged in loud conversation simultaneously about two different topics. They would go to the store and return with a couple bags of groceries each. Sometimes they would stop and lie down on a curb at an intersection to gently sweep up trash and debris from the storm drain into little plastic baggies, which no one ever knew what they would do with. Like Bill Williams and others, they had become part of the cadre of lost souls roaming the streets of Spring Dale.

Jack returned from his thoughts about the former residents of Linhurst and realized they were standing square at the entrance to Linhurst. He began to stare down the road in awe.

"You all right?" Celia asked, puzzled.

Jack didn't reply. He looked up at the massive stone buttresses that flanked the entrance. Though they were crumbling from neglect, the architectural features had never seemed as distinct and powerful as they did today. Each held a series of randomly placed signs warning trespassers not to enter. The name of the hospital was scrolled in an arc of rusted iron overhead.

"You're not thinking of going in there," an ominous voice said from behind them.

Jack jumped and turned around to see Aunt Edna, another of the town's former Linhurst residents. Edna was an icon of Spring Dale, usually camped out on her favorite park bench on Bridge Street near the river, watching cars and walkers passing by. Aunt Edna loved cigars and could usually be found working her way to the end of one.

For the first time Jack could remember, Aunt Edna had no cigar in her mouth as she hobbled up the sidewalk toward them.

"It's not a safe place, you know," the old woman's voice was frail and scratchy, "especially for children."

Aunt Edna's hair was gray and horse-like. Her skin was ashen and wrinkly. She walked with a slight hunch and a limp in her step, slightly dragging one foot behind. Her clothes were ragged and neutral in color. She stopped just feet away from them, her warm, cigar-drenched breath disrupting the cold morning air with puffs of water vapor.

"Lots of children have gone in there over the years. They want to see what's inside or mark up the place with spray paint and litter. Yet they all come running out like they've seen a ghost."

"Are there ghosts in there?" Jack asked compulsively.

"I'm certain there are," Aunt Edna replied mysteriously. She huffed another cloud of warm air. "Where there are the dead, the buildings remain alive."

Celia shivered. "What do you mean the buildings are alive?"

"Most people around here don't pay it much mind. To them, it's just a dark time in the history of their quiet little town. But the ones who left us with this should be punished. They kicked us all out one day and those buildings just sit there, heavy with the curse they left."

The old woman leaned in even closer to Jack and Celia and began to whisper in an eerily raspy tone. "Linhurst is forever cursed—alive with a spirit of all that went bad in there."

"Do you mean the way they treated those poor people?" Celia asked.

"Of course, they treated us terribly—everyone knew this," replied Aunt Edna. "It was something else."

"What else?" Jack pushed.

"I was put in there when I was a little girl," Edna began. She stood up tall for a moment—as though she was remembering being younger and stronger—then returned to her hunch after a deep inhale. "I will tell you that Linhurst is no place for children. Those people were supposed to be running a school, but I barely remember opening a book. Some of my friends were left to small rooms where they paced in circles all day. I was luckier than most. When they realized I didn't need any special care, they put me to work on the grounds because I was quite capable. I gardened, helped build storage sheds, helped keep up with all the laundry. Thank goodness they put me to work—I saw how some of my first friends toiled away in madness, trapped inside for hours each day."

"What happened to them?" Celia asked

"Some were put into solitary confinement; others I never saw again. Rarely, one of them was released to help us on the grounds, but when they were, Leonard took great care of them. He was a good man."

Celia tugged on Jack's backpack. "We really need to get to school."

"Wait," he whispered back.

Jack turned back to Aunt Edna.

"You think something more happened there—more than most people know about?"

"If you sit quietly and watch closely, you can see the way the buildings come to life at night," Aunt Edna said mysteriously. She straightened up to look out toward the brick stack rising up over the trees. "The old generating station has a life of its own, which is just the oddest thing. So many cold winters, so many dark summers, and all because they couldn't keep the power going—and now you can see the lights coming on inside the station like it's trying to get itself running again."

Jack thought of the map and realized that the smokestack—standing sentry and defunct—must be part of the generating station. The nuclear power plant in the distance, which appeared to be belching out an even higher volume of steam than usual, looked mysteriously guilty.

"Let's just say there's an energy to that place that wants to come alive again. I wouldn't be getting too close if I were you. Stay out of Linhurst if you know what's good for you!"

"Thanks, but we'll take our chances," Jack said firmly to the old woman.

"No, we won't!" Celia yelped, and she grabbed Jack's hand and pulled him along to school.

Aunt Edna called after them in a grim tone, "Be careful what you go looking for in there—if you do find it, best you leave it there!"

Jack looked back to see Aunt Edna pull a fresh cigar out of her sweater pocket and light it up. She took a deep inhale and held her breath for a moment, staring at the generating station tower like she was waiting for it to do something. She exhaled a wreath of smoke around her head, then began walking along slowly again.

"Come on, Jack!" Celia tugged on him again.

They walked along quietly for a while. Soon students were approaching from every intersection, making their final turn to head up to the high school. Jack and Celia stopped at the last intersection before crossing the busy street to school and awaited the crossing guard's go ahead.

"We should listen to her and forget about that place already," Celia said. "That's our fourth warning!"

"Fifth."

"Same difference."

"Maybe she's on to something," Jack said as the crossing guard waved them across the street.

"I don't think she's onto something as much as she's *on* something," Celia quipped sarcastically, rolling her eyes.

"If we just go in there, maybe we can learn something that no one is telling us."

"You're just not listening," Celia said, exasperated. "Adults are clearly concerned about kids having anything to do with Linhurst. Aunt Edna lived there and said the same thing—don't you think she knows a thing or two about it? You can't really be considering going there?!"

"I don't see why not. They're just going to tear it down anyway," said Jack stubbornly.

Celia grunted at him, ending the discussion. Once they crossed the street, she picked up her pace, leaving Jack in the dust.

"Hey, wait up!" Jack called, hurrying after her.

Chapter 5

The Trouble with Class

They arrived to the usual logjam of students funneling through the front doors of the school to beat the first bell of the day. Jack and Celia climbed up the concrete steps to the old brick building and pushed through the large double doors with all the other bodies in a hurry to get to their lockers.

Among the sounds of locker doors banging, the halls were ringing with students swapping stories about what they were going to dress as for Halloween. Jack felt strangely removed. He had better things to do than fill a pillowcase full of candy or go to some party.

Jack noticed the school's janitor, Dr. Moseley, mopping the floor right next to his locker. The old man's long gray overcoat with big pockets and matching gray pants swung rhythmically with the movements of his mop handle. Aside from a gray cap that shaded his eyes, he looked the part of a doctor, which—Jack supposed—is where the nickname Dr. Moseley had come from. Dr. Moseley was a constant, quiet presence, always sweeping, mopping or emptying trash cans. He always wore a blank expression and never interacted with anyone other than Principal Thomson, who could be heard barking orders at the poor old man from time to time.

As Jack approached his locker, a student walked through the area Dr. Moseley was mopping. The moment she realized what she had done, she froze.

"I-I-I'm so sorry—" she stammered.

Dr. Moseley looked up slowly, eyes shaded under the brim of his hat. The student took one look at him and darted past him down the hallway. Jack saw Dr. Moseley give a slight chuckle, mop up the sneaker prints, then disappear inside his maintenance closet nearby.

"Funny old man." Jack shook his head and laughed a bit at the encounter.

He continued to his locker and began to pull books out for the morning period. As he stuffed his science book into his bag and zipped it up, he overheard a boisterous group of seniors whispering frantically just a few lockers down. Jack looked up and saw Xavier Daniels at the center of the commotion, with the full attention of his football friends.

Xavier was a senior—a strapping seventeen-year-old and the best linebacker on the varsity football team. Rumor had it he could bench press 300 pounds in the school gym, a record on the team that year.

"Twenty hours of community service?!" Xavier's friend Anthony Cappelli shouted. "Can you still play?"

"Captain Hadaway said he would leave it up to Principal Thomson whether it would affect football," Xavier replied. "I thought my dad was gonna strangle me when he found out."

"Why didn't you tell us you were going?" Mitch Davis replied. "We would have gone with you."

"I kept hearing them talk about the flashes of light at practice and wanted to see it for myself," admitted Xavier.

"What was it like?" Mitch asked.

"Dude, I'm telling you, that place isn't right," Xavier said, with a note of terror in his voice.

"What's so bad about it?" Anthony sassed. "Man, you must get freaked out easily!"

Mitch laughed.

"I'm not kidding, it's legit haunted like people say," Xavier protested.

"Haunted?!" laughed Mitch. "That's crazy!"

"My dad told me he snuck in there with friends when he was in high school and they saw a ghost boy who goes around at night looking for his parents," Anthony bragged.

"I heard that story, too," said Xavier, unimpressed.

"Do you believe in ghosts?" asked Mitch.

"I do now!" Xavier concluded.

Mitch and Anthony looked uneasy suddenly.

"All you got was community service?" Anthony asked.

"Captain Hadaway said if I ever go in there again I'll get much worse than community service," Xavier cautioned. "But you couldn't pay me enough to go back in there!"

Celia tugged on Jack's hoodie. He turned around to see she had a puzzled look on her face.

"What?" Jack whispered.

"What are you staring at?" Anthony asked Jack.

Jack suddenly realized he was frozen, facing the boys, absorbing every word of their conversation.

He looked down, plucking at his fingernails, and mumbled, "Oh, my locker... it's that way."

He turned around and shuffled over to his locker just a few feet behind him. He slammed the door shut then took off down the hallway for his first class, Celia right on his heels.

Xavier's tale was swimming in Jack's mind. Combined with the new warning from Aunt Edna, Linhurst was taking over his thoughts. He could hear her words—*the place is alive!*

As Jack and Celia arrived at their first class, creative writing with Ms. Shields, Jack yearned to be finished with his project.

"Today is Halloween!" Ms. Shields called out delightfully.

Her sing-songy voice was strangely muffled as she danced around the front of the classroom, her tablet computer with the orange case tucked under her arm. Ms. Shields had a round pale face and stood no taller than the shortest ninth grader. Some said Ms. Shields reminded them of a Hobbit—with fluffy, brown curly hair and a closetful of long brown dresses to match.

"Before you head out for trick-or-treating or the festival tonight, I urge you to complete your writing assignment that is due tomorrow. If anyone has questions or needs help, please don't be frightened to ask—I promise I won't bite!"

Then Ms. Shields gave a big smile, showing a pair of neon green plastic vampire teeth. She chuckled at her little Halloween gag and the class gave a collective sigh at another of her typically corny jokes.

A week earlier, Jack may have considered asking Ms. Shields for advice—but he thought better than to ask adults about Linhurst at this point.

As much as he would have liked to just whip up a quick tale that included all the things he had read about Spring Dale, his thoughts were consumed with questions about Linhurst. He was overwhelmed with the desire to figure it all out rather than focus on a half-hearted story for a quick A.

As the class dragged on, Jack tried his hardest to scribble out a story that didn't include the abandoned mental institution.

> *It was the hottest day of the summer. Andy and his best friend Nicole made their way into town for ice cream and a cold soda. The sun blazed overhead, causing beads of sweat to well up and pour down their faces. They couldn't wait to get into the air conditioning, but Andy wanted to get inside the store for more than just air conditioning.*
>
> *Andy's dog went missing two days ago, and since school was out for summer, he enlisted Nicole to give him a hand tracking him down.*

Roscoe was the sweetest and most loving dog any boy could ask for—he just wasn't the smartest. Every so often, Roscoe got away but he always came back. Now that Nicole and Andy had plastered the town with flyers, they could just sit and wait for someone to call, but they decided to be vigilant and hit the streets in search of his long-lost pal.

In just the past two days, Andy and Nicole had walked, biked, or hoverboarded nearly every square mile of Spring Dale. They looked in the town library for clues, but no one had seen him. They went to the iron foundry—nothing. They even asked around in Harry's Music but everyone was so busy loudly playing instruments it was hard to get a word in.

As soon as they stepped inside Collin's Stop & Shop, they headed right for the coolers.

Jack paused. He remembered his encounter with Lisa Lexington at Collin's the day before and reminisced, dreamily. In his mind's eye, he recalled her long, perfect hair, the scent of her shampoo, the spellbinding tenor of her voice as she so perfectly uttered those two simple words: *orange soda.*

"I found this fun little newspaper clipping for your story on Spring Dale," said Ms. Shields, rudely awakening him from his daydream. He looked up to see her holding out an old piece of paper, a naturally toothy smile on her face now. "I hope it inspires great things!"

She set the page on his desk, then made her way to the back of the class to assist other students. He picked it up and gave it a quick read. It was an old black and white newspaper article that read *Spring Dale Resident Wins Knitting Competition—Fastest Needles in the Northeast!*

Jack groaned. He knew she was trying to help, but this was not the sort of stuff that was going to encourage creativity.

"Aww... so cuuuute!" his classmate, Danny Slater cooed condescendingly. "You're writing about a knitting competition!"

Danny pursed his lips and batted his eyelashes, snatching the article off Jack's desk. After a quick skim, he turned to share it with his friend Tommy Thomson.

"Hey, Tommy, check this out—Jack's writing a story about his favorite hobby..."

Danny snorted out loud and Tommy burst into laughter as well. A loud ahem! and a stern look of disapproval from Ms. Shields immediately silenced the pair.

"I trust you two are working quietly!" Ms. Shields scolded the boys.

They dropped their heads and snickered to one another.

Danny was tall, with a build like a defensive lineman; the kind of kid husky-sized clothing was invented for. He had beady eyes and dark dense hair that accentuated his already thick eyebrows. Tommy was just as tall, but lankier; a narrow face full of freckles, a mouthful of braces and naturally red hair he wore spiked up with copious amounts of gel.

Danny and Tommy were best friends and Spring Dale High School royalty: Danny's father was Coach Slater, the school's gym teacher and basketball coach; Tommy's dad was Principal Thomson. Both boys were stars on the school's varsity basketball team, and both reveled in giving their classmates a tough time and getting away with it. Jack was no exception.

In fact, since elementary school, Jack had remained a favorite target for harassment because he never had the strength of the courage—or the interest—to fight back. Celia said they were obviously dealing with some early childhood issues, and likely feeling much worse than him inside.

The main problem with their behavior was that they usually got away with their antics with nothing more than a gentle warning—thanks to their fathers.

After he'd checked to make sure Ms. Shields wasn't looking, Tommy crumpled up the knitting article in his hand.

"Catch this, Grandma!" he sneered, then tossed the crumpled ball at the back of Jack's head.

Danny laughed out loud as the wad of paper bounced off the top of Jack's head and dropped back onto his desk.

"Leave him alone!" Celia exploded from a few desks away.

"What is all the commotion here?!" Ms. Shields demanded as she headed to the front of the room. Both Danny and Tommy were already sitting innocently at their desks. She gave them both a stern look—even though she never caught them, she knew they were up to no good, as usual.

"Everyone back to work," she demanded. "We have five minutes until next bell."

Tommy and Danny gave a last snicker then buried their heads in their work, if one could call it that.

Celia took a deep breath after giving the bullies a final glare.

Jack picked up the wad of paper and opened it. After giving it another glance, he crumpled it back up again and stuffed it inside the desk. Not helpful.

He returned to his writing.

> *As soon as they stepped inside Collin's Stop & Shop, they headed right for the coolers. That's when Andy realized the poster of his dog had gone missing. Just the day before, Mr. Collin agreed to let them hang it on the glass door of the sodas in hopes that someone might recognize his missing pup, Roscoe.*
>
> *Who would take down the sign?*
>
> *He thought about all the places they had been in search of his long-lost friend. The library, the music store, the fire hall, neighbors' houses, even the knitting shop.*

Jack sighed. What a terrible story.

That's when it dawned on Andy—the only place they hadn't looked was Linhurst State School and Hospital.

Jack paused and looked up. *What am I doing?!* He couldn't include that in his writing—he'd never hear the end of it. Think! Think! He just wanted to be done with the assignment and stop worrying about it.

Riiiiing! Jack was startled by the end of class bell.

"Remember, your paper is due tomorrow!" Ms. Shields called from the front of the class. "I know you will all do a great job. Happy Halloween!"

She turned on her projector and an animated Happy Halloween gif made of dancing spiders appeared on the whiteboard. The class sighed collectively, shaking their heads as they picked up their books and bags and headed down the rows of desks out the door.

Ms. Shields seemed oblivious to the eye rolls and general adolescent snark filling the air.

"Hopefully I will see some of you tonight at the Spring Dale Fire Hall Halloween Fest!" she announced.

Jack and Celia made it through Algebra without any disruptions and headed off to lunch. They found themselves pressed into the furthest corner of the spacious lunchroom with no other table to call home. They couldn't sit with the athletes, the math whizzes, or the wood shop guys. Jack did get an invite to sit with the science crew, but after winning at the solar competition, John Mason was very jealous and very rude to him. So, they stayed with their usual spot.

"Did you guys hear what happened yesterday?" shouted Nate Salamone as he flopped down at the long cafeteria table with Celia and Jack.

When Nate's tray hit the table, a few peas spilled off and rolled right over to Celia, where they stopped at the edge of her tray. She glared at him, scooting them back in his direction with her fork.

Jack's friend Nate sat with them most days of the week. The only time he didn't was when the guys at the baseball table accepted his request to sit with them, which was rare.

Nate fantasized about being a star pitcher on the varsity team, but he was a much better benchwarmer. Nate wasn't exactly terrible at baseball—well, maybe he was. But he really enjoyed it—no, obsessed about it—and knew practically every statistic since the dawn of the sport. In the end, Jack figured Nate probably enjoyed watching from the bench more than he actually wanted to be on the field. Plus, he was far too athletically unmotivated for most positions.

Jack had met Nate in second grade on the T-ball field. Their parents had signed them up for the town league the same year, and both were positioned in the outfield. When they weren't on the bench, the pair spent most of their time in the field swatting at flies, telling jokes, and swapping video game tricks. If a ball ever came their way, they would scramble uncoordinatedly, nearly running into one another to fetch it. And neither of them had the arm to get the ball all the way back to the infield.

Since that first year, they had been friendly. Yet while Celia got along great with Jack, she and Nate didn't always see eye to eye—he was a bit too high strung and loud for her taste.

"I just heard that Xavier Daniels snuck into Linhurst and got arrested—how cool is that?!"

"Yeah... I saw him in Hadaway's car," replied Jack.

"The captain?!" Nate replied excitedly. "What did he look like?"

"What did he look like?" Celia pounced. "Like a guy in the back of a cop car. What a stupid question, Nate."

"No, it's not!" Nate bit back. "I heard he saw a ghost—I bet he was totally freaked out! I would have loved to see the look on his face."

"I don't know, maybe," said Jack. "I mean, I didn't really get a good look—he was in the back of the car."

Which was a bit of a lie. Jack remembered very clearly making eye contact with Xavier, and he definitely looked shaken.

"Xavier says it's haunted in there," said Nate, shoveling food into his mouth. "I can't believe he went in there! And so close to Halloween! It wasn't even on a dare or anything."

Food fell out of Nate's mouth and onto his tray as he mumbled through a mouthful of peas.

"Gross…" Celia grumbled, curling her lip. "Nobody wants to see your half-eaten lunch. Seriously, it's like you're regressing to a former version of yourself from pre-adolescent childhood."

Jack cleared his throat to interrupt Celia's psychological assessment.

"I wonder if anyone else from school has ever gone in there." Nate spoke rapidly while shoveling more food and milk into his mouth, completely unfazed by Celia's disgusted glare.

Nate continued, talking through a mouth full of peas, "You don't really ever hear anyone talk about Linhurst. I asked my folks about it once and they told me to never talk about it again. They wouldn't tell me anything. Though my dad did say that when he was in high school he and his friends went there once and it's just a bunch of old buildings. They didn't even go inside but one of his friends went in another time and found a padded room and straitjackets and stuff. You know, because there were lots of mental people there."

"Ugh, you're so insensitive!" said Celia. "They were people! Human beings like you and me and Jack. You can't just call them mental—some of them suffered from real mental illnesses and were born with disabilities. But guess what… some of them just needed a pair of glasses so they could see! That was their only problem! They couldn't help being there. It wasn't even their choice…"

Nate choked on some milk, then wiped it off his face with his sleeve. "How do you know so much about the people who lived there?"

"We found an article about it," said Celia confidently. Jack kicked her under the table. "Ouch! What?! Jeez…" she yelped, rubbing her shin.

"An article? About Linhurst?" Nate stopped chewing and his eyes grew wide as his mouth hung agape. For once, he was speechless.

"Yeah, just an article about how it closed, is all," Jack began carefully, trying to make it sound as boring as possible. He was Nate's friend—but Nate had a big mouth.

"Where did you find it?" Nate asked excitedly.

"In the library when I was doing research for Ms. Shields' writing assignment," Jack replied.

"Research?" Nate laughed. "Jack, you are such a nerd! I wrote mine in one night. I didn't do any research."

"That's why your work is always so sloppy," Celia scolded.

Nate made a face at her.

"Seriously, guys?" Jack looked from one friend to the other.

Nate gulped down a bunch of milk and shoveled more food into his mouth. Jack and Celia took the chance to change the subject.

"I wrote mine about animals of the Amazon," Celia said, "and I did my research. What was your topic, Nate?"

"Speech is Silver, Silence is Golden," he replied, sweeping his hand through the air dramatically. "Good title, right? I wrote it about a guy who learns to speak up for himself more and, in the end, he's better at making friends and sports and stuff. I think it's A-worthy." Nate sat back, crossing his arms proudly over his puffed-out chest and smirking confidently.

Jack and Celia bust out laughing.

"What's so funny?" Nate replied.

Jack and Celia just shook their heads.

Chapter 6

Hard Lesson in Gym

After lunch, students emerged from the locker rooms and out to the shiny wooden floors of the gymnasium. The bright industrial lights and exposed metal framework hung high above old team jerseys displayed along the concrete block walls painted in the school's signature blue and gold. A large icon of Spring Dale High's horned mascot encircled by the words *Go Rams!* was emblazoned on the center of the carefully buffed maple floor.

Jack lingered on the edge of the court, waiting with Celia and other classmates for Coach Slater to arrive. Tommy Thomson and Danny Slater were hanging out at midcourt, standing firmly in their usual spots. They dominated on the varsity basketball team, and gym class was just playtime for them.

Jack saw Lisa Lexington and her friend Marcy—in their Rams lacrosse tees and short shorts—jog out from the locker room to the middle of the gym to join the class. Jack wasn't the only one watching. The girls, perched solidly atop Spring Dale High's ladder of popularity, were usually the center of attention in any room and were drawing the usual gazes, both adoring and envious.

"So, I was thinking if we met at my house we could do lunch at Crystal Cafe and go to the mall for a while," Lisa chirped as they joined Susan Wheeler at the opposite sideline. "My mom can drive us—she's getting a manicure in the afternoon. You should go with us, Susan!"

"Ouch!" Jack shouted as Celia punched him in the arm.

"Are you going to just stand there staring, or would you like to drool a bit, too?" she whispered sarcastically.

"Why'd you hit me so hard?" he replied, rubbing his arm.

Celia rolled her eyes. "To snap you out of it. Look around, Jack."

She jerked her head toward Tommy and Danny. Jack stole a glance over his shoulder at the pair, who were smirking and sharing conspiratorial chuckles as they gazed in the direction of Lisa, Marcy, and Susan. Jack turned back and noticed that Nate was bending Matt Peterson's ear about something, but his eyes were also fixed on the same trio of sophomore girls.

"Lizard brains," Celia growled.

A loud whistle sounded, and all conversation ceased.

Coach Slater hobbled to the middle of the court, looking agitated as usual. He was a short, burly man with a cranky disposition. His mustache was thick, well-groomed, and completely covered his entire upper lip. His eyebrows were impressively dense, with some of the longer hairs projecting outward from his face. He wore a faded blue tracksuit with orange stripes down the sleeves and pant legs; the decades-old material still retained enough elasticity to accommodate his protruding potbelly. He wore a blue and gold Rams cap—which covered his shiny bald head—and a whistle and stopwatch around his neck.

Coach Slater stopped at the Rams logo in the center of the court and blew his whistle. "Good afternoon, class!" he bellowed.

A half-hearted good afternoon came from the students, all tired and overfed from lunch.

"I said, good afternoon!" Coach Slater shouted, eyes wide, demanding a more respectful and energetic response. As the words exited his mouth, a drop of spittle caught on his mustache. It shivered timidly above the corner of his upper lip as if it was afraid to let go.

"Good afternoon!" the students yelled at attention.

"That's better," Slater replied.

He folded his hands behind his back, thrust out his chest, and paced slowly around the Rams logo in the middle of the court, taking in deep breaths through his nostrils.

Jack inwardly rolled his eyes. He knew better than to display any outward expression of dissent, but it was clear that Coach Slater was about to begin one of his famous lectures, which typically amounted to berating and belittling the entire class.

"You know, when I attended Spring Dale High as a student, it was much different than it is today," the coach began in a low, gruff voice. "As I look around at all of you here today, I can't help but long for the time when Spring Dale Rams were truly a force to be reckoned with. We were champs!"

He looked up and motioned to all the jerseys hanging overhead.

"Today? Not so much."

He looked around at the students and shook his head.

"You? You're all slow. Weak. Lazy. You kids these days spend all your time in front of the computer, binge-watching shows and shooting bad guys. In my day, we were out on the court and in the field whenever we weren't in class. We worked hard to beat the other team. It was our greatest passion to be the best of the best."

"Sir, yes, sir," Nate whispered under his breath.

"Come again, Salamone?!"

"N-nothing, sir," Nate stammered.

Jack grimaced as Coach Slater made a beeline for his friend, grabbed Nate by the shirt collar and dragged him by his side to the center of the court.

"Here's a fine example," said Slater, letting go of Nate's shirt.

Nate stood frozen, his face deep red, visibly quivering as he stood before his classmates.

"I give you Exhibit A—Nate Salamone, our would-be JV pitcher," Slater mocked. "Poor kid couldn't throw a strike over the plate if the mound was a foot away."

The class stood silent, nervous and fidgeting.

Coach Slater laughed out loud. "I'm not going to mince words. Nate is one of the reasons Spring Dale just plain sucks at sports these days, kids. We have a school full of losers."

He shoved Nate. "Back to your spot, Salamone. No hard feelings about the pitching thing, right? Just keep your water-pouring hand strong!" Coach Slater chuckled, winking sarcastically.

All eyes were on Nate as he shuffled back to his spot between Celia and Susan Wheeler—shoulders slumped, head low, and cheeks pink in a posture of absolute defeat and embarrassment.

Jack was furious about the obvious abuse of power they had just witnessed. His fists were clenched and his breathing heavy. He despised Coach Slater.

"Thankfully, today we have our two star players who are—as usual—going to show us how it's done," Coach bellowed. "Pick teams! Move it!"

The students lined up at midcourt for selection. Coach Slater chose his son Danny as one team captain and Will Jordan—the best matchup against Tommy under the net, though Danny always overpowered him—as the other team captain. Danny went first, picking his best friend Tommy; Jack couldn't remember a game where they weren't on the same team.

The captains went down the line until Celia—who was always picked second to last—went to Danny's team. Jack—who was always the last pick—found himself on Will's team.

"All right, everyone," Coach Slater yelled, "let's get this game going!"

Coach blew his whistle and threw the ball up in the air, giving it a nudge in the direction of Danny and Tommy. He had no qualms about showing favoritism for his star players, who treated gym class as a way to get in some extra shooting practice.

Jack was not particularly adept at sports, but he was especially unskilled in basketball. He wasn't the shortest in his class—he just lacked the hand-eye coordination that counted on the court. Play after play, Jack and his teammates found themselves out-gamed by either Danny or Tommy, while Will Jordan, who played center on the school's junior varsity team, did his best to keep up with the brutes, and encouraged his fellow teammates even better.

While they rarely won against Tommy and Danny, there were unexpected breaks during every game—like midway through the first few plays of the game when Jack found himself with the ball.

"Shoot it, Jack!" Will shouted excitedly. "You got this!"

Jack wrestled with the decision—should he get rid of the ball like he always had or try to shoot it? That's when he saw Lisa looking at him from the opposite side of the court. She had a hopeful look on her face and smiled at him encouragingly. He decided to go for it.

Just as Jack was about to take the shot, he was hit hard from behind and instantly found himself at eye level with the floor. Tommy, who'd knocked Jack off his feet, laughed out loud as Danny scooped up the loose ball and took off with it. Jack watched helplessly from his prone position as Danny headed down the court and made another basket.

"Solid layup, son!" called Coach Slater, then turned to Jack. "On your feet, Alexander!"

Celia came to Jack's aid and helped him off the floor. As he scrambled to get up, he could see Lisa running back down the court and wondered how much she'd seen of the embarrassing incident.

"Getting help from your girlfriend?" Tommy sneered as he jogged by.

"Don't listen to him," Celia scoffed, brushing off Jack's shirt. "He's obviously dealing with attachment issues stemming from having an unloving and overbearing father figure."

Jack screwed up his face.

"Are you okay?" she added.

"Back to your zone, Sheila!" Coach Slater yelled at Celia; he had never bothered to learn her name.

The teams moved the ball up and down the court, Jack's team looking for breaks to actually beat Danny and Tommy. For the first time Jack could remember, his team was keeping pace with a close score of 24-21. This seemed to be affecting Coach Slater's constitution, and he was turning redder by the shot. He found reasons to blow his whistle anytime Danny and Tommy were overwhelmed by other players. After what felt like an eternity to Jack and his exhausted teammates, Coach Slater blew his whistle once more and hollered over the energized students.

"One more minute!" Slater bellowed, his booming voice echoing throughout the large gymnasium.

The ball came back into play and Keith Sawyer lost control of it—it bounced right into Susan Wheeler's hands, and she made a basket to bring the score to 28-28. The ball made its way down the court and into Danny's possession, but Will was able to snag it and get back up the court for another point before Tommy could block him, bringing the score to 30-28. Jack's team was winning for the first time!

Danny passed the ball inbounds to Tommy as everyone made their way back down the court while Coach Slater hollered for them to get moving. Tommy was pressured by Ron Carey's excellent defense. He passed the ball off toward Keith Sawyer, who fumbled the ball into Will's hands. That's when Danny grabbed hold of Will's arm and punched the ball out, then shoved him a few feet. No whistle from Coach Slater. The ball bounced to Lisa, and Tommy yelled, "Pass it now!" He was standing right under the net with an open shot. Will was back on his feet and got a hand up to block the shot just in time. Revenge! thought Jack. Celia now had the ball and she fumbled it off to Amy Jones who dropped it but was quickly picked up by Jared Hadley on Jack's team.

"Traveling!" Coach Slater blew his whistle furiously, clearly tired of watching the ball being endlessly passed around. His face the shade of an heirloom tomato, he grabbed the ball and handed it directly to Danny. Everyone—including Danny—knew this was wrong. Everyone also knew better than to argue with Coach Slater.

Tommy passed the ball to Danny and almost immediately raced to the basket and made another point.

"Game tied 30 to 30!" Coach hollered. He whistled and motioned for Danny and Tommy to join him on the sideline. They dashed over to him and huddled up. He whispered something, blew his whistle, then they rejoined the game. Tommy stood just feet from Coach Slater while Danny positioned himself near the net.

Coach Slater wandered over and grabbed the ball from the opposing team. Then he walked back to the sideline. "Final point!" he bellowed.

He blew his whistle and tossed the ball inbounds—right into Tommy's hands.

Now this was clearly unfair—illegal in fact—and infuriated Jack and his teammates

For once they were doing well and had a chance to win. Now, all they could do was play on and hope gym class would be over soon.

Tommy immediately passed the ball to Danny, but Will was onto their game and arrived in time to block the pass. He snagged the ball and headed up court with it.

Danny and Tommy pursued him in an instant. Jack's team furiously applied offensive maneuvers and the ball was passed around several times until it ended up with Tommy, who was hotly covered. Tommy passed to Danny, who attempted a wide-open longshot from the three-point line.

"You got this, son," Coach Slater yelled triumphantly. "Finish it!"

Danny shot the ball, but it hit the backboard and came back into play. Will grabbed the ball and the entire team raced up the court with a renewed energy.

"Come on, Danny!" Coach Slater screamed at the top of his lungs. "Quit being a retard!"

Jack's team passed the ball cleverly, getting Tommy and Danny to zigzag all over the court. Suddenly the ball made it into Jack's hands and he found himself with a clear shot to the basket once more.

With the game still tied, this could be the winning point. As if in slow motion, he could see Lisa standing nearby, staring at him fondly—or so he hoped. He saw his chance to show her he wasn't like all the other students longing for her attention. Just then, out of the corner of his eye, Jack caught a glimpse of Danny charging for him. He kept his focus on the basket, even as he saw Tommy bearing down on him from the opposite side.

Jack felt the ball release from his hands and watched as it traveled in a high arc, a beautiful illustration of the laws of physics. Time practically stood still. Everything slowed as he watched the orange orb spin freely in the air, traveling toward the basket that, if it made it, would give his team the win. He could see Lisa smiling and cheering with the others. He could also see Danny and Tommy still coming at him full speed, clearly unwilling to slow their trajectories.

Just as the ball ended its descent by dropping into the net with an intensely satisfying swish, he jumped back a step just in time for the pair of knuckleheads to collide midair at the spot where he made the shot. They hit the floor with a hard thud. Suddenly, time was back to normal speed and Jack came out of his trance-like state.

"Nice shot, Jack!" some called out. "You did it, Jack!" cheered others. "We won!" cried Susan Wheeler. Jack felt a wave of excitement and embarrassment rush through his body—but the feeling was soon squashed. Coach Slater rushed over and blew his whistle repeatedly.

Jack turned to Coach Slater, wondering what it might be like to actually be congratulated by him for once. Instead, he found himself the target of wrath.

"What did you do, you idiot?!" He scowled at Jack angrily, pointing toward the two large boys slowly peeling themselves off the floor. "That's a technical. Three foul shots!"

"I didn't do anything!" Jack pleaded.

Coach Slater pulled Danny and Tommy to their feet and gave Danny the ball.

"Take your foul shots, Daniel… now!" Coach Slater fumed impatiently at his son. Danny squirmed nervously in place, then slowly moved toward the foul line with his dad.

"But… I…" Jack stammered. "I didn't do anything… they just…" He couldn't understand how he was being accused rather than rewarded.

"Wait… Dad…" Danny interrupted.

"Danny!" Coach Slater screamed. "Take your shots."

As the pair stood rubbing their clobbered noggins and regaining awareness, Coach Slater yelled right in Jack's face, "You tripped them, I saw you, you little—"

"I didn't!" Jack hollered back, flabbergasted. "They ran into each other!"

"Don't you speak to me that way!" Coach Slater's voice grew menacing.

Rather than shrinking back, the obvious injustice fueled Jack's anger, emboldening him, and he let loose. "You're a cheater!" Jack blurted.

Jack's words echoed off the walls of the gym, and for a moment, the court was as silent as the vacuum of space. Then, every student in the gym gasped at once.

Celia, who was standing just feet from Jack, let out a small yelp, before covering her mouth. Jack's momentary rush of triumph was quickly overshadowed by intense fear. Coach Slater's face changed colors, beginning a pasty white then flushing the deepest shade of red then purple. His eyes looked like they were about to pop out, and his forehead was covered in beads of sweat.

Jack looked sideways to see a look of utter surprise on Celia's face. Her shock wasn't unexpected, but what was odd was that she was pointing at his shirt.

Jack looked down to see a green glow coming from under his shirt where his mother's necklace rested against his chest. A moment later, it went dark.

"What's the meaning of this?!" Slater bellowed, looking at the lump beneath Jack's tee shirt where the necklace rested.

"I... I...," Jack stammered. He pulled the amulet out from under his shirt and held it in his hand. It was warm to the touch.

"Some sort of trick necklace?" Coach snapped. "You know you aren't supposed to wear jewelry in gym class!"

Jack looked up, his head spinning. He'd just gone from making the winning shot, to giving up foul shots to Danny, to having to explain why his mother's necklace was glowing. It was a lot to take in.

"Jack Alexander…" Coach Slater inhaled an enormous amount of air through his flaring nostrils. He yanked Jack's necklace over his head and squeezed it tight in his hand. "Principal's Office!" he bellowed. "And I'll be keeping this gizmo." The fuming coach shoved Jack's necklace deep into his sweatpants pocket.

Jack slunk toward the gym doors, burning to escape the embarrassment of the moment while trying to play it cool for just a few more moments.

Coach Slater cleared his throat and gave a loud ahem! Jack turned. "Forgetting something, Alexander?"

Coach Slater grunted and pointed toward the lockers. "Get your stuff and get off my court!"

As Jack went to retrieve his backpack, his teammates looked after him, simultaneously exhilarated, deflated, and bewildered by the turn of events that had given their team the win one moment and seen their unexpected hero sentenced to certain doom the very next.

When Jack returned from the locker room with his bag, he saw Danny toeing the free throw line, ready to take his unfairly awarded foul shots. Jack could tell by Danny's uncharacteristically subdued manner that even he knew this wasn't fair—but he wasn't about to question his father.

Jack reached the gym doors and turned one last time to see Danny sink the ball in the basket. Coach tossed him the ball and he made the second shot. Danny and Tommy's team win again. Shocking.

Jack sighed. It had felt good to win one game, if only momentarily.

Without realizing he was doing it, Jack found his eyes seeking out Lisa Lexington who—to his surprise—was watching him leave the gym. As their eyes met, she mouthed *I'm sorry* and Jack quickly turned away, blushing. A wide smile unfurled across his face.

The doors closed behind him with a bang, and the school hallway felt suffocatingly silent as he began his slow march to the principal's office.

Chapter 7

This is the End

Jack approached the principal's office and reached for the door handle slowly. Just as he was about to make contact with the cold metal handle, it swung open wildly, nearly knocking him over. He stumbled backward as a woman emerged hastily.

As he regained his bearings, Jack realized that he was already acquainted with the woman. With a long brown dress, fuzzy sweater dangling past her waist, glasses slightly askew, and a stack of books under her arm, it was none other than Ms. Beck, the town librarian. She faced Jack abruptly, startled to see someone standing there.

"Excuse me, young man!" she gasped apologetically.

As she straightened her glasses and took a closer look at Jack, her eyes narrowed in recognition and her lips pressed together in a disapproving line. "Oh, it's you again! Up to no good, I'm sure."

"I'm here to see the principal." The foreign sentence fell out of his mouth as if from a nightmare.

"I'm quite sure you are," Ms. Beck said imperiously. "I hope he gets this whole thing straightened out."

She turned on her heel abruptly and marched down the hallway then out the front doors of the school.

How did she know about the basketball game already? It just happened!

Jack made his way inside Principal Thomson's office, where the principal's assistant, Debra Dean, was slouched behind a large old computer monitor, tapping away furiously on the keyboard. To the right of her desk was a massive mahogany door fitted with an oversized gold plaque reading Principal John Thomson. Jack could hear his heart beating in his ears.

Ms. Dean stopped typing and looked up at Jack. "Can I help you?" she questioned in a nasally voice. The extreme disinterest displayed on Ms. Dean's face was completely at odds with the level of anxiety and apprehension Jack was experiencing.

"Coach Slater sent me to see the principal," he replied, wincing as his voice cracked.

"Very well," she replied with acute boredom.

Jack wondered how many students she saw at her desk throughout the day as she picked up her phone and intercommed the principal, whom Jack could clearly hear reply from the other side of the door, "Send him in."

Ms. Dean hung up the phone and nodded to the door then returned to her typing. Jack approached the massive mahogany door and reached for the knob with great trepidation, willing each second to stretch out just a bit longer. He'd seen fellow students emerge from this place in emotional tatters; tear-stained, red-faced, and thoroughly undone by whatever kind of verbal dressing-down they had been forced to endure. Jack had only seen the inside of Spring Dale High's Principal's office in his most anxious and terrifying dreams. Today, the nightmare was about to come true. As his fingers connected with the cold metal of the old brass doorknob, the whole experience felt surreal. He watched his own hand grip the knob and slowly turn, silent at first, but as the latch slipped out from its socket in the frame it clicked audibly.

"Come in," the principal called from inside.

Jack stood frozen, knowing there could be no turning back now. He gritted his teeth and pushed.

A shelf along one wall held a few awards, education degrees, and certificates. A few large framed posters and newspaper articles were just beyond that. Photos of various sizes dotted the room—a snapshot of Principal Thomson handing out Christmas gifts to children at the local hospital. Another photo showed him posing with teachers, all in gym gear, and Coach Slater laughing and holding Thomson in a headlock. A family photo propped on a bookshelf showed Principal Thomson with his son and wife cheerfully standing atop the most challenging trail at Hawk Mountain.

The principal's college diploma was proudly displayed in an oversized frame on the wall behind the man himself, who was seated in a huge crimson leather chair behind a glimmering mahogany desk, scribbling a note on a pad of paper.

The window blinds were half drawn, casting horizontal shadows across everything in the room. The air smelled distinctly of coffee and hand sanitizer, with a touch of pungent aftershave like the brand Jack's grandfather wore. A small chrome desk lamp gave off a faint glow of yellow-orange light that illuminated the principal's face and accentuated his square jaw.

He looked up at Jack and motioned for him to have a seat in the lone chair positioned in front of the giant desk.

"I will be with you in a moment," Principal Thomson said with a slight smile, then turned back to his note.

Jack slid into the chair uneasily and lowered his bag to the floor.

He had never been this close to Principal Thomson. Of course, he'd seen him speak in the middle of the gymnasium during assemblies, passed him in the hallway from time to time, and observed his interactions with teachers and other students from afar. But there had been no need to interact with the man one-on-one.

He was not looking forward to this new experience.

Jack replayed formative memories of Principal Thomson in his mind. The time Brice Lee had been caught scrambling to locate his history book in the depths of his messy locker three minutes after the class bell rang. Principal Thomson hollered at him for a whole minute about how being late and disorganized could change one's entire path in life. Every student in Jack's homeroom had watched the entire incident through the open class door.

As Principal Thomson continued to scratch out a note, Jack remembered another time the principal lost his cool. Mrs. Payne, the algebra teacher, forgot her tuna casserole bowl in the back of the staff refrigerator for a week, and Principal Thomson read her the riot act in front of the entire cafeteria, sending the poor woman fleeing into the hallway in tears.

Jack realized that, despite what he'd seen and heard, the principal didn't really seem all that terrifying up close. He was in his late fifties or early sixties, Jack guessed. His reddish-brown hair was peppered with white, and he wore horn-rimmed glasses, round frames softening the angles of his face. A brown tweed jacket over a light blue shirt and mint-green tie was his signature outfit.

Jack glanced up at one of the framed newspaper clippings on the wall behind Principal Thomson. It was dated 1977 and read *Town Approves Nuclear Power*. It featured a photo of Thomson among a group of men all shaking hands and smiling widely. Why was he in the photo?

"That was a proud day for Spring Dale," said the principal, following Jack's gaze.

He set his pen down gently on a blotter pad in the center of his tidy desktop, devoid of a computer.

"Lots of hard work went into bringing the nuclear power plant to our town, Jack," Principal Thomson began softly, catching Jack's gaze upon the nuclear power plant article. "Yes, there were a handful of protesters, all worked up about toxic waste and threats of meltdown; all sorts of silliness. But they needn't have worried, Jack. Nuclear energy is safe and clean. Sure, we toyed around with the idea of alternate energy—wind, solar. Why, we even had a renowned scientist recommend fusion energy, but folks weren't up for any of that. So, you see, you have folks like us to thank for putting an end to the rolling blackouts Spring Dale faced in those days, a time that it felt like we were living in the dark ages of energy. We were all saved by nuclear power, Jack!"

Jack adjusted himself in his seat, nervous to hear Principal Thomson say his name repeatedly.

"Without the plant, we just wouldn't be where we are today. And we knew, even back then, that it was an investment in our future… your future. Now with energy prices so high and fossil fuels growing scarcer every year, a new plant will bring a fresh start to Spring Dale."

Principal Thomson stood up and leaned forward on his desk, looking Jack over. "Now, Jack, let's talk about what brings you here."

Jack swallowed hard, took a deep breath, then dove right in. "I was in gym, and I made the last shot, and Danny and Tommy collided and fell on the floor and—"

"Whoa, whoa!" Principal Thomson interrupted with a chuckle. "Slow down, Jack."

Jack stopped abruptly at the command, feeling panicked.

Principal Thomson leaned in and gave him a reassuring look. "Relax, Jack. I'm sure that whatever happened at gym was not your fault. After all, Coach Slater can be pretty tough."

Jack was taken aback. *Is Principal Thomson making fun of his son and his son's best friend?*

"And believe me—I know how aggressive Danny and Tommy can be when it comes to sports, especially basketball. You should see them when they practice at the house—I'm constantly having to break the two apart!"

He chuckled heartily. Jack was incredibly relieved. The principal gave him a generous smile, then sighed.

He stood up, put his hands in his jacket pockets, and turned to gaze out the window between the blinds, a serious expression overtaking his face.

"Let's talk about the real reason I asked you here," Principal Thomson continued, horizontal lines of afternoon light hauntingly bisecting his face.

Asked me here? Jack was thoroughly confused. Coach Slater sent him here from gym class.

Principal Thomson turned back toward Jack, fixing him with an intense stare.

"That's right—I asked to see you this afternoon, Jack. We need to get square on something, you and me." He reached down and ripped the note from his pad and walked around his large desk, taking a seat on the corner facing Jack. "It has come to my attention that you are doing some research for a class assignment."

Jack nodded nervously. *Here we go again! Another adult is unhappy with me researching Linhurst.*

"I understand you've been tasked with writing about our old town here. Is that right?"

"Yes, sir," Jack replied, trying to quell the irritation broiling inside him.

"I hear you've come upon some things pertaining to Linhurst State School and Hospital, have you?"

Not sure it's any of your business. Though the thought hadn't materialized as words or actions, Jack was conscious of a shift taking place inside him. He was partially terrified but partially exhilarated by this newfound side of himself that seemed to be blooming at a crossroads where what those in authority wanted didn't coincide with his inner sense of justice and the need for truth.

"Yes, sir, that's right," he replied politely, though his thoughts were pricklier and less agreeable.

"That's what I was afraid of," Principal Thomson sighed. "I'm dying to know, Jack—what piqued your interest?"

"Ms. Shield's writing project. My subject is about Spring Dale and I thought it would be good to include Linhurst since it's such a big part of our town. I found a piece of paper at the library—"

"Yes, you did… very good!" Principal Thomson interrupted.

Thomson leaned back over his desk, opened the top drawer, and pulled out the map and article Jack and Celia had stumbled upon. He held it up for Jack to see for a moment.

As Jack stared at the article facing him, he was feeling ripped in half by emotions, both anger and distrust. How did he get his hands on this? Then something else struck him: Principal Thomson was one of the men in the photo from the Linhurst article he'd found the day before. With such a distinct jawline, there was no mistaking it. As soon as that piece of information clicked into place, Jack realized

Ms. Beck was also in the photo—a much younger woman, but undeniably her.

Ms. Beck brought this to him! Principal Thomson must have been the person she phoned from her desk at the library!

"Well, let me just begin by saying that many young folks like yourself have heard about Linhurst State School and Hospital, and have been understandably drawn to the mystery that has grown up around it over the years since it closed. Sometimes in small towns like ours, folks amuse themselves by spinning tales and spreading baseless rumors. I'm sorry to disappoint you, Jack," Principal Thomson inhaled a calming breath, "but there simply is no mystery to Linhurst."

"Then why is it such a secret?" Jack decided to chance a question. "Why won't anyone talk about it?"

Principal Thomson sighed heavily. "It's simple, Jack—there is nothing to talk about."

Principal Thomson rolled up the map and article page and tucked it inside his jacket. "The long and short of it is this—Linhurst had been open for over half a century when it came under the microscope. People began to question whether it was fair to keep the residents on the property. People with no training in such matters, and no knowledge of our clientele. Our residents were safe, cared for, and loved. They had nowhere else to go, no place as safe and secure. Linhurst was home for them, but in the end, those from the outside who felt they had the moral high ground dug their heels in, and the whole affair devolved into a power struggle that eventually led to the closing of the property and release of the residents. Now, those who once were residents are free and Linhurst is just a bunch of old buildings that are coming down finally. That's the whole story. Nothing more to know. If I were you, I would stick to the other great things about our town and leave that old place alone."

Jack was anything but satisfied with this answer. It was basically the same story he'd gotten from every other adult. He felt compelled to reason with Principal Thomson. As the head of the school, he had it in his power to help uncover the real truth, especially if he had once worked there.

"Principal Thomson, I'm sure there's something more to this; something that people should know about. It just doesn't make sense. What are you so afraid of?"

"Afraid?" Principal Thomson repeated, his voice suddenly rising from the placid tone he'd maintained up to that point. "Afraid of Linhurst? No, no. It's not that, Jack. We aren't afraid of Linhurst—we're terrified of it!"

"T-terrified?" Jack stammered, suddenly baffled.

"Yes, terrified!" said Principal Thomson. "Terrified of the mistakes!"

"What mistakes?" Jack pushed, seeking answers.

"Those people didn't deserve what happened to them," Principal Thomson began again.

"What did you do to them?" Jack interrupted.

"That's none of your concern!" Thomson barked.

"Everyone has a right to know the truth about Linhurst and what you people did there," Jack yelled, then sat back, shocked at himself. He knew he had crossed the line.

Thomson was fuming—he had no words.

"Why won't anyone tell me the truth if it's just going to be demolished anyway?" Jack decided to try reason, throwing caution to the wind.

Principal Thomson rose to his feet, straightening his jacket. "I think we are just about through here," he cautioned, voice edging toward hostility. He reached up to loosen his tie slightly.

Jack was certain that detention, or worse, would be the next thing out of the principal's mouth. As Jack prepared to face the music, Principal Thomson sucked in a deep breath, returned to a seated position at the corner of his desk, then lowered his face until he was nearly nose to nose with Jack.

"Demolition begins first thing tomorrow morning, and every one of those buildings will be brought to the ground."

Jack gulped—the principal's voice was crackling with restrained rage.

"This deal has been years in the making. It will be a proud day for Spring Dale, returning the town to its former glory, and the past will stay buried in the past—where it belongs."

The two shared an uncomfortable stare for a moment. Jack noticed that tiny beads of sweat had risen on Thomson's forehead, as if they were trying to escape his madness. Jack's fingers trembled as they dug into the arms of the chair.

Principal Thomson closed his eyes, took another breath, then jumped to his feet. "It's settled!" he declared, sounding suddenly cheery. He walked over to his office door and swung it open. "I will work with Ms. Shields to find you a new topic, and be sure to give you an extra week to complete it!"

Jack was stunned. He blinked at Principal Thomson. The man who only seconds earlier had been berating him and staring daggers into his skull from those beady eyes behind the coke-bottle lenses was now smiling broadly at him like they were best friends.

What just happened? Jack blinked slowly, flabbergasted.

The principal gave Jack a wink, then motioned for him to exit. Jack picked up his backpack and headed for the door, slightly unsteady on his feet.

"I checked your grades before you arrived, Jack Alexander. Seeing that you are such a bright and clever student, you're certain to get a terrific grade on the assignment, no matter the topic."

The school bell rang loudly overhead, signaling the change of periods. Principal Thomson put out his hand for a shake, and Jack nervously obliged.

"Jack, I appreciate your cooperation in putting all this behind us," said the principal, squeezing his hand just a bit too firmly. Then, when he knew Jack had enough of the death grip, he peeled Jack's hand open and slipped the note from his desk into his palm.

"I'll email a copy to your father—this one is for you to hang onto."

Principal Thomson returned to his desk and began writing a new note. "Be sure that door is closed on your way out."

Jack looked at the folded note in his hand then turned to close the door behind him. As he grasped the handle, he felt a reckless urge to slam it, but politely pulled it closed with a gentle click.

Jack shook his head as if he could wake up from what felt like a terribly unhappy dream. He felt very relieved to be back in the principal's waiting area and out of the lion's den, though a great frustration was racing through his veins.

Ms. Dean was still noisily tapping away at her keyboard. She cleared her throat and looked to the person seated in the row of chairs across from her desk.

"Mr. Mayor, John will see you now," she said, looking lazily at the man seated in the middle chair across from her.

The mayor replied with only a slight smile. He leaped to his feet, a newspaper rolled tightly in his hand, and marched right up to Jack and stopped. He cleared his throat for Jack to move away from the door, and Jack pressed himself against the wall.

"Thank you, young man," Mayor Helowski barked, then opened the door with a jarring, "What are you trying to prove?!" and slammed it shut.

"Off to class," Ms. Dean droned, making an apathetic shooing motion at Jack without looking up from her computer.

Jack couldn't have been happier to oblige.

Chapter 8

Mose's Clues

As Jack headed for Mr. Urbach's science class, he stopped at his locker amid the bustle of students shoving books, slamming locker doors, and chattering up a storm. The early afternoon energy was palpable, the students ready to be done with class so they could get out and prepare for Halloween.

For a moment, Jack found himself longing to be a kid again, jealous of his old self—the one who didn't care so much about Linhurst.

As he stood under the glowing fluorescent light overhead, he opened the note from Principal Thomson.

October 31
Jack,

> *There are some things in this world that don't lend themselves well to journalistic inquiry— Linhurst is one. Ms. Shields will provide you a less challenging topic, and I am confident you will heed my warning.*

> *As a clever young man, you will see, to forget the past will set you free.*

> *The choice is now yours, you'll remember, of course—*

> *It is wise to leave these things be.*

Principal John Thomson

Jack was immediately angered, deflated, and nauseous all at once. The condescending note—the one Jack had watched Principal Thomson scribble down right there in front of him—was less a strong warning and more a thinly veiled threat.

Jack found his perception of the world warping and shifting. Had the simple town of Spring Dale he thought he knew merely been floating on the surface of its checkered past? He shook his head in an attempt to clear it. Just a day ago, the thought that he'd be capable of earning the displeasure of every adult in town, let alone a handwritten threat from the school principal, would have been laughable; something from a strange dream. But the note in Jack's hand was undeniably real and he suddenly wanted nothing more than to take everything back and erase the recent past, burying his obsession for Linhurst once and for all.

Jack shook his head one more time, shoving the note to the bottom of his backpack. As he reached into his locker to retrieve his science book, Celia ran up behind him, breathless.

"Jack!" she whispered loudly. "What happened in there?!"

As Jack summarized his conversation with Principal Thomson, Celia's eyes grew wide, and he wondered if she was experiencing the same swirling conflicting emotions he felt while attempting to process everything that had just occurred.

"Wow... Jack... that's... I mean... Principal Thomson is..."

She let out a long sigh as he looked down to zip up his backpack.

"At least you are finally over it now, right?" Celia begged, searching Jack's face for agreement.

"Over it?" Jack yelped. "I'm far from over it!"

"Please, Jack, he gave you a new assignment and an extra week. What if I help you with it?"

"Celia!" Jack snapped. Students rushed up and down the hall around them; a bustling, noisy river of bodies.

"Jack... I just don't understand."

"You're right, you don't understand, Celia," said Jack bluntly. "But I am done talking about Linhurst."

Celia stepped back, a mix of surprise and confusion on her face.

"It's time I actually do something about it," Jack said resolutely. "I'm going there tonight."

With that, Jack turned before Celia could utter a rejection. But before he could make a quick retreat, he collided with someone blocking his path. When he looked up, Dr. Moseley, the school janitor, was standing there like a statue, staring down at him, mop handle in hand. Jack could see the rolling trashcan and janitor's cart behind him. Jack started to mumble an apology, but the elderly man's wrinkled hand clamped down upon his shoulder.

Jack felt panic rise in his chest.

Dr. Moseley leaned in with terrifying slowness, and moved his face uncomfortably near to Jack's; the tip of his stained gray cap nearly touched Jack's forehead. "Did I hear you say Linhurst?" The old man's voice was cold and raspy.

"I—I—we—" Jack's words escaped him as he wilted beneath Dr. Moseley's piercing gaze.

"Why are you talking about Linhurst?" Dr. Moseley pressed.

"I just want to know what happened there," Jack squeaked.

Dr. Moseley drew back a bit, a look of surprise touching his expression, then he squinted more discerningly.

Most students had already made it to their classes, and the stragglers were hustling to make it before the bell rang. Celia's eyes darted back and forth from Jack and Dr. Moseley to the classroom they should be hurrying to reach. Jack hardly noticed the ramifications he was about to face as the last door closed and the bell echoed through the building.

The hallway was silent.

Dr. Moseley leaned in more closely, mop handle blocking Jack's escape.

"Why do you want to know what happened at Linhurst?" the old man asked.

Jack trembled slightly, his eyes wide. For once, he had no reply. Celia stared on in horror.

The janitor pulled back a step.

"It wasn't always desecrated ruins," he said in a harsh whisper. "At one time, Linhurst flourished, living up to the vision of its founders—an institution meant to help people who couldn't help themselves." Dr. Moseley straightened up a bit and his face seemed to soften. "Linhurst was a safe and sound place long ago—somewhere you might call home. It was surrounded by flourishing lawns and beautiful gardens overflowing with the biggest blooms. It was a place where the residents and staff could roam and enjoy one another's company together, where people were people. Patients, doctors, and caretakers—we all walked together on warm sunny evenings and crisp autumn mornings. There was a casual grace that lifted the worries for those poor souls who just needed a little bit of special care. And they celebrated all the best holidays together in fine spirits, and enjoyed one another's company with high hopes that one day things would be better for everyone."

"It sounds lovely," said Celia dreamily.

"But things wouldn't be better," said Dr. Moseley glumly.

"Oh." Celia frowned.

"How do you know all this?" Jack asked.

"I was there."

A confused look crossed Jack's face. Dr. Moseley was a janitor at Linhurst?

"When things were hopeful, when we had a bright future ahead—with new discoveries in medicine and societal attitudes about people with mental illness and intellectual disabilities beginning to turn a corner, I was there through it all."

The janitor inhaled deeply as he pulled off his cap and wiped sweat from his brow with his sleeve. Though the top of his scalp was bald, he had plenty of hair around the circumference of his head, and bushy sideburns, all pure white. His face appeared much gentler without the hat, which obscured his eyes and shaded his expression.

After he replaced his hat, Dr. Moseley stepped back so that he could look at both Jack and Celia.

He leaned on his mop handle, continuing, "The people of Linhurst... they were beautiful souls. It was just that the world had rejected them for one reason or another. They didn't deserve what happened. By the end, we were basically herding people like they were cattle. Some of the residents grew very angry and had to be restrained, locked in rooms and placed in straitjackets."

Dr. Moseley looked down and reached inside his jacket pocket, searching for something.

Celia shifted impatiently on her feet. "Okay, well, thanks for the info... we gotta go," Celia said awkwardly, smiling at Dr. Moseley and shuffling over to Jack's side.

"We should go," she whispered through clenched teeth in Jack's ear. "We're late for class."

"Just a minute, Celia," Jack replied.

He was suddenly comfortable with the old janitor and wanted to hear more about his time at Linhurst. It seemed he'd stumbled upon an adult who wasn't scolding him for talking about the place. Jack was hungry for more detail, and Dr. Moseley clearly had a very good memory of it all.

"I can get you to class," Dr. Moseley said as he looked to them with a warm smile, handing them hall passes.

After that, he finally retrieved what he'd been after in his coat pocket—an old photo, creased and crinkled. He stared at it tenderly for a moment, then looked up again at Jack and Celia.

"So many wonderful people," said the janitor, his voice growing hoarse. "We needed help, but there were just too many residents—and those monsters just didn't care. They only wanted money and power. They wanted control."

Jack felt his stomach flip at this new information. "Wait... who do you mean? Who are they, Dr. Moseley?"

"Please, call me Mose," Dr. Moseley replied pleasantly, as though the trio were old friends.

Jack felt a wave of vertigo as another crack formed in his former worldview—the one where Dr. Moseley was scary and unapproachable, Mr. Thomson acted like a normal principal, and librarians were just librarians. Whether he liked it or not, this new world was becoming increasingly familiar.

Mose handed Jack the photo, who in turn held it gently while giving it a glance.

"The people who ran Linhurst... they accepted everyone who came to them," Mose continued, interrupting Jack's attention on the photo. "Now it doesn't sound like such a terrible thing to want to help others in need, but they didn't do it to help people. The more residents they brought in, the more money they received. We had 450 people in a building that only fit a hundred residents. They did it for the money—not to help others, but to help themselves. They filled the place until there was no room… then they filled it some more."

"Why would they do it if they knew it was wrong?" Jack asked.

"That's just it… why did they do it?!" Mose shouted. "We begged them to stop when we were at maximum capacity. We tried to show them that some of the residents didn't belong there, and the ones who did belong there weren't receiving proper care because we were so terribly understaffed. We also didn't have the right people—they hired anyone who walked through the door as long as they worked cheap."

Mose's voice was rising still. It was clear his experiences at Linhurst had stayed with him. Celia was looking rather disturbed by his agitated state. Jack wanted more information.

"What am I thinking?" Dr. Moseley said, suddenly. "I don't mean to burden you kids with all of this." He pulled back a bit and motioned his mop handle as if to point Jack and Celia to class. "Be careful who you talk to about Linhurst."

"We will!" Celia barked as she grabbed Jack's arm. "Let's go," she whispered feverishly, but Jack shook her hand off his elbow.

"Wait!" Jack demanded. "Nobody will tell us anything about Linhurst, but you know so much and want to share!" Jack became stubborn. "I'm not leaving yet. Celia, you can go without me."

Celia stomped her foot. "Come on, Jack," she pleaded. "Let it go already!"

"Let what go?" Dr. Moseley inquired.

"He's been trying to write his assignment about Linhurst but Thomson stopped him and he should just listen. He's been obsessing about it."

"I promised someone I would find out what's behind those walls... and I'm not going to stop until I do."

Mose smiled admiringly at Jack. He leaned back in, more careful now, and a little quieter. "It was supposed to be a school, a place for people to learn and grow, but we became people herders and babysitters. So many of us worked tirelessly day in and day out to keep the residents clean and fed and attended to. There just weren't enough beds, hands or time to do it all."

Mose looked off into the distance as his eyes welled up with tears. Ashamed to be staring at him, Jack quickly turned his attention to the photo in his hand. He unfolded it to see a black and white portrait of a little girl with long blond hair standing outside in the sun, an open field behind her and a vast line of trees in the distance. She was dressed in a white gown and holding a daisy in her hand. A group of men—some older, most very young like teenagers—dressed in matching button-down shirts and work pants stood around her.

"There certainly wasn't enough time to treat her," Mose said, clearing his throat and wiping the tears away.

"Jack!" Celia pointed at the photo, her eyes wide. "Do you recognize her?"

He squinted at the photo. "Yes!" Jack replied with excitement. "It's the same little girl from the newspaper clipping."

"Newspaper clipping?" Mose chirped.

"We found it in the library," Jack replied. "It fell out of an old book and had a map on the other side."

"I see… with a map, you say?" Mose's eyebrows raised.

"A map of the entire town," said Jack. "Including Linhurst, with every building drawn and labeled and a red line through the middle."

"That's a curious thing," said Mose. "How did you find it?"

"I'm writing a story about Spring Dale," Jack began. "Or I should say I was going to write a story about Spring Dale."

"Principal Thomson told him he can't write the story because he was going to include Linhurst," said Celia matter of fact. "I agree… he needs to stop and go with his new subject."

"That old coot!" Dr. Moseley interrupted.

Celia's jaw dropped. Jack couldn't help the smile that spread across his face at the sound of Mose ragging on Principal Thomson.

"Of course, he would prevent you from looking into it. He's one of the men who brought that place to its knees. He was the one who—"

"Principal Thomson was involved in the closing!" Jack interrupted.

"You got it!" said Mose with a snap. "From what I could tell, he was the main culprit... red all over his fingers!"

Jack's mind raced back to the photo in the newspaper story—he could picture the little girl lying in the bed with all the people standing around her. He pulled his phone from his pocket and opened the snapshot of the article, then zoomed in on the faces.

"Principal Thomson is in the same picture as this little girl," Jack said.

"That's right," said Mose. "He was an administrator. The director of the hospital. His policies had a big part in shaping the culture of Linhurst. The only care he ever had for the residents was how much money they'd bring in from the state. Walking dollar signs... that's all they were." Mose shook his head. "They've let those buildings rot for years, and tomorrow they're going to put the final nail in the coffin—tearing it down to the ground. Complete eradication... that's exactly what Thomson and the others want. They've worked hard to make this town forget about the sins of the past, but it's always been there haunting them. When it's gone, it'll be much harder to get anyone to remember or care about what happened under their watch."

"Look... there's Coach Slater and the librarian, Ms. Beck!" Celia interrupted, pointing over Jack's shoulder at the photo from the article.

"Yes, that's them, all right," said Mose. "Hilda Beck was the special projects manager. Slater was activities director, but he was more like a prison guard. He had all the healthy residents working around the clock. Thomson didn't have a clue how to run the place, and he was even worse as mayor of Spring Dale!"

"He was the mayor?" Jack puzzled, then remembered the photo on the principal's wall. "That's why he was pictured with the article about the nuclear power plant approval!"

"He was very instrumental in bringing that monstrosity to our town," said Mose, shaking his head. "I think Thomson started out with good intentions, but he got off track somewhere along the way."

"The little girl in the photo from the article," Celia began, "she looks just like the girl in your photo, Mose."

"That's correct," Mose replied gently. "Her name is Heather… she's my daughter."

The old janitor smiled slightly. Mose's daughter was a resident of Linhurst, too?! Jack looked at the photo for a closer look at the man standing by the bed.

"That's you!" Jack exclaimed. "You're the doctor in the photo!"

"That's me," said Mose. "I was one of the few doctors who worked at Linhurst. We put in tireless hours each day trying to improve the lives of our residents."

"You were a doctor at Linhurst?!" Celia replied in surprise. "Now you're a janitor? All these years we thought you lived at Linhurst!"

"I did live at Linhurst," Mose laughed. "And I may as well have been a patient! I was there so often I took a bed for my own so I could be on call at all times. When I look back at it all, I wonder—I don't know that a person of sound mind would have made the same decisions I did, continuing to work under such crooked leadership, in such horrendous conditions, without calling down the law."

The old man laughed hysterically, and Jack began to wonder if maybe Mose was crazy after all.

"I gave everything to Linhurst, and in the end, it ruined my reputation. When Linhurst closed, no one would take on a doctor who had worked there. Wouldn't interview any of us with a ten-foot pole… as if we were the ones who created those horrid conditions. I spent several years out of work. Finally, Thomson offered me the job here; he said it was a favor to a former colleague. I knew the real reason—he wanted to keep me close, knowing what I did about how they ran that place. But I have my own reasons for being here. He's watching me, and I'm watching him. Thomson and his buddy Slater have misguided our town for years, and though they were never indicted, I'm certain they are the reason for Linhurst's failure. They think they can do whatever they want in this town, but I'm here to make sure someone holds them accountable. I made a mistake at Linhurst—keeping my head down, keeping quiet until it was too late. When I catch them, I'm not going to stay quiet this time."

Dr. Moseley suddenly stopped himself. Jack was feeling a bit uneasy hearing so much frustration and anger.

"Listen to me going on," Mose said more lightheartedly, trying to break the tension.

Jack chuckled nervously while Celia stood beside him, fidgeting with the straps on her backpack.

"Why was your daughter there?" asked Jack. "Was Heather sick?"

"Heather didn't belong there," said Dr. Moseley. "Her mother died when she was very young, and when I took a job at Linhurst, I soon found myself trapped in Building C day in and out. If Heather wasn't in school, she was with me at Linhurst. I eventually decided it was more practical for her to have a bed there while I worked late at night, so I brought one into my office and that is where she lived through the end."

Jack thought about the lettered resident's buildings labeled on the map. He could picture Building C in his mind.

"At first, she did well," continued Dr. Moseley. "Linhurst became her home. She made lots of friends and helped out around the property. It was nice to see her become part of the fabric of the place."

Dr. Moseley sighed heavily, trying to keep his composure.

"Eventually there were just too many people. Building C became so overcrowded, the stench and the noise were overwhelming. The sounds of people moaning, crying, calling for help all day. It was too much for a little girl—I should have seen that, but I was absorbed with the overwhelming needs of the residents. By winter, she confined herself to a corner of the room, away from the madness."

Dr. Moseley took another deep breath. Jack was growing uncomfortable hearing the story.

"It was one of the coldest and snowiest winters we had ever seen—we were all trapped inside that wretched building. We had a blizzard every other week for two months. They didn't have the money to keep the heat up, and the hospital's generating station could only put out so much power, despite having a set of hands working on it nonstop.

"Heather came down with something—a virus. I thought it would move on quickly, but it lingered. She spent a lot of time lying in bed that winter. I couldn't tend to her like I should have. I could have done more, but all day every day I was tending to the residents. They called for me constantly: 'Dr. Moseley! Dr. Moseley!' while Heather lay in bed with a sickness that refused to leave her body."

"Poor little girl," Celia said softly.

"Who are the men in the photo?" Jack asked, changing the subject. It was too hard to hear about someone lying sick in bed without thinking of his mom.

"Heather helped these guys around campus—gardening, painting, and other odds and ends," said Dr. Moseley. "The tall one is Leonard. He was her favorite. A kind man, he was always willing to lend a hand. And you can see by his size how he would be helpful in so many ways. The photo was taken that summer before she became ill. When Heather got sick and she couldn't spend time with them anymore, I never saw them again."

Jack handed the photo back to Dr. Moseley, whose eyes were glassy as he tucked it back into his pocket. He pointed to Jack's phone.

"I remember the day they took that photo for the newspaper," said Mose, dabbing at his eyes with his sleeve. "It was for a new brochure to share about progress and updates at the hospital. The leaders at Linhurst—namely

Thomson, Slater, and Beck—were coming under intense scrutiny for how things were being run. They insisted all was well and decided a little public relations would get the public off their backs.

"They wanted me in the photo to represent the hospital staff. They said I had a kind face. With Heather sick as she was at that point, at first I refused. But they continued to pressure me and I told them I wouldn't leave her side. That's how she became the center of attention in the photo."

Dr. Moseley paused then leaned in toward Jack.

"May I see the photo more closely?" Dr. Moseley asked kindly. Jack handed his phone to Dr. Moseley, who held it out at arm's length. "Wish I had my glasses," he chuckled.

He scanned over the photo for a few seconds. "Heather was too sick to even stay awake by the end of that very week," Dr. Moseley said quietly.

Jack swallowed hard, and Celia wiped a tear from her eye.

Dr. Moseley's expression shifted from grief to anger. "It was all their doing," he said, pointing to Thomson, Slater, Beck and the others gathered around the bed.

"Why are you telling us all this?" Celia asked, bewildered and concerned. "We are just kids and Jack needs to stop looking into this."

"Something tells me you will use this information wisely," Dr. Moseley replied. "And somebody needs to know about this if anything is going to change… especially our youth. Everyone in this town deserves to know what happened in there. I will go to my grave before anything like that is allowed to take place again… which is exactly why I put the article in the library in hopes that someone would find it."

"You put this in the old book?!" Jack exclaimed.

"I found the map before they closed Linhurst and tucked it away in a box. Things happened so quickly when the state came in and shut us down, I simply forgot about it. I hadn't seen it again until just a few months ago, while going through my old things. That's when I decided to slip it into a historic book in the new library. Hilda Beck guards her fortress with great prowess, ensuring the information that goes in and out is personally approved by her.

"I figured the only way to get something as sacred as an old Linhurst article in there was to hide it in the historical archives where students rarely go—Beck would be less concerned about keeping up with that section. I was certain a resourceful academic or someone with sway might find it and make something of it."

"What's the red mark?" asked Jack.

"I was always curious about it, but never had a chance to find out what it meant. But I always found it terribly odd the red line goes right through Building C—there's nothing there!"

Suddenly a door slammed nearby, startling all three of them. When they turned to find the source of the sound, they saw Principal Thomson headed toward them. A frustrated Mayor Helowski rushed down the hall in the opposite direction, madly racing for the front doors of the school.

After the mayor disappeared around the corner, Thomson made his way toward them hastily.

Mose quickly grabbed his mop with both hands and began wiping the floor.

"Be more mindful next time!" Dr. Moseley began in a loud voice, pretending to be flustered. "Careful where you walk, or things can get very slippery." He gave his two new friends a wink.

"Shouldn't you students be in class?" Principal Thomson demanded as he rapidly approached. "Especially you, Alexander!"

"Yes, sir!" Jack yelped.

He grabbed Celia's elbow, and they took off down the hall.

Chapter 9

It's a Science

Jack and Celia dashed into science class together, very late and slightly embarrassed.

Celia took the first aisle and slipped into her seat. Jack bumped and fumbled his way up the middle aisle, kicking desk legs and scuffing backpacks all the way to his back-row seat. "Hey!" screeched Susan Wheeler as Jack tripped over her foot, which was hanging out into the middle of the aisle.

When he finally reached his desk, Jack slumped down red-faced in front of his friend Nate, who was sound asleep on his open textbook in a typical post-lunch hibernation state.

Thankfully, Mr. Urbach paid no attention to the late arrivals. The ninth-grade science teacher was furiously scribbling out notes on the whiteboard, in full swing as usual.

The room was heavily decorated: colorful 3-D models of atomic particles hung from the ceiling, a large poster of the periodic table of the elements took up most of one wall, and several different-sized plasma globes fizzled and sparked with colorful veins of electricity. Mr. Urbach was the most animated teacher at Spring Dale High School, though few students appreciated his energy and enthusiasm for science as much as Jack.

"Energy… What is it all about?" Mr. Urbach turned and threw his hands out to the sides, making large circles in the air. "Energy is all around us. It is a part of us. It is everywhere. Our universe is made of energy and it is fundamental to the existence of everything! Einstein said energy cannot be created or destroyed. It can only be transferred from one body to another. It can change forms, but the total energy remains the same."

Mr. Urbach was a squat man with long, fine hair that drifted away from his head as he danced around the classroom, adding additional flare to his charismatic movements. Each day of the week he wore a different brightly colored polo shirt, moving through the color spectrum systematically—Monday red, Tuesday orange, Wednesday yellow, Thursday green, Friday blue, and Saturday violet, which Jack only know because he attended Science Saturdays. On Sundays, students who attended mass at the same Catholic church as Mr. Urbach said he wore a pure white polo.

Mr. Urbach was passionate about his field, often losing himself in excitement for a topic, sometimes standing on a chair for added emphasis, or punting a whiteboard eraser across the room to be sure everyone was paying attention.

"Now, back to fusion energy," he exclaimed, coming to the center of the classroom and picking up a pair of orange and blue sponge balls. "Imagine if, as opposed to splitting an atom in half through a process of fission as they do in nuclear power plants, we were to fuse the atoms together as one."

He gently held the sponge balls in each hand before suddenly pressing them together with all his might—gritting his teeth as if the effort was straining him immensely and looking around the room with wide eyes.

"Impossible, you say?!" he queried the room.

"Not at all!" He gestured out the window. "The sun itself runs on fusion power! That's right, class, if we could sustain the kind of energy that is produced by the sun," Mr. Urbach whispered as he meandered between student desks, "that would be free energy!"

Mr. Urbach paused for a reaction. None came.

"Now, there are some technical issues to be resolved… The sun's immense gravity can contain the plasma needed to produce the energy. In order to replicate that kind of power here on earth, we would need to use powerful magnets."

He stopped pressing the balls together, and his eyes wandered around the room, a delighted smile on his face. Most students were dozing off or very loosely paying attention. Jack, on the other hand, was completely engaged—he was fascinated by the topic of energy.

Mr. Urbach's smile faded a bit, and he took a deep breath and smoothed his hair down, seeming to sense that the subject was a bit advanced for the class. He returned the sponge balls to his desk, before circling back to the center of the classroom and leaning on an unoccupied chair.

"Consider our own nuclear power plant," he began in a more subdued tone. "It was built years ago, at a time when scientists knew that fusion was a safer, cleaner, and much more powerful process for generating energy than fission. Splitting the nucleus of an atom—which is exactly what they do with uranium at the plant—can give us quite a bit of energy, but at what cost? Radioactive waste, the threat of nuclear meltdown..."

His voice began to rise.

"It's happened before at plants across the world, and it can and will happen again. A meltdown could spew radiation into the atmosphere and destroy the entire town. We'd all be subjected to radiation poisoning, which would lead to mass deaths, birth defects for generations."

He clapped his hands together loudly. The entire class jumped in their seats, except for Nate, who was quietly snoring behind Jack.

Mr. Urbach stopped for a moment to compose himself, patting his hair down and adjusting his green polo.

"With fusion energy," Mr. Urbach continued in a more normal tone, "fuel sources are safe and abundant—there is no risk of meltdown, no greenhouse gasses are produced, and any radioactive waste products are short-lived. It's truly the perfect energy source."

"What a load of garbage," Tommy guffawed loudly.

A few gasps came from the class. Danny chuckled.

Mr. Urbach, whose mouth was still forming around the word he'd been starting to say before Tommy's brazen interjection, turned to face the insubordinate ninth grader—a look of surprise slowly morphing into one of determination.

"Oh, no, dear boy," said Mr. Urbach, pointing a shaky finger at Tommy. "We could have fusion energy today."

"Oh, yeah? Then why don't we?" Tommy asked.

"Some of the greatest minds—scientists, mathematicians, and engineers—have been working to produce a fusion reactor for decades. But the current fission-based nuclear industry is far more powerful… and corrupt. They won out with their money and power. Did you know we even had a renowned fusion scientist living right here in Spring Dale? Professor Vidar claimed he could build a fusion reactor. Unfortunately, the stress of it all—working against the nuclear establishment with barely a dime to support his research—pushed him over the edge. He was eventually placed in Linhurst."

"Then he was probably crazy!" Tommy yelped. "If it's as good as you say it is, they'd be building a new fusion plant instead of adding more towers at the nuclear power plant."

"First of all, young man, Max Vidar was a genius!" shouted Mr. Urbach, his eyes bulging out, and his face turning bright red. "He was on the verge of a breakthrough. He just couldn't find the right interest in his project."

"Pshhh… are you saying if he had, he would have built one of those in Spring Dale?" Tommy sneered. "Then you must be crazy, too."

Danny snickered at the exchange. It wasn't new for Tommy to challenge teachers, but his tone was unusually defiant even for him. The rest of the class was on the edge of their seats, anxious to hear the heated conversation.

"When the nuclear energy company came to Spring Dale offering us an alternative form of power, many of us were very opposed to it," Mr. Urbach replied carefully. "We were outspoken about it. The dangers that are presented by nuclear power far outweigh the benefits in many minds. We protested when the leadership in this town agreed to the nuclear deal."

"My dad helped bring the nuclear power plant here!" exclaimed Tommy. "It gave people jobs and it's what kept Spring Dale alive!"

"That's just what your father would say—and he's the one who brought that awful scourge to this town when he had a chance to make the right choice."

A collective gasp spread over the class.

Mr. Urbach continued, just inches from Tommy and Danny. "He should have prioritized the health and well-being of others, but instead, sacrificed our future to turn a profit!" Mr. Urbach's eyes were wide, his hands balled up in trembling fists at his side.

Complete silence filled the room.

Tommy looked like someone had slapped him square in the face. The color began to drain from Mr. Urbach's expression as he regained his composure and realized his mistake. He swallowed hard, spun on a heel, and retreated to his desk.

"Page 128, please!" he said, voice wavering slightly. "Answer questions one through twenty and hand them in before the end of the period!"

He sank into his chair and opened his laptop, its screen obscuring his face from view. The room was completely silent except for the sound of rustling book pages as students flipped to their assignment and began to read.

"What was that all about?" Susan Wheeler whispered to her neighbor.

"What's going on?" Nate mumbled, bleary-eyed.

"Quietly please," Mr. Urbach mumbled from behind his laptop.

Jack flipped to the page in his textbook and read the title: *Free Energy, Fact or Fiction?* It featured a photo of Professor Max Vidar, the scientist Mr. Urbach had just proclaimed to be a genius. Jack read the caption under the photo.

Credited with advancing fusion reactor technology, Dr. Vidar retired from the field shortly after his experiments led to the successful fusion of two atoms.

Jack thought it was strange that the book said Max Vidar had retired when Mr. Urbach had just told them the scientist had been placed in Linhurst.

The reference turned Jack's thoughts to Linhurst again, and he began to replay everything Dr. Moseley had shared in the hallway. He felt a wave of empathy as he thought about Dr. Moseley's tireless work to help care for the residents and his daughter's untimely death.

Why hadn't Thomson, Slater and the others stepped in to help? Why didn't they care that it was overcrowded and that people were suffering?

The sadness Dr. Moseley carried felt achingly familiar to Jack. He understood what it meant to lose someone the way Dr. Moseley had. Jack's hand instinctively went to where his mother's necklace would have rested on his chest, but he ran his thumb over his shirt and a lump began to rise in his throat when he remembered it had been taken from him.

He shook his head, trying to clear his mind of any thoughts of his mother—too painful, especially at school. He turned his attention back to the textbook assignment.

A fusion reactor (also known as a fusion power plant or thermonuclear reactor) is a hypothetical machine that produces electric power by the energy released during nuclear fusion.

Nuclear fusion is the process by which the nuclei of two atoms are fused together. Every nucleus has a positive charge, meaning the nuclei of two atoms automatically repel one another. Therefore, nuclear fusion requires a significant force to overcome this natural repulsion. This requires a combination of high temperature and extreme pressure.

It was first discovered that the sun produces energy through the process of fusion in the 1930s. The sun's natural energy comes from two atoms of hydrogen fusing (combining as one) to create a single helium atom. During the process, some of the mass of the hydrogen is converted into energy—the heat and light of the sun.

Though most scientists and investors consider nuclear fusion technology a pipe dream, fusion scientists are hopeful that a successfully operational fusion plant could run constantly, powering entire cities on just a few liters of seawater. The hope is that fusion energy reactors would replace all forms of energy today, potentially reversing global warming in a substantially short period of time.

Jack's head spun as he read the entry. *I hope this isn't on the final.* Luckily, the questions were simple enough to answer without having a degree in astrophysics.

The end of the class period came sooner than Jack expected. The bell rang, signaling the end of the school day, and Jack's mind began to race again.

There wasn't much time left—the demolition of Linhurst was scheduled for first thing the following morning, and if he was going to uncover anything, it would have to be tonight.

Jack packed up his things and headed to the front of the class. He handed his answers to Mr. Urbach.

"Discover anything new today, Jack?" Mr. Urbach appreciated feedback from his star student.

"It was interesting to read about another process of creating energy," Jack replied. "I kind of get it, but it's a bit confusing. Do you think it's really possible?"

"I believe it is very possible… just needs more attention and cutting through the political red tape to make sure research dollars are directed toward it. It's all about the funding, Jack. The only other way nuclear fusion energy is going to come to fruition is by some strange miracle." Mr. Urbach shook his head wistfully. "Maybe it's something you could plan to work on one day."

Jack blushed to think Mr. Urbach had so much confidence in him. "Maybe!"

"Have a great day, Jack. Happy Halloween."

Jack smiled and left the classroom.

As school let out, Jack could feel the energy. Halloween was officially in high gear for the students of Spring Dale High. Every kid, from toddlers to teenagers, anxiously awaited sundown and the various festivities the small town had to offer, from trick-or-treating and costume parties to the town festival.

Jack's mind, however, was elsewhere—and he had work to do.

Chapter 10

Bullies Show Their Cards

The halls were empty in a matter of minutes, save for papers and fallen decorations. Celia caught up with Jack at his locker, her arms full of books and papers.

"Sorry your subject didn't work out for you." Ms. Shields' voice echoed down the hall before Celia could say anything. They both looked up as Ms. Shields approached rapidly, balancing a stack of books and papers in her arms.

When she reached Jack and Celia, she removed one of her arms from the precarious pile to hand Jack a small slip of paper.

"Your new assignment, Jack. And no worries… you have an extra week to complete it."

Jack stared at the paper in his hand, then looked up and faked a smile.

"Are you all set with your paper, Celia?" Ms. Shields asked.

"I finished mine on Tuesday!" Celia bragged.

"Excellent!"

Jack frowned, and Ms. Shields reached out and patted him on the shoulder. "I'm sure you'll pass, Jack." She smiled.

Jack nodded.

"Happy Halloween!" Ms. Shields chirped, smiled and winked, then awkwardly dashed down the hall toward the teacher's lounge with the leaning tower of books in her arms.

Jack looked back down at the paper and read aloud, "*New Topic: Lost at the Museum.*"

Wow, that's lame.

"That should be easy enough," Celia said, peering over his shoulder.

Jack shoved the paper into his pocket. "I could care less about the stupid assignment at this point," he barked.

Celia stepped back, eyebrows raised.

Jack sighed. "Listen, I just have a lot on my mind now. Especially after what Dr. Moseley said."

"Jack…" Celia comforted. "Are you sure we should believe everything he said? If it's all true, why aren't Principal Thomson and the others in jail right now?"

"I don't know, but it sounds to me like they should be locked up!" Jack replied, anger simmering.

Celia looked around nervously. "Jack, that's what I'm saying. Don't you think if there was anything to prove, it would have been proven by now?"

"Dr. Moseley wasn't faking it, Celia. He's definitely upset by what happened there. I don't know… maybe he does hold a grudge against them for something, and that's all there is to it. But I don't think so."

Celia sighed, exasperated. "What do you want to prove, Jack? I don't get why you're so hung up on this. Can't you let it go?"

Jack turned to look his friend in the eye. "It's about keeping a promise, Celia."

"Keeping a promise to who?" she asked, confused.

"My mom was working on a story about Linhurst before she died. She started to dig up some stuff—she was onto something—but she never had the chance to finish it. We were going to go there together when she got better, but we never had the chance." Jack sighed and took a deep breath. "I can't just let them bury it all, Celia. My mom knew something wasn't right about what was happening there. Now, after everything that has happened these last couple of days, you're right, I can't forget it. I have to go there… for her."

Celia's eyes were wide with concern. Jack could tell she was surprised to hear him talk about his mother so openly, since he rarely did.

"I understand the grieving process, and… and sometimes it doesn't follow a set path…" Celia paused. "I'm sure you must really miss her, Jack…"

Jack slammed his locker door. He knew Celia was trying to help, but it only frustrated him more.

"You don't know what it feels like… how much Dr. Moseley cared about Heather. She died because of people like Thomson and Slater. It's just not fair that they—"

"I know it's not fair," Celia interrupted. "But what can you do about it now? Heather's gone. Your mom is gone. You can't undo what happened in the past."

To this, Jack fumed and stormed away.

"Jack!" Celia begged. "Please… I didn't mean that."

Jack walked furiously down the hallway toward the school's front entrance with Celia running to keep up. They were the only students left in the building.

"Jack…please wait for me!"

Jack stopped dead in the middle of the hallway and turned to Celia just as she caught up.

"I am going there tonight," Jack said. "It's my last chance. While everyone is celebrating Halloween, I am going to get in there and discover the truth about Linhurst!"

Jack gave Celia one final furiously determined look then turned and pushed through the front doors.

They were greeted by the cool afternoon air, drifting leaves… and two towering figures that appeared out of nowhere.

"You're going to try and sneak into Linhurst, aren't you?" asked Danny Slater, grabbing the front of Jack's sweatshirt.

"That's trespassing, dweebs!" Tommy Thomson chimed in, blocking Celia, arms crossed.

Jack and Celia were cornered.

"Didn't you hear about Xavier!" said Danny.

"Yeah, I was the first to hear about it. I saw him going to the station with Captain Hadaway," Jack said confidently.

"Then you know what happens when you go snooping around in places you're not allowed," said Danny.

"Who says he's going to Linhurst?" Celia asked, defiant.

Tommy turned to her and poked a finger in her shoulder. "Who asked you?"

"Leave him alone." Celia stood her ground. "You're a bully."

"Oh, is that right?" Tommy sneered, bringing his face level with hers. "I don't take orders from whiny little girls, Milk Dud." He turned back to Jack. "My dad told me to keep an eye on you. He says you've been sticking your nose in things that are none of your business."

"Your dad isn't in charge of me," said Jack. "Especially outside of school."

"What exactly are you trying to prove, Alexander?" Danny asked.

"You wouldn't understand," Jack answered, staring Danny in the eye.

Danny smirked, then turned to Tommy. "He couldn't handle Linhurst anyway, right, Tommy?"

"True story… it's haunted!" Tommy confirmed. "You'd lose your mind in less than ten seconds."

"How would you know?" Celia asked, folding her arms across her chest.

"Because we've been in there, Squealia!" said Tommy.

"And you wouldn't believe what we saw," said Danny.

"Then what's it like, if you know all about it?" Jack quizzed. He wanted details.

"Ha! He wants to know what it's like," Danny laughed. "Fine… we'll tell you." Danny gripped Jack's shoulders tightly then leaned in toward him, his mouth forming into a menacing grin. "If you could even make it past the entrance without chickening out, you'd have to go down the long dark road that winds through the woods."

"Once you get to the old generating station," Tommy chimed in, glaring down at Celia, "you have to decide: do you want to take the creepy road to the left or the creepy road to the right."

Jack could picture the road and the generating station on the map. He was making mental notes as Danny and Tommy talked.

"Sounds kind of scary," Jack egged them on, pretending to be nervous. "What comes after that?"

Tommy lowered his voice, taking on a cinematically sinister tone. "Once you choose your path, either way, it feels like you're going to be swallowed up by evil. You could die in those woods and no one would ever find you."

"If you made it through the woods, you couldn't just walk into a building. You have to find a way inside," Danny added. "Every building on the property is boarded up solid."

"It's super scary," Tommy whispered nervously, exposing his genuine feelings about Linhurst.

"Quiet!" Danny growled between gritted teeth, stomping on his comrade's foot. He turned back to Jack. "Then, if a little punk like you could manage to find the courage to make it inside one of the buildings—which you wouldn't, by the way—it is pitch black. And flashlights don't work in there the way they should, so pretty soon you're just feeling your way around in the dark."

"The whole place makes sounds," Tommy said, a faraway look on his face. "It feels like you're being followed…" He looked around nervously, as if talking about the place might conjure up something unpleasant.

Danny punched his sidekick in the arm. "Dude… focus!"

Tommy attempted to regain composure; he was clearly growing more nervous by the sentence.

Danny cleared his throat and continued. "Every turn is another hollow room or rotting hallway. Then… the scariest part of all… all the underground tunnels."

"Tunnels?" Jack puzzled. *I don't remember anything about tunnels.*

"It's like an entire road system down in the tunnels, connecting underground to every building. Pitch black… concrete walls… no windows… no ventilation. Dripping water sounds like footsteps… something running at you," Danny shivered. "Something moving all around you…" He swept his arm through the air dramatically, eyes on his fingers as they trailed across the sky above him. "But are they footsteps?" he whispered, eyes locking with Jack's. "Or is it just your imagination? Every step you take could be your last!"

"Don't forget the ghosts!" Tommy blurted out.

"Ghosts?" Celia echoed, swallowing hard.

Danny stepped back from Jack, crossing his arms smugly. "Yes. Ghosts. Hundreds of them," he replied darkly.

"I'm sure you didn't see any ghosts," Jack said dismissively.

"Oh, yeah?!" said Danny. "I know what I saw, Alexander. There's an evil one in the tunnels. It calls itself King."

"You're full of it," Jack cut him off. "I'm sure you didn't even make it past the generating station."

Danny gritted his teeth, then twisted a fistful of Jack's sweatshirt in his meaty hand. "That's it, Alexander... I'm gonna—"

Before Danny could finish his sentence, Tommy let out a holler, and the next thing Jack knew, the bully was flat on his back. Danny turned to see what had knocked his friend over just before he too hit the ground hard.

Jack spun around to see Dr. Moseley standing over the bullies, the handle of his long push broom grasped firmly in both hands.

"Hey, old man, what's the matter with you?!" Danny yelled.

"Guess you should watch where you're standing," said Dr. Moseley nonchalantly.

"Watch it, Grandpa!" Tommy growled. "My dad owns you."

"Good luck finding yourself a new job!" Danny added. "When our dads hear about this, you're totally sacked!"

"I think it's high time you two snots learned some manners," Dr. Moseley said, looking down at Danny and Tommy, who both remained seated on the ground, looking flabbergasted.

"Some people have to learn things the hard way." Dr. Moseley's voice was calm and deathly serious.

"You don't scare us," Danny blustered, though he couldn't look Dr. Moseley in the eyes.

A slightly crazed look fell over the janitor's face as he leaned over the two bullies. His eyes were completely in shadow under his cap, orange afternoon sunlight silhouetting his tall, lanky figure. He came cap to forehead with Danny and, in a soft, hollow voice, said… "Boo!"

Danny scooted backward, then looked nervously at Tommy, who just shrugged.

Danny glared at Dr. Moseley, then grabbed Tommy and they pulled themselves up off the ground.

"Weirdo!" Danny shouted, his voice cracking. He turned to his friend. "Come on, Tommy, we're done here… for now."

Danny shot the trio a threatening look before he and Tommy took off down the front steps of the school. He stopped halfway down the sidewalk and shouted, "Stay out of Linhurst!"

Jack, Celia, and Dr. Moseley watched as the two disappeared around the corner, turning down an adjacent street, high-fiving each other as though they had just won something. They rounded the bend and were out of sight when Mose started chuckling.

"Don't pay them any mind," said Dr. Moseley, fixing his cap and brushing off his jacket. "They'll get what's coming to them, all in good time."

He gave Jack and Celia a wink then reached inside one of his tall jacket pockets and pulled something out, holding it firmly inside his fist, then motioned it toward Jack.

"What is it?" Jack asked.

Mose opened his hand and an object tumbled out, suspended by a silver chain. Dangling before him was his mother's necklace. Jack opened his hand and Mose set it down on his palm gently.

"Where did you find it?" Jack asked, surprised and relieved.

"I saw it in Principal Thomson's office and knew it belonged to you."

"Thank you, Dr. Moseley," Jack exclaimed, fastening the necklace around his neck.

"Just Mose!" the old man insisted.

"Thank you, Mose!" Jack laughed.

"Have a good night, you two," Dr. Moseley said with a friendly smile. "Happy Halloween!"

He slung the broom over his shoulder and whistled his way back inside the school.

As Dr. Moseley disappeared down the hall, Nate came blasting out of the doors, running straight for Jack and Celia.

"What was that all about, you guys?!" he inquired, breathless and energized.

"Nate, don't tell me you were watching this whole time," said Celia incredulously.

"I was afraid to come out," Nate replied. "I thought you guys were gonna get pummeled!"

"Glad you had our backs!" Celia groaned sarcastically. "Why didn't you step in or get someone?"

"I did... I found the janitor for you guys," Nate replied courageously. "You know... I'm just glad you guys are okay."

Jack shook his head.

"Okay, so anyway, what time are you guys going trick-or-treating?" Nate changed the subject. "Let's meet up!"

"I'm not going trick-or-treating," said Jack.

"What? Why not?" Nate whined, terribly disappointed. "Come on... don't do that lame 'I'm too old' thing. We always go! It's like a tradition! It's gotta be our last year. Nobody would give out candy to tenth graders! And who doesn't like free candy?"

"Nate, chill!" Jack stopped Nate's rambling. "I'm not going. I have something I need to take care of."

"Something to take care of? Can't it wait?! It's Halloween!"

"I'm going to Linhurst," said Jack.

"No way!" Nate gasped, stunned.

"He is," said Celia, elbowing Jack. "And I can't believe you just told him."

"You're going there, too?" Nate yelped nervously. "What's gotten into you guys? Didn't you hear about Xavier Daniels?! Community service?! Captain Hadaway took him down to the police station and charged him and everything! He got fingerprinted! His folks are pissed!"

Celia shrugged, nodding toward Jack. Nate stopped talking and stood frozen in place for a moment, fiddling with the straps on his backpack. Jack waited to see if his old, obnoxious pal had run out of steam.

"Well, count me out!" Nate said, with finality. "There's no way you could get me in that place! Forget it! It's haunted! I wouldn't go in there if you paid me! You guys are seriously nuts. What'll you do if you get arrested... or if..."

"We didn't invite you, anyway!" Celia groaned.

Nate frowned. "Oh... I know... I'm just saying I wouldn't go even if you invited me... that's all."

"Have fun trick-or-treating, Nate. Sorry we can't go," said Jack, and he began to walk away from the school.

"Wait for me!" Celia called, hustling after him.

"Okay," Nate called after them. "I guess, like, just text me if you change your mind or whatever!"

Celia and Jack began the trek toward home, walking side by side quietly, lost in their own thoughts.

"Do you guys even have costumes?" Nate's voice echoed in the distance after a few minutes. They stopped and looked back to where he stood atop the steps of the school, right where they'd left him. "I have extra costumes if you want to borrow them!"

"That's okay, thanks, Nate!" Jack called back, and he and Celia turned and continued walking away.

"I have a vampire cape with teeth," Nate continued, yelling across the distance, "or my Flash costume from seventh grade! I think it could fit one of you all right. There's a pirate costume my brother only wore once. Let's see... umm... Captain America? French Fries? A mouse caught in a trap? Oh yeah! Charlie Chaplain, too! I think my sister's got some stuff that might fit you, Celia!" As they continued walking, Nate's voice grew too faint to make out any more of the costumes in his collection.

Jack lifted a hand up to wave at his goofy friend, and he and Celia shared a chuckle.

As they laughed, the loud roar of a sports car cut through the quiet neighborhood, growing closer. Jack knew who it belonged to immediately. The car raced down the street toward the stop sign where they were about to cross, and Celia clenched Jack's arm.

"Oh great, look who it is," she grumbled.

The cherry red 1970 corvette, shimmering with a new coat of wax, slammed to a stop with its bumper just over the pedestrian line. The window was down, though the evening was already quite chilly. The driver stared straight ahead, bulbous nose poking out from under his gold and blue Rams cap, mouth set in a frown below a thick, bristly mustache.

"You two watch yourselves," said Coach Slater, without turning toward them. "I've got eyes on you."

He peeled away, leaving a trail of smoke.

Jack scoffed at the man's antics, rolling his eyes, but Celia's grip on Jack's arm tightened as the scent of burning rubber lingered in the air.

Chapter 11

Gearing Up

Celia and Jack continued walking in apprehensive silence. The day's events weighed heavily on their minds.

How could it be that so many adults didn't know, or care to know, what had happened at Linhurst? How had everyone turned a blind eye for so many years as the enormous campus—once such a central feature of Spring Dale—fell into ruin while its former residents roamed the streets? And if Thomson and the others were really responsible for allowing all this to occur, how did they get off scot free?

Now they were simply going to tear the place down without answers? *Something is definitely not right about this whole thing.* Jack stewed. He was convinced of it—especially thanks to the new information they'd gleaned from Dr. Moseley.

When they reached Jack's house, he ran up the steps to the front door and held it open for Celia. After a moment, he realized that she was taking longer than usual, and turned back to see her standing at the foot of the steps with a hesitant look on her face.

"What's the matter?" he asked.

Celia shook her head.

"What?" he asked, feeling suddenly uneasy about her disposition.

"Jack…" she started, looking down to her shuffling feet.

"Celia, what is it?"

"I can't go with you!" she blurted out.

"Why?!"

"I realize you're curious what happened there, but I'm afraid we'll get in trouble or hurt. Or worse… Maybe we'll find out something we don't want to know. Or something someone else doesn't want us to know…" Her words faded as she saw the disappointment on Jack's face.

Jack nodded as his face turned stoic. "I understand."

"Please don't be mad at me," Celia pleaded. "As much as I don't want to go in there, I don't want you to go either—but I know it's something you have to do."

Jack nodded again, without heart. "I guess… have fun trick-or-treating or whatever," he said, unable to keep an edge of bitterness out of his voice.

He turned sharply and disappeared into his house, slamming the door tightly behind him.

He stood for a moment in the darkened hallway in the same house he had entered countless times since his earliest days. Memories of happier times returning from the park or the zoo—his mother and father at his side, leading the way to a talkative family dinner after a fun afternoon outing—suddenly flooded his mind.

He remembered coming home from his first science fair win—trophy and ribbon in hand, the prospect of a celebratory treat of ice cream before bed firmly at hand.

And he easily recalled—as much as he had tried to forget—all the times he had entered that very same hallway, ready to drop his bag at the foot of the staircase and race up to see his mom, hoping she would magically look and feel better "this time."

His heart sank deep inside his chest, the sense of loss palpable. People he loved were no longer at his side, and he was truly alone in an adventure he knew he must complete.

He sucked in a deep, angst-laden breath, filling his lungs with air he hoped was loaded with courage.

Then it hit him hard: *I am actually going into Linhurst tonight.*

He really had no idea where to begin; he was certainly not prepared with anything beyond his instincts and an old map to help him find his way around.

Supplies! I have to pack supplies!

A sudden burst of energy struck Jack and kicked his mind into high gear. He dashed up the stairs to his room and shook the contents of his backpack out on the bed, completely emptying it of books, pens, and papers. He pulled a basket from his closet and plucked out a couple of headlamps and flashlights.

It's going to be dark.

He tossed the lights into the bag.

He pulled out his phone and checked the battery—it was at seventeen percent.

I need to charge this!

He grabbed the cord on his desk and plugged it in. As the phone charged, he opened the map photo on his laptop and made a fresh printout to take along. As he looked again at the photo of the doctors and nursing staff surrounding Dr. Moseley's daughter in her bed, fresh determination gripped his heart.

I am going to find out what happened.

Jack went back to his closet and dug out his favorite pair of hiking boots.

Better tread than these old sneakers.

He picked up a pair of gloves from the floor of his closet and pulled them on. He had a few bottles of spring water on his desk, leftover from the last time he went on a hike and didn't use them. He tossed them in the bag.

Stay hydrated… who knows how long I'll be in there.

He pulled off his favorite gray hoodie and flung it over his desk chair, then grabbed a warm, long-sleeved flannel shirt from a hanger and pulled it on over his tee shirt. He stepped in front of the mirror and took a look.

Okay… what else?

His mind raced.

Wait—it's Halloween! I've gotta look convincing!

He dug back into his closet and found Halloween makeup from the year before, then hurried into the bathroom and applied black and white makeup to his face, blackening his eye sockets, smearing streaks of fake blood across his cheeks, and messing up his hair.

"Close enough," he said out loud, looking in the mirror at what was, in reality, a lousy costume—but one that made a convincing enough zombie.

With one last deep breath, Jack pulled on his striped hoodie, then grabbed his backpack and was out in the hallway.

As he reached the top of the stairs, he paused. Something was pulling at him. He felt the sensation often but always ignored it.

His eyes landed on the door to his parents' bedroom. It was always closed. Jack hadn't been in the room since the day his mother had died. Sometimes, he would catch a glimpse inside as his father was entering or leaving, but he didn't have the nerve to look closely, and certainly not to enter. But tonight, the feeling that always seemed to be pulling him toward the room—toward his fears and sadness—was stronger than ever before.

Jack turned and walked slowly back up the hall. He put a hand around the knob and held it for a moment. His insides were turning. He was trying to convince himself he could do it this time—he could look inside the room. All he had to do was turn the knob. Then push the door open. See the bed where she once lay, telling him stories, laughing. See the rocker where he would read his homework to her and tell her about science class, trying to keep her awake and talking because he was afraid that if she fell asleep she might never wake up.

All he had to do was turn the knob to their bedroom door... but his head dropped, followed by his hand. He sighed and swallowed the lump in his throat, struggling to press it back down to the pit of his stomach where he'd learned to keep his sadness.

He shook his head, growled at his cowardice, then took off down the hallway and dashed downstairs in angst.

He made for the front door and, just before he reached for the handle, it swung open toward him.

"Hey, buddy!" His dad smiled, pulling Jack into a big hug, then holding him out by the shoulders so he could take in his son's costume. "Cool! I like it!" Dad said, messing Jack's already unruly hair. "Zombie Jack!"

Jack was taken off guard by his father's unexpected appearance.

"What's the matter, bud?" Dad asked, noting Jack's startled expression as he entered the living room and set his briefcase by the door.

"I didn't know you were coming home early today," said Jack, trying desperately to keep his nerves in check.

"Getting ready for the fire hall Halloween fest tonight." Dad paused and looked at Jack, who was acting rather suspicious.

"Hey..." Dad started. "I hope you're not trying to sneak out early without having dinner first."

Jack chuckled and sighed nervously. I thought he was on to me.

"Of course not." Jack smiled. "Just getting ready to go. You know how much I love Halloween, Dad!"

Jack tossed his backpack by the front door and headed to the kitchen to heat up leftovers for dinner.

He had no sooner scooped reheated mac & cheese onto his plate than he was scarfing it down with reckless abandon, feeling time slipping away with each passing bite.

"Slow down, Jack!" Dad chided. "You'll be sick before you even get your first piece of candy!"

Jack gave a half-hearted laugh and slowed his pace—but only for a few moments.

"Anything new I should know about today?" Dad asked.

Jack nearly choked on a bite of elbow noodles at the question; had his dad seen the email from Principal Thomson already?

"Nothing special," Jack replied, avoiding his father's eyes.

Dad paused for a moment. When Jack finally looked up, he gave his son a concerned look. Jack just shrugged.

After he cleaned his plate, Jack turned to his dad and gave him a quick hug then dashed for the front door.

"I assume you and Celia are going trick-or-treating with Nate?" Dad called after him.

Jack's eyes widened as he turned on his heel.

"Yes, Dad!" he hollered into the kitchen, feeling terribly uncomfortable about the lie.

"You guys have fun," said Dad. "Keep your cell phone on in case I need to call."

Jack immediately felt around for his phone. *It's charging!*

He ran up the stairs to his room and pulled the cord from the phone, then clicked it on. It was at sixty-seven percent—close enough!

He dashed down the steps to see his dad seated on the living room sofa, turning on the laptop to check his email as he did every night after dinner.

"When you're done trick-or-treating, come down to the fire hall. They convinced Mayor Helowski to climb in the dunk tank—should be a hoot! Think I might throw a few balls myself after hearing about the new power plant deal he pushed through."

Jack returned a nervous smile and stood staring at his dad, who was patiently waiting for the laptop to fire up. *He's going to see the email from Principal Thomson… I gotta get out of here.*

A knock at the front door startled him.

"Trick-or-treaters already?" Dad asked as he looked toward the door. "Would you mind, Jack—the candy is there on the table."

Jack turned to see a bowl filled with Baby Ruth bars and mini packs of M&Ms in a pumpkin-shaped bowl atop his grandmother's end table. He picked it up and carried it to the door, growing ever more anxious to slip away. As he approached the door, he could see a figure through the frosted glass. Whoever it was seemed much taller than the average trick-or-treater. He turned the knob and pulled the door open.

"Hi, Jack! Nice costume… I guess you're a… zombie?"

"Lisa?" Jack gasped as his face immediately flushed a deep red. Thank goodness for zombie makeup! His pulse quickened.

His palms began to sweat around the bowl of candy. He couldn't understand why Lisa Lexington was standing right there on his own front porch—but there she was, dressed in a black and white 1920s flapper dress with a feather headpiece circling the crown of her head.

"I wanted to say I thought it was brave of you to stand up to Coach Slater today," she said softly, breaking the silence.

Jack couldn't believe his ears.

"I think he is such a bully," Lisa added as Jack struggled to regain the ability to speak.

Jack had no idea what to say. Why on earth would Lisa Lexington come all the way to his house just to tell him she liked how he'd shouted at the gym coach and gotten sent to the principal's office?

The Principal! Principal Thomson! his brain shouted at him. *Oh no! The email! Dad will see it any moment now.*

"Oh, I… um… thanks, Lisa… but I should go," Jack fumbled over his words and began to close the door, but Lisa quickly put her arm out to stop it.

"Wait, Jack!" she yelped. "I wanted to ask if you'd like to go trick-or-treating with me and Marcy then we can check out the Harvest Fest afterward?"

Jack stopped dead: had Lisa Lexington just asked him to hang out with her? Had she just asked him to accompany her to a public place where they would be seen together?

"I… um… I… ahaa…" Jack cringed inwardly as he scrambled for words. His brain was apparently short-circuiting.

He needed an out, though he so badly wanted in. Lisa smiled nervously, waiting for him to respond. Jack couldn't think—should he skip out on his plan to go exploring the huge, dark, abandoned and haunted insane asylum in search of who-knows-what, or should he go trick-or-treating with Lisa Lexington, whom he'd had a crush on since sixth grade?

"It's just that… I was going to… it's just that I have to go to, um…" Jack fumbled more, rubbing his neck nervously with one hand, clenching the bowl of candy tightly with the other. Lisa stood in place, nodding and waiting for him to reply.

"Hey, Jack—can you come in here, please?" Dad called out from the living room. Jack's heart sank and a huge lump welled up in his throat. *He read the email from Principal Thomson. It's over. It's all over.*

"Jack, is everything okay?" Lisa asked.

"I'm sorry, Lisa… I have to help hand out candy!" Jack shrugged and laughed nervously. "I'll take a rain check!" he said stupidly, his face beet red beneath the paint and fake blood.

He dug a fistful of wrapped treats out of the bowl and held it out in front of Lisa. She looked down at it, looked up at Jack, then down again, then held out the old pillowcase she was using to collect candy for the evening. Jack dropped it in, smiled, waved goodbye, shut the door, and went halfway down the hall before sliding to the floor against the wall of the entryway.

Through the frosted glass, he could see Lisa's figure lingering on the front porch for just a moment, before slowly disappearing down the steps and out of view.

Hand out candy?! I'm such an idiot! Jack berated himself, feeling sick to his stomach with nerves.

"Jack, are you all right?" Dad asked quietly from the sofa, where he was hunched over the laptop.

"Oh, yeah, sure... all good," Jack laughed nervously and placed the bowl back on the table by the door.

"Who was that?" Dad asked.

"Oh, uh... just someone from school," Jack answered.

"I see," said Dad. He paused for a moment, then shook his head. "What's the Wi-Fi password again? I can't seem to get online."

The Wi-Fi password?! That's what he wanted?

Jack tried to remember the password, fumbling around for the letter and number combination he had once memorized, but before he could speak again, Dad hopped up.

"Oh, silly me! What am I thinking!" He went to the door and picked up Jack's backpack, bringing it to his son and helping put it around his shoulders. "You're trying to get out of here. Don't let me hold you up—I'll look for the password on the modem!"

Jack felt an enormous weight lifted from his shoulders as his father set the backpack on them.

"Thanks, Dad," he said, running for the door before anything else could slow him down. When he reached the front door, he turned for a moment to say a quick goodbye.

Though a pang of guilt struck him at his current deception, Jack felt a wave of deep love and affection for his father, as well as a certain pride at his strength and sensitivity, both of which had kept them afloat as they tried to figure out how to navigate life without Mom.

"Love you, Dad," Jack said.

"Love you too, son," Dad replied heartily, increasingly puzzled at his son's behavior. "Remember... not too much candy!"

"Yeah, yeah." Jack rolled his eyes, and he was out the door.

The sun was hovering just over the horizon, casting golden-red rays of late daylight over the rooftops of Spring Dale as the sounds of exuberant children filled the air. It was Halloween night and costumed characters of all colors, shapes, sizes, and species were beginning to gather for one of Spring Dale's most beloved holidays.

Jack checked his phone for the time—it was 6:00 on the dot.

A group of children dressed as Frankenstein, an evil king, a vampire, a ghost and a football player passed by. Another crew comprised of skeletons and hockey players raced toward a row of homes across the street to get their first treats of the night. The disguised children were in such a hurry they nearly bumped Mam and Pap Saunders off the sidewalk and into a hedgerow. Mam barked a few obscenities and threw a flurry of offensive hand gestures before continuing on her way—Pap just kept his head down and marched on. Jack watched as a mother with a young baby in a stroller, led by a throng of energized toddlers, hastily crossed the street to avoid Mam and Pap. She threw an uncomfortable glance over her shoulder at the odd couple. The unwarranted fear and disrespect filled Jack with sadness and frustration.

Just down the sidewalk, among the gathering throngs, Jack spied one more figure—Lisa Lexington. She was on her own, and Jack supposed she was heading toward her friend Marcy's house. He felt a huge lump rise in his throat when it dawned on him—had he just given up the girl of his dreams? When would she ever look at him again, let alone ask him out?!

Jack made his way to the corner of the front porch, where his rusty blue bike with the peeling orange pinstripes rested against the wall behind the swing. His mom had gotten him this bike for his birthday just before she died. Though it was banged up and much too small for him now, Jack carried it down the steps, feeling comfort in knowing it would be carrying him on his journey throughout the night.

He carried it down the steps and set it on the sidewalk. Between the massive old sycamore trees lining his street was the occasional street lamp. As he climbed over his bike, he saw the bulbs inside the old iron lamps flicker to life. He thought of how dark it would be in Linhurst and flipped the switch of the headlight on his handlebars then hopped on.

As he rode down the block toward the entrance, he passed more trick-or-treaters. They were filled with exhilaration as they ran from house to house, scoring their Halloween loot. He envied them in a way, but Jack knew he'd never be happy until he'd worked to find justice for Heather, Mose, Mam, Pap, and all those Linhurst had left behind.

When he arrived at the entrance to Linhurst—the same one he and Celia passed every day on the way to school—he stopped and straddled his bike.

Jack recalled the look on Xavier Daniels' face as Captain Hadaway drove away. He'd looked terrified, and Jack knew it wasn't from being trapped in a police car. It was something else. Was it the same thing his mother's friend Barbara had seen? Had he seen a ghost? Or had he just let his imagination run wild?

Jack stared hard into the space beyond the large stone buttresses plastered with warning signs.

Tonight, I'm going to ignore the signs and find the truth.

White steam poured from the nuclear power plant in the distance, filling the sky with puffy, clouds and creating a thin veil over Linhurst.

As he took one more deep breath, Aunt Edna's words came back to him: *"Be careful what you go looking for in there... and if you do find it... best to leave it alone."*

He wondered what he would find—and whether he would leave it alone or find the courage to disturb it enough to change things.

He mounted his bike and looked around. Most of the trick-or-treaters were now up the street a bit, and he saw no one else was in sight nearby.

"Now or never," Jack whispered aloud.

He looked down at the road to Linhurst, pushed forward on his bike and began his journey into the unknown.

Chapter 12

Into the Unknown

Once he'd cleared the entrance to Linhurst, Jack pedaled fast as he could. He wanted to get as far from the street as quickly as possible, to avoid being seen.

He focused doggedly on the surface of the road, swerving to avoid rubble, sticks, and potholes. The jungle on either side of him loomed heavily. He looked back to the main road and caught a glimpse of a few trick-or-treaters racing past the entrance. Though the stone buttresses seemed far enough away, Jack was sure that if he could still see people, they would be able to see him if they chose to look in his direction.

The fear of detection propelled him forward and he pedaled faster, his breathing growing heavier by the second as his heartbeat accelerated.

He bumped along over the cracked road, listening to the hum of his tires and the spin of the chain, the air chilling him as it rushed over his body.

The moon was rising to his right. Daylight was dwindling fast on his left. His mind was focused on the task at hand, trying to predict what might lay in wait beyond the entrance to Linhurst.

He looked back again quickly, continuing to pedal forward. His view of the street was now obscured, the road behind him disappearing into the dark woods that flanked him.

What would happen if he got caught? What would his dad think? What would Captain Hadaway do to him? What would everyone at school say? Principal Thomson would surely come up with a painful punishment for denying his orders.

A wall of trees with twisted branches strangled by climbing vines soared overhead. The tangled canopy was crawling with imaginary shapes—snakes, monsters, and all sorts of menacing creatures. Jack kept riding, trying to shake the images out of his head. At one point, he swore he saw a human figure standing at the base of a tree staring out at him coldly. *Just my imagination*, he reasoned, speeding up a bit. Suddenly, ahead of him in the middle of the road, the leaves began to stir as though a small twister was rustling them up.

Not again! Jack slowed.

The leaves flew up into a great mass and formed the shape of a giant hand. Unlike the day before, when he'd first witnessed this strange phenomenon, the hand formed a different gesture; palm out and fingers stretched open wide as if to say "Stop!"

But Jack didn't stop. He wouldn't. Not now. Not after he'd come this far.

He pedaled harder, determination welling inside of him. The hand sucked in more leaves, growing denser and larger. More leaves were suctioned from the ground and a second hand appeared and motioned for him to stop.

Jack pedaled harder, anger boiling inside him. *I am not stopping now. It's just leaves! Leaves and wind!*

As if in response to his thoughts, a great wall of wind formed in front of him, pushing against him and tearing across his body. His eyes began to water and he could feel his throat filling with dust, but he kept pedaling, though he could see he was getting nowhere fast. He looked down to see his tires spinning in place against the road.

As he gritted his teeth and braced himself to push even harder, a faint green light appeared on his handlebars. Jack looked down briefly to see that it was coming from the amulet again. His balance wavered, and he almost tumbled off his bike. The leaves had transformed into massive fists. They were flying toward him, ready for a knockout.

Jack's necklace grew brighter, illuminating the oncoming fists—just feet away from him now. He closed his eyes tightly a moment before the leaf-knuckles reached him—when the mass suddenly dissipated and he was smacked by the face full of dying autumn. He opened his eyes and continued coasting along the bumpy road. He turned back to see that the great mass had fallen gently to the ground; only a few small leaves fluttered down like snowflakes.

He looked down to the amulet. The silver symbol lay dark on his chest.

Jack was baffled by what he had witnessed, but after the last few days, he was starting to grow accustomed to extraordinary occurrences.

He pedaled onward. *I must be close to the generating station.*

Out of nowhere, a strange sound pierced the air. A low, ominous howl.

Is that my bike making noises? He dubiously glanced down at his brake pads. They seemed to be functioning correctly.

The howl came again, louder this time. Jack's blood turned to ice. It was clearly coming from behind him. Jack looked back. The winding road flowed behind him, faintly illuminated in the dusk like a river through the forest.

"Aaa!" the howl called out.

He picked up his pace, ears tuned to the blood-curdling sound behind him.

"Aaaa!" it cried again, closer this time. He couldn't bring himself to look back again.

He pedaled faster, sweat beading up on his brow, legs burning from the effort to outrun the thing.

"Aaaaa!" it howled again. Jack's thoughts bounced wildly from the normal to the paranormal. Could it be an injured crow? A dog? What if it's a lost spirit with a grudge!?

"Jaaaack!"

Jack's stomach twisted as he realized the horrifying truth—the voice was calling his name!

"Jaaaaaack!"

It screamed, shrill and tortured. It was perfectly clear now, and he knew with certainty it was coming from directly behind him.

"Jack... please... don't go any farther!"

I know that voice! He slammed on his brakes.

"Look out!" the voice screamed in his ears.

He whipped his head around and was immediately met by another bicycle flying toward him in a blur.

He leaped from his bike and landed in the brush at the edge of the road, narrowly missing a giant tree. He started to pull himself up when he was smothered in a bear hug.

"Jack! Are you okay?"

Celia was right on top of him.

"Celia?!" he shouted, utterly bewildered to see her hovering over him, as he lay on the ground along the road into Linhurst.

He pushed her away to be sure the face matched the voice. She jumped to her feet and put out a hand to lift him out of the brush. They stood staring at their bikes lying in a tangled heap in the middle of the road.

"Is that how you're going into Linhurst?" Celia asked, puzzling at his costume.

"I just needed to convince my dad," he replied, skeptically eyeing her torn jeans and faded pink hoodie. "What are you supposed to be?"

"It was the best I could do on short notice." Celia pulled her hood up over her head. "See... I'm a ghost."

Jack rolled his eyes at her poorly executed disguise, though his zombie costume wasn't much better.

"Wait... Celia... why are you here?" Jack asked.

"Oh, Jack, after I thought about it, I knew I couldn't let you go all alone. This…" she gestured to her outfit, "is just to convince my parents, too. "

"Wait, you're not going trick-or-treating?" Jack asked, confused.

"I followed you this far… what do you think?!"

"And your folks actually believed that as a costume?"

Celia punched him in the arm.

"Ouch!"

"I'm here to help! Give me some credit for that at least!"

"Did you see me go into Linhurst?" Jack asked nervously.

"I didn't," she confirmed. "I just figured I could find you if I was on my bike—so much quicker to get around."

"Great minds think alike!" he replied. "And you made sure you weren't spotted before you entered?"

"I'm pretty sure," she replied confidently.

Jack searched her face, anxious about the potential of being discovered. She interrupted his questioning eyes.

"Okay, where do we go from here?" Celia asked ambitiously.

"We stay on this road and we're in. You sure you're ready?"

"I'm not, but let's do this thing!"

She was looking a little pale despite her lack of zombie makeup. Jack pulled his bike away from Celia's and set it on its tires.

Celia put her hand on Jack's arm. "Promise we'll be careful and turn around if we're ever in danger?"

"I promise we'll be careful," he replied. "Let's go!"

Celia pulled her hood over her head, and Jack followed suit. She lifted her bike and mounted it. They nodded in unison and started down the road.

For a few minutes, they rolled along in silence, side by side through the darkness. The autumn air was cold against their faces, thick with the scent of wet leaves, occasionally punctuated by the distinct earthy odor of a murky puddle.

The woods finally thinned as they broke into a clearing. The open space was occupied by a hulking building seated in shadow at a fork in the road. Jack stopped his bike and skidded to a stop through loose pebbles. Celia pulled up beside him.

"What is it?" she whispered, breathless.

Jack pointed up, and Celia removed her hood to look.

"The smokestack," she whispered in awe.

Jack nodded.

"The generating station," Jack said, staring up at the familiar tower from his new vantage point.

The large generating station was decaying, its bricks and beams giving in to the elements of time. Determined plant life encroached from the overgrown woods surrounding the multi-story building and covered layers of graffiti. Through the broken windows, they could see a few sets of metal staircases, a network of pipes, and pitch blackness beyond.

The smokestack climbed high above the rest of the station, reaching toward the sky turning a royal purple over a brilliant orange. Having learned from Dr. Moseley that it was the building where men worked to keep the power on at Linhurst, Jack imagined a column of smoke pouring out the top many years ago—long before the nuclear power plant spewed its steam all day long.

Jack swung his bag around and pulled out his printout of the map.

"Here's where we are," he said, pointing at the drawing. He looked up and pointed to a dark, overgrown path through the woods. "That way will take us to the main buildings."

Suddenly, a loud snap echoed through the adjacent woods.

"What was that?" Celia yelped with a start.

"Probably just an animal," Jack replied, unfazed.

"You sure?" Celia squeaked, eyes wide.

"I've been in the woods around Spring Dale plenty of times," Jack said. "Could be squirrels or rabbits. Maybe a fox… but he wouldn't bother with us."

"How can you be so certain?"

He pulled out his flashlight, flicked it on and shined it into the woods until he located a set of glowing eyes peering out at them from the underbrush.

"What is that?" Celia trembled.

"Just a raccoon," Jack said confidently.

The creature ambled away, its fuzzy striped tail disappearing into the thick brush. Jack flicked off his flashlight and dropped it into his bag, then pulled out two headlamps.

"Let's put these on," he said to Celia, handing her a headlamp then putting one on himself.

Another strange sound cut through the air—something completely different from the rustling and branch-snapping of the woods. Celia froze, petrified, and Jack paused to listen. The sound was much louder and more difficult to define, as if it coming from all around them. To Jack, it sounded like an inhale followed by an exhale—the breath of a sleeping lion. The long low roar rattled their bones and shook the ground. Jack thought he saw a quick flash of light in tandem with the sound but quickly brushed it off as his imagination.

"Did you hear that?!" Celia whimpered.

"Yeah," replied Jack. "It sounded like a lion yawning."

"Oh, great..." Celia replied. "Now there are lions in the woods?"

"Let's go that way," he declared, pointing his flashlight up the road that branched to the right.

Before moving on, he pulled his phone out to check the time—6:20.

He opened the camera app and snapped a few photos of the generating station.

"Might as well get some photos while we're here." Jack glanced at Celia, who was looking very unsure of things. "Good to have a record before this is all gone."

The rumble came again, along with a flash of green light that appeared to radiate from inside the windows of the darkened generating station.

"Did you see that?" Celia asked nervously. "What was it?"

"No idea," Jack replied.

"Maybe the flash from your phone?" Celia suggested, unconvincingly.

"The flash is turned off," said Jack. "I'm trying to make sure we aren't spotted."

Celia wrapped her arms around herself and shivered. They waited in silence for more movement or sounds. All was very still and eerily quiet as they stood over their bikes in the clearing, the generating station looming in darkness above them, the woods surrounding them like a massive wall inside a castle yard.

Jack cleared his throat.

"Probably just a flash from a car's headlights or something," he offered, though they were nowhere near the road; he was trying to reassure his friend… and himself.

They mounted their bikes and started up the road again, which took them back into the darkness of the woods. It was a steep climb, and their path was barely visible under a blanket of branches, leaves, and dirt. On either side of the road, tall trees struggled against a vast network of vines, tangled like prey in a spider's web. As Jack and Celia pushed their way farther into the forest, the road narrowed, and the air grew dense.

They came to a bend and as they headed into the curve, the branches and vines from the woods appeared to close in on them.

"It's a dead end!" Celia called out as she slammed on the brakes. Jack skidded to a stop beside her.

As Jack shone his flashlight ahead, looking for a way through, he couldn't believe his eyes—he swore he could see the woods moving and changing shape.

"We're trapped!" Celia yelled.

The branches and vines appeared to be twisting, reaching, growing over the road and winding around one another. They looked back to see more of the same.

The low, giant lion's growl came again, followed by another. They felt the ground beneath them shake and rumble. A green light flashed through the trees from behind them.

"The green light!" Celia said.

"I saw it, too," Jack replied.

"Make it stop!" Celia moaned, closing her eyes and covering her face with her hands.

As Jack watched in awe and terror, another flash of green pierced the dim forest, this time from his mother's necklace. The tangled mass of vines and branches suddenly retreated, gracefully unwinding themselves and withdrawing to the shoulders of the road.

Jack looked down to find the necklace still glowing brightly. It felt warm against his chest.

He turned to Celia to see her reaction, but she was still covering her eyes. She was holding onto her bike's handlebars with all her might as she mumbled, "Please, please, please," under her breath.

"Celia, it's okay," Jack whispered calmly.

"Please, please, please..." she stopped and opened one eye at Jack.

"It's okay... look," Jack said, pointing ahead.

The path was open again, and what little remained of the setting sun cast a faint orange glow around the opening of the once seemingly endless tunnel.

Jack looked down at his necklace again to show Celia, but the light had gone dark and the metal was now cool to the touch.

Did I imagine that, too?

"That was crazy, Jack!" Celia said, voice shaking. "I've seen enough... we should go back!"

Jack shook his head.

"It'll be okay," he said, thinking of the necklace and the retreating vines. "Trust me."

"You promised we would turn back at the first sign of danger, and that..." she pleaded, lost for words. "What was that?!"

"Trust me... I have a feeling about this."

Celia rolled her eyes and sighed. By the look on her face, she was not happy—and maybe slightly queasy. He could relate to her feelings because he was feeling the same way.

She swallowed hard, then put a foot on a pedal and forged ahead. Jack ran his fingers across his mother's necklace for comfort, then got moving.

They rode up the steep incline through the last of the forest tunnel and out into a new clearing. Jack immediately spotted a brick building on a hill to their left, set off the road and almost completely masked in vines and brush. It was a large four-story structure with rows of massive windows, every pane broken and shattered. The exterior—once a stately red clay—had weathered to a charcoal brown. Jack squinted through the mess, looking for an entrance to the building as they pedaled along slowly.

"Look, Celia." Jack pointed to a sign hanging over the main entrance of the building. Though the weather-damaged wood of the marker nearly rendered the lettering illegible, they could still make it out: *Building A.*

"This must be the main area where all the residents lived," he said as he spotted more brick structures scattered throughout the area. "Dr. Moseley worked in Building C, the same place where the red line is marked on the map," Jack added excitedly.

"If this is Building A, we must be close!" Celia responded, a measure of excitement returning to her voice.

They pedaled through a large open area and looked across the great expanse of crumbling asphalt and neglected landscape. They passed an abandoned car, its tires flat and its windshield shattered. Short runs of rusted chain-link fence protruded from dry earth and overgrown grass. Thick black trash bags were torn open, tossed along the side of the road amid other scattered litter; old soda cans, shreds of plastic, scattered paper, broken pens. Scrap metal of every shape and size was strewn about as if a load had been dropped from a plane. A twisted sheet of metal guardrail was wrapped around a giant, blackened oak tree as though it was working to snuff the life out of it.

Jack spied street lamps set along the crumbling road every ten feet or so, with the occasional light box twisted off. A few lamp posts were bent and twisted completely to the ground. As Jack passed one of the posts, he looked up to see a light bulb still set inside the housing. The sight of such a familiar, functional object struck him as odd in this desolate place. The people of Linhurst had left everything where it was—just up and left one day and never looked back. As he passed another post, he saw the words Made at Spring Dale Iron Foundry emblazoned on a plaque fastened to the base.

They continued along the bumpy road, feeling the earth-shaking rumble again, followed by another. They seemed to come in twos.

"There it goes again," said Celia nervously.

This time, they saw no flash of green light. Jack looked down at his necklace... nothing.

They came to a fork in the road.

The road to their left stretched up a long hill toward the western horizon, where the sun had retreated for the remainder of the night. The sky was a deep blue with only a thin band of light above the tree line. At the top of the hill was the water tower, its silhouette like a sentry guarding the valley where Jack and Celia rode.

The road to the right was a straight shot back into the dark woods. Jack could see several other large buildings sitting closely together.

"Let's go that way," Celia said, pointing to the road on the left.

"There's nothing up there," Jack replied. "We need to go that way to find Building C." He pointed up the road to the right that would lead them back into the dense woods. Celia gulped.

Dead center of the fork in the road was an open area of overgrown grass surrounded by an aged white picket fence. A massive, gnarly oak tree stood tall in the center of the clearing, its roots like twisted fingers gripping the earth. Jutting out from the ground all around the base of the tree were small white wooden stakes and stones.

Jack and Celia rode their bikes up to the edge of the picket fence and came to a stop.

"It's a cemetery," Celia whispered nervously, pointing a shaky finger at the tree and headstones.

Jack pulled his phone out and snapped a photo.

"Isn't this creepy?" she asked.

Jack laughed under his breath as he turned and snapped a photo of Building A in the distance behind them.

"Why is that funny?" Celia questioned. "People died here, Jack."

Jack turned to Celia. She was clearly distressed. He tried to see things from her perspective.

He thought about Tommy and Danny's tale of ghosts—which he'd previously dismissed. Then he considered how his mom's friend Barbara was never the same again after sneaking into Linhurst. He recalled Xavier Daniels and his oath to never enter Linhurst again. Clearly, death and the paranormal played a part in the mystery of Linhurst.

"People die… it's just how life is," Jack said calmly. "I don't think it's creepy."

He looked more closely at the crosses and stones and noticed they were all faded.

"You can't read the markings on the memorials," Jack said. "It's like these poor people never existed."

"They're all forgotten," Celia said, her voice swelling with emotion.

Jack nodded blankly.

"You know, not everyone who dies returns as a ghost," Jack said matter-of-factly, trying to reassure Celia.

"Says who?"

"It's common knowledge," he added hastily.

She shook her head and raised her eyebrows.

"People only return as ghosts when they have unfinished business," Jack added. "That's what all the stories say, right? There's Casper… The Headless Horseman…"

"Thanks a ton, Jack!" Celia interrupted. "The Headless Horseman is the last thing I want to think about right now!"

She looked all around, nervously checking for any hooded, pumpkin-toting apparitions.

"We need to get to Building C." Jack refocused on the task at hand.

Celia nodded hesitantly and they started up the road past the cemetery and back into the woods to the other buildings. Jack's headlamp shone along the road in front of them, creating a faint circle of light.

Before they could reach their destination, they were stopped short by a massive tree lying across the middle of the road. Jack got off his bike and peered ahead into the darkness.

"We'll have to walk from here," he whispered to Celia.

He could see a number of large brick buildings beyond, set back off the road, nestled within the strangling forest. Jack laid his bike against the downed tree and Celia followed suit.

"What now?" she asked.

"I want to figure out where we are."

Jack pulled the map out of his bag and traced their route from the entrance to the generating station, then up the road to Building A. He ran his finger along the road past the cemetery to the spot where he guessed they were standing. The buildings formed a semicircle on the map around his finger.

"Aha!" he declared. "According to the map, if we are here..." he tapped his finger on an unmarked spot along a road on the map, "...then Building C is that one."

He ran his finger along the map to the drawing of Building C, then pointed straight ahead.

Directly in front of them, fifty yards into the darkness, stood a building resembling Building A.

"Look at this!" he exclaimed, his finger on the map. "The red line from the administration building to the generating station crosses this road almost exactly where we are standing. I don't remember seeing another road along the way, do you?"

Celia shook her head then looked around to reconfirm the fact that they were indeed still surrounded by nothing but forest. There was no sign of another road or path. Jack shrugged and rolled the map up, then stuffed it back into his bag and slung the pack around his shoulders.

"That map was drawn in 1984. I bet that line called The Best Route is buried under all this," Celia proclaimed, gesturing to the vigorous plant life and healthy layer of leaf detritus on the ground. "Maybe we can start calling it the worst route!"

Jack nodded, then climbed over the fallen tree and started off along the road leading to Building C.

"Do we just leave our bikes here?" Celia questioned with great concern in her voice.

"Yes, they'll be fine!" he called to her without turning around.

Celia sighed heavily, climbed up over the log, and ran to catch up with him.

As they walked through the silent night along the debris-covered ground, the sounds of twigs snapping and leaves crunching under their feet seemed more like sparklers and small firecrackers. They could only imagine what they were awakening in the darkness.

They came upon a long-rusted fence—damaged and twisted in many places, covered with dead vines, and a large open area beyond. The fence ran alongside a crumbling concrete sidewalk that Jack began to utilize immediately.

Better to take the walkway than continue with all the noises we're making.

As they walked along the fence line, Jack spied a sizeable opening in the chain link and peered through. On the other side was a swing set for small children; rusted, twisted, and sitting quietly alone in the middle of an open yard; more residential buildings cloaked in the darkness behind. A single swing rocked gently forward and back, though there was nothing there to move it—not even the wind.

Jack thought the better of pointing this out to Celia. A chill ran through him, and he turned his careful walk into a steady jog. Celia was right on his heels.

Everything around them was eerily calm as they drew closer to Building C. Jack's attention was laser-focused. He pictured himself walking right up to the building, opening the front door, walking inside, and somehow finding exactly what they needed to prove what happened here. The answers felt so close he could practically taste them.

Jack could make out the windows of the front of Building C now, and what looked like a porch atop a short run of stairs. The branches and foliage of the woods pressed up against it—on the verge of swallowing the entire structure into nonexistence.

What will we find inside? An open safe with hidden secrets? Jack chided himself internally. *No... that's ridiculous.* Maybe something that would tell them more about the red line on the map. Or something Thomson left behind. That's more reasonable.

He located a weather-damaged sign hanging over the entrance.

"Building C," Jack whispered to Celia, pointing his light to the red sign with peeling white letters on crackled wood.

They had arrived.

Building C resembled Building A. It had a once-grand wooden porch, and supporting columns coated in sheets of peeling white paint. Its sagging, rotted roof looked as if it had ceased protecting the inside from the elements long ago.

Sets of twelve-panel windows on either side of the entrance were completely shattered—shards of glass the only thing remaining in the frames. The second-story windows were in the same condition.

Jack recalled Danny's description of the boarded-up buildings and difficult entry and shook his head. Never count on Danny to tell the truth about anything. Building C's large double doors—coated in large strips of peeling red paint—were partially ajar.

Jack took a step forward. It was almost too easy. The only thing that would make it even easier would be if they could just go inside and flip on a light.

Suddenly, something fluttered across one of the windows. It was so fast, he thought his mind was playing tricks on him again. Jack thought he caught a flash of white.

"Did you see that?" Celia shrieked, confirming his vision.

He nodded. His mind raced back to the time he found himself lost in the woods at the edge of the Linhurst property. The memory of the dancing curtain in the window and the strange object that floated by made him shiver involuntarily.

"Please tell me you don't still want to go in there after that," Celia whispered, her voice trembling.

Jack turned to her. Her eyes were wide and full of fear.

"You still want to go in there." She answered her own question in a flat tone.

"Celia, I'll admit I'm pretty scared right now," said Jack. "Here we are out in the middle of the woods surrounded by these old empty buildings on an abandoned campus where we could get arrested for trespassing."

Celia nodded her head energetically, looking at him hopefully.

"And even with all that, I'm not ready to give up. I still want to go in there and see what we can find out."

Celia shook her head furiously. She was mystified by his persistence.

"I know how this must look," Jack said. "I'm sure you think I'm crazy. But you have to trust me."

"Jack, we're just kids!" Celia pleaded. "This is too much!"

"I promised you we would turn back if things got bad," Jack replied. "I'll tell you what—why don't you hang out here while I check it out inside?"

"Wait out here?!" she replied quickly. "I would much rather stick with you than stand out here in the total darkness with who-knows-what creeping around me!"

He laughed, then looked around hesitantly and flipped his light back on.

"Can we just take it slow?" she pleaded.

"Yes, we'll go slow."

Jack pulled his phone out and checked the time. It was 6:36. Plenty of time.

He snapped a few pictures of their surroundings, including the very dark Building C. He stuffed his phone back into his sweatshirt and they quietly made their way up the long, crumbling sidewalk to the foot of the short staircase and up onto the porch landing, taking careful steps along the way.

Once on the porch, the entire structure creaked and snapped as they traversed the splintered boards, making for the doors, which were set slightly ajar. The opening beyond was pitch black.

Jack shone his light around the porch, then inside to see a long, vast hallway stretching into total darkness where his light wasn't strong enough to reach. The floor was covered by a plush maroon carpet, bunched up in many places with thick, undulating creases and tears. Remnants of the walls and ceiling had broken loose over the years, creating a confetti of paint chips and dirt on top of the ruined carpeting. The hallway was littered with scattered papers, pens, Linhurst employee ID tags, a rusty black stapler, broken pairs of scissors, and more debris than they could quickly categorize in just in the first twenty feet alone.

Jack stepped over the threshold. As he set his foot down, a howling creak rose up from the ancient floorboards. He took another step, and the floor groaned ominously.

"Be quiet!" Celia shrieked under her breath.

"I'm trying!" Jack snapped back.

He took another step, and the floor groaned more intensely.

Step. Creak! Step. Rip! Step. Crackle!

On his seventh step, Jack's foot went right through the carpet, swallowing up his entire leg. He collapsed to the floor, bringing a large piece of odorous maroon carpet with him. A cloud of dust encircled his body in the faint glow of his flashlight, which had fallen by his side. He was trapped to his knee in carpeting.

Celia dashed inside—creak! rip! crackle! —and grabbed hold of Jack's arm. She tugged and pulled, but his leg stuck fast beneath the floorboards.

"Jack, help!" she hollered at him.

He pushed hard on the floor, trying to lift himself out of the hole. Finally, the carpet let go. Once he was back on his feet, he brushed himself off.

"We have to be careful where we step," she whispered in a motherly tone as she brushed off his back.

Jack chuckled and nodded in agreement.

"Jack, your leg!" Celia yelped, pointing to a rip in his pants.

He bent down and looked inside the tear in his jeans to see a cut several inches long, blood oozing out slowly.

"Ugh, my dad is going to kill me!" he said in frustration.

"That's a bad cut!" Celia said, bending to look at the wound.

"No—my jeans. They're only a month old!"

"Are you kidding me?" Celia groaned. "We have more to worry about right now than a rip in your jeans."

She unzipped his backpack quickly.

"What are you doing?"

"Looking for something to clean up this cut."

"It's not a big deal," Jack replied.

"We have to clean it up," Celia insisted.

"I have water in there," Jack said, wincing a bit at the pain.

Celia pulled out one of the small bottles and furiously twisted off the cap, tossing it into a corner with all the other litter.

She tore open his jeans a bit more and poured the water over the cut to wash off any debris.

"Hey!" Jack yelped.

She handed him the bottle. "Drink!" she commanded.

"It's just a scratch," he laughed, watching his mild-mannered friend suddenly transform into an ER doctor.

Celia grabbed hold of his flannel shirt with a firm fist and tugged on it with the other. She ripped off a piece victoriously.

"What are you doing now?" Jack leaned away, confused.

"Hello, genius... I'm wrapping your leg to stop the bleeding!"

She knelt and tied the torn piece of flannel tightly around his leg, covering the cut.

"Wow, you're serious about this!" Jack marveled.

"My dad took me on a backpack survival trip one time. I know how to handle these things. You don't want that to get infected, believe me!"

Jack chuckled and downed some more water.

She pulled the bottle from his lips. "Don't drink it all!" she yelped, then finished off the bottle. "Wow... I was thirsty!"

She crushed the bottle, tossed it back in his pack, and zipped it up tight.

Suddenly, the moment was broken, and they remembered they were inside Building C of Linhurst, closer than Jack could have ever imagined to finding out about the place. Fixing Jack's leg had momentarily distracted them, but the eeriness had returned, and they both turned silent.

The air inside the building was thick.

Peering down the long dark hallway with just their headlamps and flashlights, Jack and Celia could see a series of open doorways alternating on either side, spaced about every ten feet. Every moldy, rotted doorway framed a hollow rectangle of blackness.

Small particles of dust and dirt floated softly in the beam of their lights. Deafening silence engulfed them.

"Let's investigate these rooms," Jack whispered, though the thought of even looking inside any of them filled him with dread.

"Okay, let's go already," Celia whispered, giving Jack a little shove.

The pair walked slowly and carefully down the narrow corridor to the first open doorway. They leaned around the edge of the doorframe, shining their flashlights inside. The room contained overturned desks and chairs, filing cabinets with open or missing drawers—contents spilling out—and paperwork blanketing the floor beneath shattered windows boarded up to the outside. A shred of white, sheer curtain hung dead on a rusted rod above one of the windows.

In the center of the room, an old typewriter and television sat on a desk, looking as though they were waiting to be used at any moment. Furniture, cabinets and medical equipment were left to decay as if everyone in the building had just gotten up and walked out the front door one afternoon.

On the far wall hung a large oval mirror, completely shattered, a few bits of its original reflective matter clinging to the edges. Hanging nearby were several framed black and white photographs.

Jack stepped inside the room for a closer look. The first photo showed residents of the hospital alongside nurses and doctors. The patients looked listless, standing aloof in a line, all wearing simple white gowns. Another photograph showed a group of small boys sitting in a line on a wooden bench. The boys were in an empty room without sunlight;

they were all staring down at the floor, their hands neatly folded in front.

The last photograph was of people working in a garden—a girl with thick curly hair held a garden shovel in one hand and a fistful of tulips in the other. Though she appeared to be about ten or twelve years old, she, like the adults in the photo, proudly held a cigar tight in her teeth.

"Aunt Edna!" Jack exclaimed.

"This must have been an office," Celia whispered, pointing her light to an open desk drawer with pens and other supplies still inside.

"I think you're right," replied Jack. "Now it's like a ghost office."

"Don't say ghost!" Celia squeaked.

As Jack approached the filing cabinets for closer inspection, the great inhale came again—only this time it was deeper and longer. Peeling paint flaked off the walls and fluttered down around them. The creaking floorboards rattled under their feet. Celia grabbed Jack's arm to regain her footing. The exhale came very quickly, and soon it was quiet.

"No flash of light," Jack whispered.

They waited a moment for more surprises, but none came. Jack stepped back inside the doorway and shone his flashlight down the endless hallway. He waited for movement or sound. Nothing. He walked out into the hallway, careful of his steps. Celia followed, holding tightly to the back of Jack's sweatshirt.

A small crashing sound echoed from a room just down the hall. They shined their lights toward the source of the commotion.

"What was that?" Celia whispered.

"I don't know," he answered nervously.

They waited, listening intently, when suddenly a pair of small glowing orbs appeared along the baseboard and dashed down the hallway toward them. A long tail zipped around the corner through a doorway.

"Just a rat," Jack sighed in relief.

"Just a rat?" Celia replied sarcastically. "Raccoons, lions, and rats—I wonder what else is living in here."

They moved a little faster through the building, sweeping their lights inside each open doorway. Every room was more of the same: abandoned offices, the contents of desk drawers strewn across the floor, empty shelves and rotting furniture.

As they approached the end of the hall, it appeared to be a dead end. Jack felt deflated. This was not what Mose described, and it didn't look like the large room from the photo of Heather.

He ran his hand along the wall into the darkness to see that the hallway continued onward despite the lack of doorways. Eventually, their lights fell on a large dark opening with rusted metal caging framing either side of the corridor. They made their way through to the other side, and there it was—the massive room with tall windows reaching toward the ceiling. The room from the photo. The space seemed to travel upward endlessly into darkness—farther than their lights could reach. Long wooden floorboards traveled away from them into emptiness, broken only by floor-to-ceiling pillars cutting through the middle of the open space.

"This is not at all what I expected," Jack said quietly, noticing the vast amount of debris.

He tripped over something and looked down with his headlamp to see a ragged child's doll, dirty and disheveled. Celia grimaced.

"Of course, I don't know what I expected," Jack continued. "These buildings have been abandoned for so long, I can't believe there's even as much stuff left as there is."

Jack pulled out his phone and took a few photos of the vast room, this time with the flash turned on. The entire room was littered with old beds, mostly overturned. Twisted piles of wrought iron bed frames and chairs lay everywhere. More furniture, medical supplies, and office equipment were smashed up against the wall and bent badly out of shape—casualties from trespassers and vandals throughout the years. As they walked carefully through the room, they found themselves snaking around wheelchairs, bed pans, and hospital gurneys. Straitjackets rested amid the clutter as though troubled souls had been lifted from their bodies and cast to the floor.

Jack and Celia moved through the room methodically, carefully inspecting everything, looking for clues of where to go next.

"This is definitely the room from the photo of Dr. Moseley and his daughter," Celia whispered.

"This must be where all the Building C residents lived—where Mose and his daughter lived."

Jack was growing anxious. They had arrived at Building C, but where were the answers? *Where to next?* he wondered anxiously.

The walls were covered in graffiti from former trespassers. Spray paint tags were everywhere and included warnings like *No way out*, and *All Souls Lost*. Jack pointed his light up to a sloppily-written tag that read *Danny & Tommy Were Here*!

"Looks like they did explore this place after all," said Celia.

Jack nodded. He wasn't surprised.

"Now where?" she asked.

"That's what I'm wondering," Jack replied impatiently. "Let's investigate the far end."

Jack stepped carefully toward the edge of the room, shining his light all around. Celia continued to hold tightly to his sweatshirt.

When they arrived at the farthest reaches of the great hall, Jack's light fell upon a large metal door. He reached for the handle and gave it a tug. It didn't budge. He pulled harder. Still nothing. Then Celia grabbed hold and they both pulled and tugged, but it wouldn't open.

"There must be a way through here," Jack said.

"It's just an old building that people completely destroyed," Celia sighed. "I just don't think there's anything left that's worth looking for—can we please get out of here?"

Celia's right.

Suddenly, his emotions crashed from excitement to defeat in a heartbeat. He looked down and leaned his head against the door, his headlamp shining a circle of faint light at his feet. They had come all this way and risked life, limb, and reputations for nothing. Linhurst was just a wasteland of abandoned buildings that weren't giving up their secrets—if they had any to tell at all. *Nobody wants to talk about Linhurst because it's old and uninteresting, and everyone's moved on to better things. There is no story. End of story.*

Tears welled in Jack's eyes, and his bottom lip quivered as he held back a wail. Standing still with his head against the door, he began to sob quietly, shoulders shaking with deep emotion.

Celia placed her hand on his back and rubbed gently. "Jack... it's okay," she whispered calmly. "You tried."

Jack's head was swimming as he stared down at the ground. The flashlight's glow was blurred by tears, giving everything a starry glimmer. Celia continued to rub his back, the only thing that kept him from sliding down the door and curling into a ball on the floor.

He wasn't sure how long he'd been weeping when the sobs began to change form, becoming laughter-like—at first just a chuckle, then a full-on laugh. He stood up straight, wiped the tears from his eyes, sniffed heartily, then turned to Celia. She was staring at him as though he had completely lost his mind.

"Are you all right?" she asked.

"It's just that... now that I really think about it..." he could hardly get the words out around his mixture of laughing and crying, "…I think the only reason I did all of this was because somewhere deep down inside I thought it would bring my mom back."

"What do you mean?" Celia probed, concerned.

"It made me feel closer to her—pursuing this adventure we promised each other. To try and help the people she wanted to help way back then. But look where we are! This is crazy…"

He spun around, waving his hands madly at the post-apocalyptic scene around them.

"There's nothing here! There's nothing to prove! She told me we would do this together but she knew she was dying. She knew she would never make it long enough to come here with me." Jack was growing hysterical. "It was just a silly, empty promise to a little kid who was about to lose his mom!"

"Jack, we don't have to give up yet if you aren't ready. We came this far," Celia whispered calmly. She was deeply concerned about him.

"It's just that... I made a promise to my mom to find the truth... but there's nothing here. It was all a waste of time! I miss her so much, Celia!"

Jack began to sob again. Celia took a deep breath. She was holding back tears.

Then she stepped back, a look of determination on her face. "Let's try to find our way to the Administration Building where the red line starts," she announced. "I mean, we came all this way already. Let's at least check it out before we leave."

Jack sniffed hard and wiped a sleeve across his face, then stood up tall. He turned to Celia and looked her in the eyes. Her great compassion had suddenly and completely replaced all fear. He gave her a big hug. He couldn't have chosen a better companion for this adventure that was already turning out to be both more and less than he'd hoped for.

Jack wiped the tears from his eyes with the sleeves of his flannel. He chuckled and sniffed. "Anything to get us away from this door!" he replied, embarrassed by the scene he had created.

With a new destination in mind, they started back to the entrance of Building C, retracing their path around the flipped beds and overturned wheelchairs. They were halfway through the room when Celia let out a bone-chilling scream. The pair stopped dead in their tracks.

"Look!" she cried out.

She pointed her light at a rusty wheelchair that looked like it was rocking in the middle of the floor. Before Jack could respond, it began to roll toward them.

The chair inched toward them slowly, its large black wheels bumping along over the rotted floorboards and debris.

"It looks like someone is pushing it," Celia said shakily.

"Who's there?" Jack called out, flashing his light madly in every direction.

There was no response. The chair continued to roll toward them.

"I can tell you for the first time tonight that no animal is doing that!" Celia trembled.

"What's moving it?" Jack was frozen in place, his curiosity only slightly outweighing his fear.

The chair came to a stop as it bumped into one of the busted beds holding a stained mattress. The chair was just within reach. Jack and Celia huddled together closely, holding onto one another fearfully, the sound of their breathing the only sound in the large cold room.

Then it happened.

Chapter 13

A Ghostly Experience

A great blue streak of light bisected the beams of their flashlights. It shot straight up from the seat of the chair toward the ceiling, forming in a single column. The column faded for a moment then suddenly exploded into a cloud of glowing bluish-green. The cloud condensed until it was the size of a human head, then floated down and hovered gently above the chair.

Jack and Celia held tightly to one another, eyes wide; shivering, shaking, and breathing faster by the heartbeat.

"What's happening?" Celia barely managed to get the words out, squeezing through her narrowed vocal chords brought on by a great fear rising in her.

Jack could not recall a time when he'd been more terrified in his entire life. His stomach was twisted, his entire body clenched tightly. He could feel Celia's fingers digging into his arm.

The bright orb moved from the chair to the head of the bed. The entire room was now faintly lit by the soft glow emanating from the unidentified shape.

He thought of the shape he saw inside the window of Linhurst, of Xavier Daniels swearing to never come to Linhurst again, and Danny and Tommy certain of spirits inside Linhurst. He thought of his mother.

Suddenly, the ethereal shape changed color and glowed a soft green. He looked down to see that his amulet was glowing a similar soft green.

The necklace, uncontrolled by batteries or other electrical forces, seemed to be reacting positively to their strange encounters of late. As he focused on the amulet, his breathing slowed and his trembling ceased.

Jack very gently disentangled himself from Celia's grip and took a step forward.

"Jack?" Celia madly whispered through gritted teeth. "What are you doing?"

Jack barely heard her, moving forward another step. His nerves had been replaced by an intense curiosity. The compulsion to move forward was irresistible.

Celia grabbed the back of his sweatshirt with both hands and pulled hard on him in the opposite direction.

"Jack?" she whispered hoarsely.

"It's okay," he assured her. "I'm not afraid." Jack was suddenly in a fearless trance as he pulled hard toward the light.

"Jack, I don't want to do this," she pleaded.

Jack tugged in the opposite direction with twice the strength. He was pulling both of them toward the light that floated hypnotically over the head of the wrought iron bed. Celia couldn't hold him anymore and released her grip. The momentum sent her backward. She lost her footing, tripped over a pile of junk, and landed in a seated position on the dusty wooden floor.

Jack turned to Celia to see if she was okay. She looked up at him in shock, pointing at his chest.

"Jack... your necklace!" Celia yelped.

He looked down to see the amulet around his neck glowing brightly, then back to Celia, an expression of wonder on his face. He brought his hand up to the amulet and smiled; it was warm to the touch. Something about his mother's necklace was helping them communicate with the spirits at Linhurst.

With his hand on the amulet, Jack turned back to the body of light and walked steadily toward it. He could see through the glowing orb to the other side of the room where it lit the space around them, illuminating the tall shattered windows that opened to the dark landscape outside. As he came to within a couple feet of the object, he could feel the air grow very cold. His breath was visible—icy vapor clouds illuminated by the green glow.

Jack reached out for the light.

"No!" Celia cried.

Jack paused with his arm outstretched. "Why not?" he protested.

"You don't know what that is," she pleaded.

"It seems friendly," he said, transfixed.

"It seems friendly? What are you saying?" Celia begged.

Just before his hand touched the light, the glowing green body drew away from him and darted to the opposite side of the bed and floated up a few feet higher. Its light faded slightly.

"We mean no harm!" Jack calmly pleaded.

At this, the orb floated slowly back toward them and grew bright again. It settled in just above the head of the bed and began to quiver rapidly, solidifying into a more solid shape.

Jack turned back and reached down for Celia. He grabbed her arm to pull her to her feet though she hesitated at first. Then she gave in and allowed it. Jack had promised not to let them get into any danger, and she trusted her friend despite how incredibly frightening this all seemed.

Jack turned back toward the glowing green orb.

"What are you?" Jack whispered. His mother's amulet was glowing brightly on his chest.

The orb danced rhythmically, elongating like a cobra before a snake charmer. It quivered from top to bottom as it grew brighter and took on a new shape.

Long, flowing strands of bright light transformed into beautiful wisps of hair. It quivered again and the bottom of the orb flowed outward like a gown. Then the shape of a girl's face—blurry and rippling as if reflecting on a pond—appeared amid the glowing strands. A soft "Hello?" emanated from the glowing body.

From the wheelchair, a piece of paper shot straight up into the air and drifted slowly down from above their heads. It glowed in the light of the body and floated like a feather to the seat of the wheelchair where it came to a rest.

Jack reached out a shaky hand and snagged the paper from the seat. He opened it and read the faded words typed across the top of the crinkled sheet:

From the Desk of Dr. Charles Moseley, M.D.

"Celia...it's from Mose!" Jack cried.

Below the header was a handwritten note:

> *Dear John,*
>
> *We need more supplies in Building C if we are to keep up. I have asked Eric for assistance without reply.*
>
> *It is also extremely cold these past few days. My daughter is very sick along with many of the others. Please help at once.*
>
> *Mose*
> *PS*
>
> *The rumblings continue and have become very distracting to the residents—please investigate.*

That's when Jack realized... the note... Building C...

Something made him call out, "Heather... is that you?"

"Heather?!" Celia puzzled aloud.

Jack turned to Celia. A sudden look of understanding transformed his expression.

"It's Dr. Moseley's daughter!"

The glowing body vibrated at the sound of Dr. Moseley's name. Jack turned to Celia quickly—her face registered complete shock.

Jack was grinning ecstatically. He turned back to the ghostly figure.

"Father?" the body cried out.

"It is her!" Jack effused. "We know your dad! He misses you."

"Jack?" Celia whimpered.

"I'm trying to talk to her... maybe she can help us."

He turned to speak with the glowing body again. "We're here to help. We want to know what happened here."

Suddenly the ghost shook madly, sputtering out sparks of bright green light. The body turned to the shape of a girl as a voice rose from out of the vapor-like form.

"Where is my father?" Her voice sounded many rooms away, like it was being carried on the wind. It wasn't entirely clear, but they could understand her.

"Dr. Moseley... your father... he helped us find you!" Jack exclaimed. "He showed us a photo of you holding a flower."

"Father..." came the echoing voice again, sounding closer now. "He tried to help..."

"She's talking to you, Jack!" said Celia with a mixture of terror and delight. "You're talking to a ghost!"

Celia giggled for a second in disbelief.

The ghost drifted along the bed toward them and settled just in front of Jack. She gazed at him for a moment, then looked down at the note in his hand. He opened his palm to show it to her.

"Your father wrote this?" Jack asked gently.

Suddenly her body writhed and shook, then spiraled into the air. The note leaped out of Jack's hand, sucked into Heather's ethereal body like a vortex. It circled inside her a few times, before exploding into hundreds of shredded pieces like confetti. The paper fluttered down upon Jack and Celia like snow.

Heather shot back down over the bed then flew right up to Jack and Celia, her face within inches of Jack. Her features took shape, and the pair could see her more clearly, like looking through a foggy mirror. She turned a brilliant orange and gave them a furious look, then pulled back a foot and her color deepened to red. Her body burst into a fireball and raced over toward the windows along the far wall, then disappeared into a dark corner of the long room.

She was gone. Only the glow of Jack and Celia's fading headlamps remained to light the room.

"No... wait!" Jack pleaded. His voice echoed throughout the large room.

"Don't go... we want to help make things better!" Celia added.

Silence was their only reply. Jack turned to Celia and looked at her in frustration. His necklace was no longer glowing.

"Where did she go? We can help her! Where is she?!" Jack panicked.

"Jack, I don't know," Celia replied desperately.

Jack spun and looked all around. He pointed his flashlight every which way, turned in circles, feverishly looking for the ghost. Just when they had actually found something—someone—extraordinarily significant inside the walls of Linhurst, she disappeared. Heather was in and out of their lives before they could even begin to comprehend what she was all about.

"We came all this way to help," Celia began quietly. "Just when we were ready to give up, we found her, and now she just disappears?"

Just then, a small light burst from the far corner and floated along the wall back toward them. Heather's spirit returned and drifted back to the bed only a few feet from Jack and Celia. The ball of light transformed once again into the shape of a small girl. A soft, glowing hand reached out for Jack. Fingers opened up from the palm like streams of glowing silk then brushed along his neck. Her hand gently drifted down to the amulet and caressed it.

Jack looked down at her glowing fingers trying to grasp the necklace, then looked back up to Heather.

"It was my mother's necklace," he said softly.

Heather smiled fondly and slowly pulled her hand away.

"My father tried to help," said Heather. "They wouldn't let him."

"Yes, we know," Jack replied softly.

"He wanted to make everyone better, but they didn't care if they died here," the ghost added with sorrow and anger in her voice.

"He told us what happened here. We know," Jack stressed.

"You don't know!" she interrupted in a scream, her voice echoing throughout the room as her figure shook and her body grew large as an adult. The glow from Jack and Celia's headlamps dimmed as her anger flared. Celia whimpered.

The ground beneath them shook and the beds, wheelchairs, and overturned junk in the room rattled. Heather seemed unfazed by the rumbling that seemed to be coming from underground.

"I'm sorry. We don't mean to upset you. We want to help," Jack pleaded. "We know they closed this place because people didn't belong here. We know that people were mistreated. We just want to know why it's still closed up? Why are you still here? Are there others?"

"They did it for power and money," said Heather. "But we are working to fix it."

"Who's we? Fix what?" Jack begged.

"Fix everything! We're going to set this place free!"

After Heather's emphatic statement, the giant inhale and exhale came as it had regularly since they entered the property—only this time something was different. Jack noticed that Heather's glow intensified to a much brighter green on the exhale. Jack looked at her curiously.

"Look, Jack... it's glowing again!" Celia shouted, pointing at his necklace.

Jack looked down just in time to see his mother's necklace fade out from a glowing green. *What is making it glow?*

"You have brought help," Heather said softly.

"Help? What do you mean?" Jack looked up at the little ghost in confusion. He could see Heather smiling fondly—and somewhat madly—at his necklace.

Jack pondered, but his thoughts were broken by a new sound—a mumbling of voices.

"They are coming," Heather said flatly. She turned and looked out toward the hallway entering Building C.

"Who's coming?" Celia asked.

The voices in the distance were coming from inside Building C's hallway where Jack and Celia entered.

They remained quiet as they tuned their ears. They could hear male voices speaking inaudibly. As the sounds grew louder and closer, Jack and Celia looked at each other in recognition.

"Danny and Tommy!" Celia whispered in horror.

"It is them!" Jack said. "How did they know we were in here?"

"They must have found our bikes!" Celia replied.

Jack turned to Heather. "Is there a way out of here?"

Heather rose calmly from her spot over the bed and turned away from Jack and Celia, then started toward the far end of the room.

"Wait for us!" Jack called. He grabbed Celia's hand and hurried after Heather.

They quickly and carefully crossed the room littered with equipment, furniture, and debris as they followed their ghostly guide.

"We know you're in here!" Danny called out more audibly. The bullies were getting closer.

When Jack and Celia arrived at the far end where Heather waited, Jack's flashlight shone through the ghost's body, illuminating the large locked metal door they'd failed to wrench open earlier.

"It's a dead end," he called out, looking up at Heather.

Heather paid no mind and went straight through, her body breaking apart and leaving swirls of vapor behind after disappearing completely on to the other side.

"Where did she go?" Celia asked.

"Through the door!" said Jack, amazed.

"What about us?" Celia squeaked. "We can't do that!"

Jack reached for the door's handle again and gave it a tug. It wouldn't budge. Celia grabbed hold and they both pulled and tugged on the door just as they had ten minutes earlier, but it still wouldn't open.

A sound came from the other side of the door. Jack and Celia looked at each other, wide eyed. It was hard to decipher at first—something like a low moan. They waited for a moment.

"What was that?" Celia whispered.

"Not sure," Jack replied. "A furnace maybe?"

Then it came again. This time it sounded like words. Like a voice.

"Leave here!" The voice was louder and clearer through the heavy metal door.

"Did you hear that?!" Celia squeaked.

"Leave here," Jack confirmed, frightened and curious simultaneously.

"We hear you!" called Tommy from down the hallway into Building C.

"Jack!" Celia whispered in horror, the sound of Danny and Tommy drawing nearer. "What do we do?"

"The door is locked," Jack replied. "We'll need to look around for another way out of here."

Jack had no sooner begun to search for something he could use to jimmy the lock when he heard a click inside the door and the handle turned. The door began to give way. The pair stared in terror, prepared for something possibly nightmarish to be revealed on the other side. The door stopped halfway.

Jack hesitated, then gave it a pull. It swung open with ease. He poked his head through and saw Heather waiting on the other side in a big open space with a railing behind her.

"Was that you, Heather?" Celia poked her head through.

"It was King," Heather replied softly. "He is gone now."

King? The ghost Tommy and Danny told them about?

Before he could get more details, his attention was drawn to their surroundings—they needed to get ahead of the bullies... and quick.

In the light of his flashlight, Jack could see that they were at the top landing of a dark, hollow concrete stairwell leading into an abyss of pure blackness. On the wall above them was a sign Jack recognized from Mr. Urbach's classroom—a poster with a radioactive symbol on it. The words *Fallout Shelter* were written across the bottom.

"That's a radiation symbol," Jack said.

"Where does this stairwell take us?" Celia asked, pointing her light down the stairwell.

Heather didn't respond, but instead turned and floated downward, descending quickly into the darkness below.

"I guess we'll have to follow her and find out," Jack said.

"Better than the alternative!" Celia replied.

"We told you not to come here!" Danny yelled from inside the great room behind them. Jack could see their flashlights bouncing around the walls.

"You won't get away with this!" Tommy's voice echoed into the stairwell.

"The door!" Celia yelped.

"Right!" Jack replied, and together they pushed the heavy door shut and locked it.

"Let's go!" Jack said, and they raced down the staircase into the darkness.

They caught up with Heather at the bottom, where her ghostly glow faintly lit the walls around her. Jack moved the beam of his flashlight left then right. They were in a dark, narrow hallway made of concrete blocks. It faded into darkness in either direction, with no visible windows or doors. Random bits of graffiti peppered the walls.

"The tunnels!" Jack determined.

"This way," Heather whispered as she floated down the left passage, her figure lighting the damp floor beneath them.

Jack and Celia followed, not too closely and not too far behind. Jack struggled to keep pace as a thousand thoughts flooded his mind, each fighting for attention. His brain had suddenly decided that now was a good time to try to process everything that had just happened in the past hour—they were following a ghost in a dark tunnel under an abandoned building on a property that they had no right to be on. What were we thinking?!

Their footsteps echoed in all directions. The sound was disorienting—every step echoed as if someone was following close by.

"I wonder where she's taking us?" Jack asked.

As they raced down the tunnel, Jack felt claustrophobic, anxious to escape. The feeling that they didn't belong was overwhelming.

"Leave now!" King's mumbled warning echoed in his mind.

As they continued, Jack's sense that the walls of the tunnel were closing in on them grew more unbearable. They were moving along so rapidly that he could only catch a quick glimpse inside the rooms as they dashed by: one held a giant machine, perhaps a printing press; one was filled with stalls and what looked like urinal troughs; another he thought had a dentist chair seated ominously in the middle of the cold damp space. He swore he saw a young boy staring back at him through one door he flashed his light inside.

The never-ending windowless passage contained a heaviness Jack couldn't define—it seemed to tug his soul downward, draining every last bit of energy, enthusiasm, and courage and replacing it with a profound and deeply discouraging sense of loss and hopelessness.

My mind is playing tricks on me. Jack pushed against the insanity. They needed to find the truth. They couldn't allow themselves to be frightened away, or become hollowed out like everyone who'd come before them. He had a promise to keep.

Focus! he hollered in his own mind. *You got this!*

Celia, however, was not faring as well. Jack could see the extreme terror in her eyes, her face strained with emotion as she pressed on by his side. Tears welled up in her eyes, wide and filled with sorrow and horror.

Jack stopped abruptly, pulling Celia to a halt with him.

"Are you all right?" he asked. She shook her head, mouth agape, eyes wide. The tears in her eyes settled in a thin stream along her bottom lids.

"Celia, what is it?" Jack pleaded with her to return to normal.

"I... I... it feels like we're going to die, Jack," she said, her voice trembling and cold.

"You have to push that out of your mind," Jack replied.

"I can't," she said. "Something terrible is down here. Can't you feel it?"

"I can, but we have to ignore it," Jack pleaded.

"I don't feel well," she said somberly.

"Let's keep moving—we'll be out of here soon, I'm sure," Jack said calmly, doubting his own words. He took her hand. She nodded and they continued on down the tunnel.

Heather was far out of view now and it took a while running through the darkness before they could finally make out her soft glowing shape again.

After a long, fast-paced dash through the tunnel, they reached another set of stairs leading up. And it couldn't have come soon enough—Jack noticed Celia's flashlight was starting to dim, flagging in tandem with her spirits.

Should have replaced the batteries.

"Turn off your light, Celia… the battery's dying," Jack whispered to her. Celia turned it off, then flicked off her headlamp, too.

Heather glided straight up through the stairwell, and Jack and Celia raced up the steps after her. Jack felt enormous relief to be out of the tunnels. Celia paused for a second, catching her breath and shaking her arms as if to rid herself of the tunnels' oppressive energy. The moon cast a cool blue beam through an open window, lighting the stairwell to this new and unfamiliar building.

They reached the top landing and headed through the open metal door that led out into a great open room very similar to the one in Building C. High windows with shattered glass, more overturned furniture, graffiti on the walls, and peeling dried paint and dirt were a strangely welcome sight.

Jack and Celia made their way through the obstacles of the room as Heather moved very quickly ahead of them, gliding along smoothly as though a magnetic field separated her from the floor.

They made their way into a grand foyer with boarded-up windows and a massive entrance covered by thick wooden doors. A vast checkered tile floor was at the foot of a grand staircase that led up to the second floor, with many open doors on both levels.

Stacks of old school desks were piled haphazardly in a nearby corner—remnants of the education that Linhurst falsely advertised while the children were locked away in rooms all day.

"Where are we now?" Celia questioned, breathless from the tunnels.

"The Administration Building," Jack guessed.

They maintained a fast jog to keep up with Heather.

"Where those people sealed our demise," Heather replied as she approached the large front doors and stopped.

Jack looked through a crack in the doors to see the lawn outside cast in pale blue from the moon above. The opening was just enough space for them to slip through.

Heather turned and stared at Jack and Celia, floating silently by the doors without expression.

"Where are we going now?" Jack asked.

"This is your way out," Heather replied.

"Our way out?" Jack yelped. "But we don't want to go!"

"You don't belong here," said Heather calmly. "None of us belonged here. Those poor people were trapped here because their families were told that nobody should have to deal with them at home. They were tortured, left for dead. Left behind and neglected. So many of us became sick and died when we could have been freed. What do you want here? You don't belong here! Leave! You are free!"

Heather's frantic tone made Jack anxious.

"Come with us... there must be a way for you to go on," Celia said hastily.

"I cannot," said Heather. "I must stay here and keep watch for them."

"Please," Celia pleaded.

"There are more terrifying people and things out there than you would ever have found in here. I must stay and help the men make things better."

"The men?" Jack asked.

"They are going to set us all free," Heather replied.

"What men, Heather?" Jack begged.

"They are working to make things right again," Heather said, a look of joy spreading across her face. "I am helping them by keeping people away." Her expression became angry. "Like those rotten boys who come in here to tear the place apart!"

Jack jumped as he felt a sensation in his pocket. He calmed his breathing as he realized it was his phone. He pulled it from his pocket. Dad showed on the screen as its buzzing and light interrupted the darkness. He quickly tapped the decline button.

"We know you're in here!" a voice echoed through the building. *Danny.* He and Tommy had found their way through the tunnel and into the Administration Building.

Jack's phone chirped and vibrated in his hand.

Where are you? read a text message from his dad. Jack sighed and flipped his phone to *Do Not Disturb*, shoving it back inside his pocket.

"Go!" said Heather. "I will take care of those boys."

"Go where?" Jack pleaded. "We need to know what happened here before they demolish everything!"

"You will find your way if you choose The Best Route," Heather replied.

Flashlight beams reflected from around the corner in the great room above the tunnel.

"Come on, Jack! Let's go!" Celia called.

Jack nodded and turned to Heather. "Will we see you again?"

Heather smiled mischievously, then dashed away. Jack watched the little ghost speed around the corner and into the great room toward the tunnel entrance. A few moments later, Danny and Tommy's screams echoed out into the foyer.

"Ghost!" the boys cried in unison.

Jack and Celia looked at each other, grinning ear to ear.

Jack checked the time. It was 7:13. He snapped a couple of photos inside the foyer, then he and Celia slipped through the opening in the large wooden front doors.

Once outside, they found themselves standing atop another grand porch with massive white pillars under a roof.

The stairs led down to a circular driveway and great lawn where a hefty lineup of orange bulldozers, garbage trucks, and a looming wrecking ball crane stood among construction fencing and signage. Jack snapped a few photos of their surroundings.

"Looks like they're ready to tear everything down tonight!" said Celia.

"We don't have much time," Jack replied.

In the distance, beyond the silhouetted trees, the cooling towers of the nuclear power plant continued pouring steam clouds into the air. Stars twinkled in the night sky beyond.

Just down the darkened road leading away from the Administration Building, Jack caught a glimpse of approaching headlights. He squinted for a better look, thinking his eyes were playing tricks on him. The lights grew brighter, coming up around the bend in the road, and casting a wide net along the tree line. Then he saw it—the red and blue glimmer of police rotator lights.

"Captain Hadaway!" Jack whispered loudly.

"We're in trouble!" Celia belted out. "What do we do now, Jack?!"

He looked to the left to see an open field lit by the moon and leading up to the very dark woods. Not that way.

To the right was a broad cement walkway, raised ten feet above ground level and lined by metal railings. The walkway linked the Administration Building to more buildings nearby and was part of a network of raised walkways crisscrossing the Linhurst campus.

"That way!" Jack called out.

"Are you sure?" Celia yelped in a high-pitched voice.

Jack pulled out the map from his backpack and opened it quickly. Captain Hadaway's car was slowly approaching.

"We are at the Administration Building here." He pointed to the building on the map, then traced his finger along the buildings laid out around them when his finger met up with the red line again.

"That's it!" Jack exclaimed. "The red line runs from this point on the map to the generating station. Heather said we must use The Best Route."

"I don't understand," said Celia, looking all around them.

"It must be part of the tunnels!"

"Ohhh... that's it! It makes sense now," Celia said, wide-eyed. "The Best Route is underground!"

Jack nodded affirmatively.

"But how will we get back into the tunnels again with Danny and Tommy right behind us?!"

"There must be another way in," Jack replied, gesturing to the grid of raised walkways before them.

Celia nodded in agreement and they were off.

Jack stuffed the map back into his bag as they dashed down the stairs of the Administration Building and out onto the open lawn cast in pale moonlight. They passed a row of construction fencing and bulldozers and crouched down behind a tall dumpster just as Captain Hadaway's car pulled up to the circle in front of the Administration Building. They could see his face in the side view mirror as he blazed a spotlight over the front of the building.

"He's looking for us, Jack," Celia whispered in horror.

Jack had no reply. He remained still, hoping Hadaway would move on past the Administration Building. But his hopes were immediately dashed—Captain Hadaway opened the door to his cruiser and stepped outside the vehicle. He pulled a flashlight from his side and flicked it on, then began to shine it all around.

Jack pulled Celia closer to him and carefully slid around the adjacent corner of the dumpster, barely peeking his head around to keep an eye on the police captain.

Hadaway started up the long walkway leading to the Administration Building's front entrance, where Jack and Celia had escaped only moments before.

"When he gets to the porch, let's slip into the woods," Jack whispered.

Celia nodded.

Hadaway continued up the walkway, shining his light across the lawn and through the building's shattered windows on the second story. Hadaway approached the staircase leading up to the front door when the ground began to rumble and shake, just as it had been doing all night. Hadaway was startled. He spun on his heel, shining his light back down the sidewalk toward his cruiser, lighting the construction equipment and narrowly missing Jack and Celia. He started back down the walk toward the circular drive, looking very cautious and curious at once.

Celia tugged on Jack's sweatshirt. He turned to look at her and could see the fear in her eyes.

What should we do?! her expression read loud and clear.

As Hadaway walked closer to the dumpster where Jack and Celia were hiding, a voice called out from his cruiser.

Captain Hadaway's two-way radio beeped and mumbled. He flipped off his light and made for the vehicle, reaching for the receiver through the open window.

"Now?!" Celia whispered.

Jack shook his head no. The captain was too close. Jack watched carefully as Hadaway finished the inaudible conversation and put the radio back in the vehicle. Then he opened the door, slid into the driver's seat, started the engine, and drove away.

Jack breathed a huge sigh of relief and turned to Celia. "Now!" he said.

They jumped to their feet and tore off toward the raised walkway connecting the buildings. They made their way up a quick set of stairs and sprinted hard down the long stretch toward the first building. After the long dash, they located a door, hoping to easily pull it open and head inside—but it was boarded up and completely impassible.

Jack turned and dashed toward the next building, Celia hot on his heels, running as fast as they could to reach any accessible entrance. The angle of the moon caused the wall of the walkway to cast a great shadow along their path, making everything in front of them difficult to see. As they reached the next building and found a door, they were crestfallen to find that it was also locked and completely boarded up. Jack turned and made his way to a window, then tried to pull one of the boards loose. It was no good— he wasn't strong enough. Even the windows on the main level were nailed tight.

"Let's keep going," Jack said breathlessly as they picked up their pace again. "There must be a way in." The cut on his leg was throbbing with every new step.

They turned the corner at the end of the building and continued in its shadow to the next open area of connected raised walkways, then turned again at an intersection.

Jack and Celia dashed up to the building's main entrance to find another locked door.

"Jack, we can't keep doing this," said Celia, breathless. "There must be another way. What if we go back to Building C and start there?"

Jack heard her but he kept moving, running along much faster than she could keep up. He was certain there was some other way to get back into the tunnels under Linhurst and he was determined to check every building until they found one—even if it meant starting over at Building C.

As they approached the next intersection in the walk, Jack made a sharp turn and ran straight into something solid standing in the middle of the walkway.

"Gotcha!" it called out.

Chapter 14

Uncovering Something Greater

Jack found his arm suddenly immobilized, caught in a death grip. He looked up to see the shadow of a man, the full moon blindingly bright behind his head.

"I finally found you two!" said the shadow.

"Dr. Moseley!" Celia called as she caught up with Jack. She had recognized his voice instantly.

"I've been looking all over this campus to find you and get you out of here," said the doctor-turned-janitor as he released Jack's arm.

"What brought you here? Are you trying to discover something, too?" Jack sounded relieved.

"Not at all! When I overheard you talking about Linhurst earlier today, at first I was thrilled that you were curious enough to try and figure out what happened here.

But as I wrapped up my work for the night and left the school, I quickly came to my senses and realized this is no place for young people. It never has been and never will be."

He looked down at their half-hearted costumes. "A zombie and a skateboarder?" he guessed, screwing his face up into a strange smile.

"I'm a ghost," Celia corrected.

"Threw something on to fool your folks while sneaking into Linhurst?" he asked.

The pair nodded guiltily.

"Listen, I know you mean well—and you are very curious—but we need to get out of here. This place has a tragic and horrible history, no good can come from the two of you being here."

"We can't leave yet!" Jack pleaded.

"You don't understand, Jack. Principal Thomson and Coach Slater know you're here," said Dr. Moseley. "They're coming for you."

"But we found something!" said Jack.

"It can wait. We have to go!"

"I think you'll want to see this," Celia added convincingly.

"What did you find?" Dr. Moseley asked, curiosity getting the better of him.

"Down in the tunnels is where we'll find The Best Route," said Jack.

"The Best Route? The red line on the map? You found it!"

"We think so," said Celia.

"We're looking for it," Jack added, "but we can't find a way back inside without crossing paths with Danny and Tommy."

"They did follow you here!" Dr. Moseley exclaimed. "That's what I was afraid of. Let's get out of here."

"But there's something else," Jack said, wanting to tell Mose about their encounter with Heather.

A loud snap off in the woods startled the group.

"It can wait... this way!" Mose took off down the walkway. They came to the end of the raised path and dashed down a set of stairs and back onto level ground. Jack and Celia followed him along the side of a building and around the back to a single door at the foot of a small staircase down into a cellar well.

The doorway entrance was covered by a nest of tangled vines and branches. Dr. Moseley feverishly pulled at the mass and cleared the door, then began tugging on the handle. With all his strength, he pulled until the door's lock ripped away from the rotted wood clinging to the frame, while the door slammed open against the concrete wall surrounding the steps.

He motioned for Jack and Celia to enter and slipped inside after them, then pulled the door shut behind them.

Once inside, Mose pulled a long metal flashlight from one of his big pockets and clicked it on. It cast a huge circle of bright light all around them. Jack and Celia turned on their flashlights and headlamps, too; though they provided less light than Dr. Moseley's industrial-strength version.

"You are prepared!" Dr. Moseley said.

The pair laughed nervously.

"Now, what exactly are we looking for?" Mose asked.

"The Best Route," said Jack. "We think it's somewhere along the tunnels."

"The tunnels! I never considered it!" Mose exclaimed.

The old man looked around, pointing his flashlight down the long-ravaged hallway. Doorways leading to blackened empty rooms stretched out before them like parallel lines of foreboding guards. It was quiet.

"I can't believe I'm entertaining this," Mose said nervously, his breath blowing vapor clouds into the cold air, accentuating the chill in his voice. "I haven't been in these buildings since the day they closed the place, and I never intended to return. I have nothing but horrible memories here. To be doing this in the pitch black is near insanity. You are a couple of courageous kids, I will give you that."

He looked down at Jack and Celia, who were waiting for him to lead the way. He sighed heavily then began down the hallway, marching into the darkness ahead. Jack and Celia followed closely behind.

They passed by dark, crumbling rooms filled with decaying objects. They were startled by a chair that suddenly spilled out of a room and into the hallway behind them.

Celia shrieked.

"Pay it no mind, kids!" Mose called out, forging ahead. "If you try to figure it out, your mind will only play tricks on you!"

They tore their eyes away from the wayward chair and continued down the dark hallway until they reached a hollow stairwell leading straight down into pitch darkness. Dr. Moseley paused and took a deep breath.

"What's the matter?" Jack asked.

"I have to admit these tunnels leave me feeling a bit queasy after all the tales of ghosts and vandals I've heard over the years. Hard to say what's really down there, you know?"

Jack and Celia shivered. They knew what to expect in the tunnels but were still nervous at the thought of going in again.

"We've done this before," said Celia, suddenly trying to be confident. "We got you covered."

Jack looked at her in surprise. *She's coming around.*

"This is Vincent Hall," said Dr. Moseley, who was standing under a fallout shelter sign with a radioactive symbol on it.

"Where is the fallout shelter?" Jack asked. "That's the second sign we've seen."

Dr. Moseley turned and shined his light on the sign above his head.

"During the war, they built these durable underground structures all over the country. They were meant to be safe hideaways in case of bombings, but they were never needed, thankfully. I was only in the shelter once during my tour as a new employee."

"It just doesn't make sense," said Jack. "If we go by this map, it doesn't look like the tunnels are connected with the red line. How can that be?"

"Let's get down there and see if we can find an entrance," said Dr. Moseley.

Jack and Celia nodded, then all three started carefully down the stairs. Each step was covered in bits of dust and glass, one lone sneaker lying eerily on the midway landing.

When they reached the bottom, they again found themselves inside the pitch-black tunnel system, with a choice of left or right.

"Which way?" Jack asked.

"Can we look at the map?" Dr. Moseley asked.

"The map is useless down here," Jack replied, exhausted. "We just need to find a path that intersects the tunnels. Or maybe it's something else we just aren't understanding."

Celia and Dr. Moseley stared blankly at Jack. They looked concerned by his hastiness.

"Left or right?" Jack demanded impatiently. Before giving Mose and Celia time to answer, he instinctively turned right and took off running. Given no other option, Celia and Dr. Moseley followed.

They came to a four-way intersection, and Jack paused for just a moment to inspect every direction; all three ways looked exactly the same.

Left! his brain hollered, and he took off running again.

As he tore down the tunnel, his fading flashlight and headlamp bouncing circles and beams of light everywhere, briefly crossing Dr. Moseley and Celia's beams, he looked for any hints of a new tunnel or corridor that could be The Best Route.

They reached another intersection and Jack turned left again without even thinking. He was following his instincts fully.

They soon found themselves at the foot of a stairwell, and Jack began to climb it straight up.

"Slow down, Jack!" Celia called out below him, but he continued, fully immersed in intuition. They were finally onto something, and he was desperate to discover it.

He hit the top landing and, to his surprise, was met with a fully open, rusted metal door. He dashed inside and found himself inside a large, dark room. His flashlight and headlamp were too dim to illuminate the space, so he waited for Dr. Moseley to arrive.

"Where are we, Jack?" Celia asked breathlessly as she joined him.

Dr. Moseley entered and as the beam of his heavy-duty light reached the surfaces of the room and its contents, it became clear why Jack's light hadn't been strong enough.

"The theater!" Dr. Moseley mused.

They were standing under the overhang of a balcony inside a large open theater. The theater's stage was dressed with tattered maroon curtains. An ornate chandelier hung in the middle of the room, high over the first floor where rows of folding movie theater chairs were lying scattered across the floor as though an earthquake had hit the room.

"We need to find a way down there," Jack said.

"Why do you want to go down there?" Dr. Moseley asked, as he caught his breath.

"We need to find The Best Route!" Jack responded, desperation growing in his voice.

"This building is self-contained," Dr. Moseley replied. "Other than this entrance, only the doors above onto the balcony can get you inside the theater."

"Then let's get out of here!" Jack said, racing back through the large metal doors and back down into the tunnel.

He backtracked over their previous route, Dr. Moseley and Celia lagging behind him as he ran at full speed, ignoring all the mysterious dripping sounds, ominous graffiti, and occasional blackened doorway.

He approached another intersection and turned left again, then soon found himself at another staircase. He waited for Dr. Moseley and Celia to get within distance of him, then raced up the stairs where the moon shone brightly through a set of high windows at the midway landing.

Jack reached the top of the steps and found a double door shut tightly. He tucked his flashlight inside his sweatshirt to free both hands and gave it a tug. Nothing.

Dr. Moseley and Celia were soon by his side and they grabbed the handle along with Jack and started to pull, leaning back and tugging hard. The door gave way suddenly and the trio found themselves lying on their backs.

They hopped up, brushed themselves off, then followed Jack through the open doors. They were inside another long corridor, this one with just a few doors, most of them closed.

Jack approached the first door and stopped in front of it. The door had a solid, rusted metal surface and a very small window slit in the top portion. He shone his light on it, deeply curious.

"The padded rooms," Dr. Moseley whispered in horror.

"Padded rooms?" Celia replied weakly.

"Some of the residents would become violent or—according to Slater or Thomson—in need of a little downtime," Dr. Moseley replied ominously. "They were sent here."

Jack tried the door but it wouldn't open.

He turned around and walked to the door directly behind him and gave the knob a turn. It clicked slowly open and he swung the door wide, then shined his fading light inside the space.

All around him, thick square cushions were laid out in an endless grid of padding from floor to ceiling and running the length of the walls. The same for the floor, where a tattered and stained mattress laid lifeless in the center of the room. A torn straitjacket was draped eerily over the mattress.

"Nothing to see in here that won't just give us nightmares," Dr. Moseley said nervously, then he pulled the door shut. "Let's move on, Jack."

Jack nodded, shook his head to clear his thoughts, then tore off for the tunnels again.

He raced down the steps and back onto their trail in the tunnel.

"Jack!" Celia cried out, far behind him. "We can't keep doing this!"

Jack ran faster and harder than he had all night. The pain in his leg was searing hot now. Sweat had formed on his brow and felt as though it was actually freezing to his skin from the temperature growing colder by the minute.

Jack turned another corner and found his light was too dim to see farther ahead than a few steps. Then his light flickered a few times and went dark. His headlamp was out, too, and Jack had to stop dead. He could no longer see anything in front of him. He put his hand out to feel for the walls of the tunnel; he couldn't make out his fingertips, even with his hand directly in front of his face.

"Jack, where are you?!" Celia cried out from behind him.

Jack panicked for a moment, unable to respond. He tapped his flashlight in his hand, hoping to get it working again. Nothing.

"Jack! Which way did you go?" Celia cried out.

Just before Jack could respond for help, his necklace suddenly grew brighter than ever. He was engulfed by a warm sensation of deep care, as if he was being cradled. The soft voice of a woman called into his ears from a distance, "It's okay Jackie. I'm with you."

"Mom? "Jack said aloud.

There was no reply. Suddenly he could hear voices again, but not the woman's voice. It was Celia and Dr. Moseley. They were getting closer.

But where is that voice coming from?

Celia and Dr. Moseley neared, their lights rounded the corner, landing on Jack, who was standing sheepishly with a dumbfounded look on his face.

"Are you all right?" Celia asked.

He shook his light at her to show that it had gone dark.

"We got you," she replied with a smile.

They continued onward a bit more and found themselves at another stairwell. Jack stopped dead and growled in frustration.

"What is it?" Moseley asked.

"We're back where we started!"

"He's right," Celia cried, pointing at the fallout shelter sign at the top of the stairwell. "Now what?"

Jack shook his head, kicking the dirt below his feet with frustration.

"What building are we in, Dr. Moseley?"

"Vincent Hall," Mose replied.

Jack pulled his map out and located Vincent Hall, then ran his finger over to the red line from the Administration Building to the generating station.

"How are we going to find this red line without a map of the tunnels?" Jack grumbled.

"Certainly, not by running around in circles," Celia scoffed.

"I have an idea," said Mose. "Does one of you have a compass?"

"I have one on my phone," said Celia.

She pulled out her phone and opened the compass app, then pointed it north.

"Looks like the red line runs directly southeast of here," said Dr. Moseley peeking over her shoulder and looking at the map in Jack's hands.

"Use the compass," said Dr. Moseley.

Jack pulled the map out again to check their bearings.

"Okay, so we should be here," Jack said with a more even tone in his voice. He pointed to the map then continued, "We need to go southeast to intersect with The Best Route."

Celia held her phone out in front of her.

"We need to go left!" she declared.

Dr. Moseley turned left down the dark hall followed closely by Celia and Jack. Once again, they could hear their footsteps echoing against the walls of the cavernous tunnel, making it sound as if someone was following them. The tunnel came to a three-way intersection and Jack stopped and asked Celia to shine a light on the map.

"We must be right around here," he said, pointing to an unlabeled area on the drawing.

"The red line crosses near here," Celia noted, looking over his shoulder at the map.

The trio searched all around, but they saw no new doorway or entrance.

"Let's try this way," Jack said, and started left down the tunnel.

Out of the blue, a loud bang roared through the tunnel. They froze in their steps.

"What was that?" Celia whispered eerily.

"Dunno," said Dr. Moseley.

He pointed his flashlight in every direction but met only with pitch black, and the hint of an occasional door ajar with an equally dark room behind.

"Who's there?" Mose hollered.

Jack and Celia were spooked.

"Please don't yell," Celia begged, her eyes welling up with fear.

"I'm sorry," Mose said calmly. "I'm hoping what we heard was something falling over on its own and not someone following us."

"Leave here," a bone-chilling voice echoed from the pitch blackness ahead of them.

It was low and hollow—barely audible, but they could understand it.

"King," Celia said, her voice trembling.

"Did you ask us to leave?" Dr. Moseley called out.

There was no reply.

"We are trying to find our way out," Mose called out again.

"LEAVE HERE!" the voice repeated, very clearly this time. It sounded furious.

"Who are you?" Mose awaited a reply. "Why do you want us out?" He paused for a response. "Can you help us find the hidden tunnel?" Still no answer.

"That had to be King," Jack whispered.

"Who?" Mose replied.

"The spirit who haunts the tunnels," Celia added nervously. "Danny and Tommy told us about him."

Jack cleared his throat. "We mean no harm, King!" he called out. "We are just trying to find our way out."

The trio waited for a moment for a reply, but there was still no response. Jack looked down and realized his necklace was glowing—but only for a second, then it went dark again.

"Let's keep moving," Mose whispered.

They began down the tunnel again, very intentionally now. Dr. Moseley walked close to the wall, running his hand along the blocks and feeling for breaks or uneven points.

"Search everywhere," Mose said. "If this Best Route really exists, there must be a hidden door or something."

Though they ran their hands along the walls and pointed their lights at every nook and cranny, they could find no sign of a door or hidden passage.

In the midst of their searching, they came upon a radioactive sign leaning against the wall, clean and undamaged.

"Does that seem odd to you guys?" Celia asked.

"Yes, it does look out of place down here," Mose replied. "And it's in mint condition—like someone left it here yesterday."

Celia shined her flashlight at the sign. As they drew nearer to it, they could see more signs stacked in a pile on the debris-covered concrete floor.

"That's a lot of radiation signs," said Jack.

"Why on earth would these be down here?" Celia added.

"Maybe something to do with the fallout shelter?" Jack questioned.

"Those signs don't say fallout shelter," said Celia.

"If I'm remembering correctly now, the fallout shelter is just ahead," said Dr. Moseley. "But that doesn't explain why these are here."

He wandered closer to the signs and pointed his light all around. As he looked down the tunnel farther, his light struck more peculiar things—piles of wood boards and studs lined the hallway. Shovels and picks stood against the tunnel wall alongside large digging equipment.

"They're making more tunnels!" Jack called out.

"Yes, I think you're right, Jack," Dr. Moseley replied with wonder in his voice. "But for what purpose? These buildings are abandoned and have been vacated for years!"

"Maybe something to do with the demolition they're starting tomorrow?" Celia said.

"Possibly. Whatever it is, it's very suspicious," Mose added.

Suddenly they heard a small sweet voice nearby. Mose didn't seem to notice it. Celia and Jack recognized it immediately.

"Father?" the voice repeated softly. A glowing blue orb floated past Jack and Celia.

Dr. Moseley still didn't hear the soft voice calling out to him—he was trying to piece together the reason for the equipment and signs they'd stumbled upon.

Jack turned to see Celia right on his heels and he smashed right into her.

"Watch out!" she snapped.

"Oops... sorry!"

Jack pointed beyond Celia. Heather's soft glowing form was appearing from the glowing orb. She paused just behind her father, her amorphous lines gracefully filling out into a clear human figure, and Jack and Celia could see that she had a gracious smile on her face.

Jack and Celia were in awe at the sight of Dr. Moseley investigating the materials on the ground and not the least bit aware of his daughter's presence.

"Maybe this is The Best Route," said Dr. Moseley, wandering around the signs and equipment, investigating with great curiosity. "Perhaps we found it—but what is it for?"

He ran his light along a framework of studs that supported freshly dug earth in the distance that looked like an old mining tunnel.

Jack and Celia giggled.

"What's so funny?" Dr. Moseley questioned as he turned around.

"That's the other thing," said Celia merrily.

He found himself face to face with the translucent glowing form of a little girl, staring up at him while floating gently in midair. He gasped and dropped his flashlight, then placed his hands over his mouth to muffle a scream. He looked like he was running out of air.

"It's okay!" Celia called out. She raised a hand in the air as if to comfort Dr. Moseley from afar.

Dr. Moseley's flashlight lay in the dirt below Heather, amplifying the little ghost's aura. He began to see a face in the glowing shape, and his eyes widened.

"Is it you?" said Dr. Moseley in a weak, trembling voice.

Heather nodded and moved closer to her father. His expression changed quickly from fear to joy to sadness, and he started to cry. He moved in to hug her but pulled back, then turned to Jack and Celia, looking bewildered and enlightened at once.

"I'm so sorry about what happened to you, sweetheart," said Dr. Moseley, beginning to sob.

"Father," Heather replied.

"It wasn't supposed to be this way," Mose continued. "I was here to help the children. You were here to help them, too! But you got sick and I wasn't there for you."

"Father—it's okay," Heather replied softly. "I am helping them to be free."

Dr. Moseley sobbed more, and Jack and Celia choked back tears. It was hard to imagine that the old man they had only recently learned was not a former patient of Linhurst was now standing in front of them speaking with the ghost of his deceased daughter.

Dr. Moseley wiped the tears from his eyes and looked to Jack and Celia.

"How did you find her?"

"She found us," said Jack.

Dr. Moseley turned back to his daughter, soft tears of joy and sadness streamed down his face.

"I... I... don't know what to say." He paused. "How are you?" He chuckled and shook his head. "That was a stupid question..."

Celia and Jack chuckled.

Dr. Moseley was trembling all over. "Heather—I miss you so much."

He reached out his hand to touch her and watched his fingers disappear through her body. Then he ran his hand down along her hair and small wisps of vapor floated off her glowing body—a few sparkles of light flickering into the air—changing her shape for a moment then coming back together. Dr. Moseley stared in awe, trying to comprehend what he was witnessing.

"Heather, we've looked everywhere but we can't find The Best Route," Jack said, carefully breaking the moment.

Heather turned to Jack and Celia then gave them a huge smile.

"Come... I will show you," she replied.

She passed the group and headed in the opposite direction of the signs, equipment, and lumber. They followed her.

"I'm coming!" Dr. Moseley called out as he picked up his flashlight.

Heather drifted down the tunnel and turned at the intersection, then stopped abruptly. She floated softly, facing the wall and staring at it.

"What is it, Heather?" Dr. Moseley asked as he caught up. "Why did you stop?"

"This is it," she replied.

"A hidden door?" Jack asked.

Heather nodded, then placed her open palm on the wall. Without a word, she drifted through to the other side.

"We certainly can't enter like that!" Mose said preposterously.

"Tell us about it!" Celia laughed.

Dr. Moseley approached the wall and began to inspect it closely. He shined his light all along the wall face and felt around for imperfections.

"Aha!" he called out.

The old man followed a deep crack in the wall, running his fingers down toward the ground. As he did this, a seam began to appear. He got his fingers inside the deepening crack and, with a good tug, he pulled an entire portion of tunnel wall open like a door. It was perfectly hidden among the long row of concrete blocks. It even had hinges. Dr. Moseley stepped back and joined Jack and Celia. All three stood in surprise.

On the other side, Heather was floating with her arms opened out, showcasing the space. Her soft glow lit a tunnel unlike the one they were standing in. This one looked hand dug, with no solid walls, just damp earth and roots.

"This is The Best Route," she said with a big smile.

"Wow," said Celia, marveling at the space. "We found it!"

"Thanks to your daughter, Dr. Moseley," Jack added.

Mose smiled proudly. "This goes to the generating station?"

Heather nodded.

"But why is it The Best Route?" Jack asked.

Before she could answer, they heard a loud bang down the tunnel.

"Because it's going to get us out of here, that's why!" Dr. Moseley proclaimed as he came up behind Jack and Celia and gave them a little nudge through the open door.

They heard voices down the main tunnel. Danny and Tommy were back.

"How do they keep finding us?!" Celia moaned.

"I'll take care of them—you kids get out of here," said Dr. Moseley.

"No, Father," Heather interrupted. "Follow the route."

"But, Heather... it's not safe!"

"I have done this before—it is my job."

Heather dashed past him and out into the main tunnel, then raced toward the stairwell until her light was out of sight. A few moments later, they heard Tommy holler, "Not again!"

"I love you!" Dr. Moseley whispered proudly after her. He turned to Jack and Celia. "Let's go!"

"Not so fast!" called a new voice.

They turned around to see a bright flashlight pointed directly at them.

"I had a feeling you wouldn't listen to your elders," the voice said as it drew nearer.

"Principal Thomson," Jack whispered.

"John?" Dr. Moseley called toward the light.

Jack, Celia, and Dr. Moseley froze in place, the principal's flashlight blinding them.

"Dr. Moseley," replied Principal Thomson as he lowered his flashlight and they could see his face. "I am not surprised to see you here helping these two—you always had a soft spot for children."

"John, I came here to get these children to safety," Dr. Moseley said firmly. "They shouldn't be here."

"I agree—they should have listened," Principal Thomson replied. "Why would you bring them here? What are you looking for?"

"I found an old map years ago and placed it in a book at the library's historical section," Dr. Moseley explained. "I was hoping someone could help figure it out—and someone did. But it was Jack and Celia here who found it. I came here knowing they would sneak inside Linhurst, but you know as well as I that this is no place for children."

Principal Thomson shined his light down the tunnel toward the signs and equipment.

"I see you've found more than you should have," Thomson concluded.

"What do you mean, John?" Dr. Moseley asked.

Principal Thomson let out a sinister laugh.

"Please, John... help me get these children to safety."

"Unfortunately, I can't do that, now can I?" Principal Thomson replied as he inched toward them.

"Wait... John... what are you saying?" Mose pleaded calmly. "You're a good man. Help me get them out of here."

"Now that you've found our operation, I can't just let you go spilling the beans. This was all supposed to be buried under the demolition. Now it looks like you will go with it."

"John, you're mad!" Mose shouted, incredulous.

"I have to hand it to you, Mose, you always were a clever one. Do you really think I don't know how you've been trying to stick your nose in our business all these years? Ever since the state closed this place and I gave you a job, you've been snooping around the school, trying to dig up dirt. Well, now you have, quite literally!"

The principal shined his flashlight down the tunnel at the equipment.

"I haven't seen it in person until tonight." Thomson sounded impressed. "I have to say it's coming along nicely."

"What have you done, John?" Dr. Moseley pleaded.

"Tell us the truth!" Celia snarled, incensed.

"What are you building here?" Jack pushed.

"There you go with that curiosity of yours, Alexander. You're just like your mother," Principal Thomson snapped as he pointed his flashlight right in Jack's face. "I warned you about this! I told you not to go snooping into other people's business."

"Leave him alone!" Celia cried out.

"But it was you, Mose." Principal Thomson pointed his light back at Dr. Moseley, sounding quite enraged. "You were one of those people who protested the nuclear power plant, but you had no idea what it came with."

"What does the nuclear power plant have to do with this?" Mose asked.

"That deal would have brought hundreds of millions of dollars to Spring Dale," Thomson raged. "One little mistake and we had to put the whole plan on hold... cover it up. Now that this place has been forgotten and lost to the ravages of time, we can finally finish the work and restore our town to its former glory."

"What kind of a deal did you make?" questioned Dr. Moseley.

"Free energy, Mose!" Principal Thomson laughed madly. "Once we demolish the buildings above and lease the property to the power plant, we have all this space to store nuclear waste. In return, we get all the power we need. With two more reactors on the way, you wouldn't believe the potential for our town!"

"I suppose Mayor Helowski had a hand in this, too?" said Mose.

"That bumbling idiot?!" Principal Thomson laughed hysterically. "He would sooner host a bake sale than strike a deal like this."

"You are going to use the tunnels to move and store nuclear waste from the power plant and you think nobody will find out?" Jack hollered.

"I knew I couldn't get one over on this boy!" Principal Thomson laughed. "You are such a smart little guy. But now let's be sure you don't go taking this secret out of here."

Principal Thomson started for Jack and Celia, but before he could take more than a few steps, a sudden flash of green light disrupted his trajectory. A massive glowing body engulfed the principal in a furious twister of light and wind, sparks flying every which way.

"Leave now!" a voice screamed from the entity.

"King!" Celia shouted.

"Sam King?!" Principal Thomson screamed in surprise. "It's true!"

Principal Thomson struggled against the ghost, his face contorted in terror. He broke free from the apparition and raced down the tunnel. The figure dashed after him and out of sight.

Dr. Moseley grabbed hold of Jack and Celia's hands.

"Come on, kids. We're getting out of here!"

Mose raced them through the open door of the tunnel. They dashed inside the earthen tunnel, and Dr. Moseley turned and quickly pulled the door tightly behind them. He spotted a large wooden beam against the wall.

"Jack, give me a hand," he said.

Together, they heaved it up and dropped it into two metal brackets straddling the door frame inside.

"That should hold them off for a while," Dr. Moseley said breathlessly. "We have to go and alert the authorities."

The pair nodded and all three took off down the handmade tunnel.

Celia's light was losing power quickly as they raced through the damp, dark tunnel. The walls, ceilings, and floors were wet, with loose rocks and roots all about. Their feet splashed through puddles as they ran against the cold, musty air. The man-made tunnel was barely wide enough for Celia and Jack to run side by side—nothing like the concrete tunnels running between the other buildings.

Does this ever end? Jack's legs ached from running for what felt like an eternity along the muddy passage.

"Finally, a way out!" Celia yelled as a faint light appeared just ahead.

The light was coming from a small opening at ground level covered by a metal grate. Jack knelt on one knee and pushed it aside, then squeezed through. He grabbed Celia's hand and helped her through to the other side. They both assisted Dr. Moseley—who became stuck for a moment—through to the other side and onto his feet. They found themselves inside the main tunnel system again, at the foot of yet another stairwell.

"Going up!" Dr. Mosely said, pointing his flashlight up toward a landing glowing in the moonlight pouring through a tall window above.

They dashed up the steps only to meet with a giant, rusted metal door. All three grabbed hold and pulled. It wouldn't budge.

"Again!" Mose yelled.

As they pulled on the massive handle of the door with all their might, the ground began to shake with the giant inhale they hadn't felt in some time. They pulled and pulled on the door as the ground shook more and more. Finally, the door started to give against the rust and dirt that had built up over years without use.

A faint glow filtered in through the crack in the door, then, once they pulled it fully open, they were blinded by a flood of green light. It lasted for only a second then the giant exhale came and went and all went pitch black and silent.

Once their eyes adjusted to the darkness, they found themselves inside the generating station. The bright full moon shone in through thin slits in the boards covering the tall windows set high off the ground. Walls of solid brick in the tall, congested warehouse held a dizzying web of rusted beams, piping, ductwork, valves and wiring.

A series of metal staircases and catwalks hung high above, nestled around the smokestack that shot outside toward the sky.

In the middle of the station stood a massive machine that looked at first like some type of new-age artwork made of old army equipment parts. Twelve missile-like projections protruded from a central spherical body. Gauges, valves, pipes, and wires covered the dull, silvery surface, pieced together with first-sized rivets. The entire contraption was held in place by a tripod of thick steel beams bolted to the floor. Several handcarts stood around the base of the machine, along with stacks of wooden pallets, spools of wire, and a tool bench scattered with various hammers, socket wrenches, and other unidentifiable tools.

Everything except the strange machine was covered with a thick layer of dust.

Chapter 15

Men at Work

At first glance, Mose and Jack jumped back—it looked like a giant man leaning in to attack them. Celia aimed the beam of her flashlight at a twisted metal structure directly in front of them.

Jack let out a sigh of relief. "Nothing to worry about," he said, though his heart was still pounding in his throat.

"We have to be careful in here," said Dr. Moseley. "These buildings are on the brink of collapse. Watch your step and don't touch anything—we just need to find a way out of the building and get to my truck."

"The green flash of light came from in here, Dr. Moseley!" Jack interrupted. "We can't leave yet."

As Jack looked around the building, something peculiar but recently familiar caught his eye. Several small blueish-green orbs began to appear, growing to the size of human heads. They hovered brightly in a nearby corner of the darkened station. At first, there were only one or two, then three more appeared. The balls slowly transformed, taking shape into a group of seven human figures.

Everything remained still for a moment. Jack, Celia, and Dr. Moseley stood frozen, taking in the eerie scene. Who are they? Are they threatening or friendly? Slowly, a few of the figures began drifting toward the trio of living humans.

"Jack?" Celia whimpered. "What do we do now?"

Jack had no reply this time—he wasn't entirely sure what to make of it.

As the spirits drew closer, they could make out distinct human faces within the glowing bodies.

"It's the men from the photo!" Celia called out suddenly.

"You're right!" Jack replied, awestruck. The image of Heather holding a daisy in her hand, flanked by a group of men in work clothes, surfaced in his mind.

"I know them!" Dr. Moseley gasped.

He reached inside his jacket and pulled the photo from his pocket. He opened it, then looked from it to the line of faces in front of him until he came upon the tallest ghost.

"Leonard, is that you?" he asked in astonishment.

The biggest ghost pulled away from the group and drifted toward Dr. Moseley, coming to a stop and hovering directly in front of him.

"Leonard—it is you!" Dr. Moseley whispered in disbelief. He looked around to the other men again. "You are all here," he said in amazement. "Sam. Jake. Henry Hanes."

Dr. Moseley looked to each ghost, then back to his photo for confirmation. Each ghost returned a nod or smile in acknowledgment.

"Ernie. Dobbs. Theo."

Theo gave a thumbs up. They were all wearing matching button-down shirts and work pants just like in the photo.

"Who are they? Why are they here?" Jack asked.

"They were all residents at Linhurst," said Dr. Moseley. "Like many of our residents, they didn't need to be here—they were all perfectly capable. Why they're here in this generating station…" he shook his head in disbelief, "…I can't tell you."

"Some of them are so young," Celia said quietly, compassion in her voice.

Dr. Moseley looked back at Leonard's ghost in front of him. Even in spirit, Leonard was an imposing figure—tall and strong. Looks like he could build bridges with his bare hands.

"Leonard was close to Heather." Dr. Moseley stared kindly at the giant. Leonard smiled back. "They called him a child of Linhurst… a child!" Dr. Moseley laughed bittersweetly, then moved closer to Leonard.

"He was a man. A kind man. And they kept him locked up, bound to this place his entire life for a simple and curable speech impediment. With help from a speech therapist, he could easily have lived on his own right in Spring Dale. Instead, Leonard worked all over this property—in the garden, in the kitchen, the laundry. I even think he milked cows in the barn!"

Dr. Moseley turned to Celia and Jack. His eyes were alight with memories.

"Bath day was Saturday, and he would help carry the immobile residents down to the washrooms. He did so much for others."

He gave Leonard a smile.

"Th- thank you, M-Mose," Leonard replied softly, his voice stuttering.

Dr. Moseley looked at each of the spirits again, trying to take it all in.

"I remember you all worked so hard around here," he said. "Like the time Dr. McKenzie got stuck in the mud delivering supplies to Building B; Henry Hanes and Dobbs dragged his truck out with their bare hands. I remember seeing Theo spend countless hours in the gardens keeping the vegetables healthy and strong. Sam and Jake, you two spent a lot of time working on the energy problems we had. You were certain you could keep this furnace up and running," he gestured around the old station, "and sometimes I'm sure you performed miracles, getting this mess to generate any heat at all!"

He turned to Jack and Celia. "Heather was quite fond of them all—she really looked up to them and admired their good spirit."

"Who is the man in the back corner?" Celia asked.

Dr. Moseley looked behind the men to the last ghost who remained in the far corner. This apparition appeared older, with a wrinkled face and high hairline. He wore a pair of wireframe glasses that rested on the end of his nose. His clothing differed from that of the other ghosts—a simple outfit of corduroys, a collared shirt, and suspenders. He was small and thin, and the suspenders looked as if they were keeping him from slumping completely forward. He twiddled his thumbs nervously.

Dr. Moseley's mouth fell open in recognition. "Max Vidar?!"

"It is Professor Vidar," replied Theo. "He will help us be free."

Vidar's ghost nodded, and Dr. Moseley worked his way across the dark, debris-ridden generating station to meet up with him, sidestepping old metal pipes and fallen boards strewn across the dusty floor. When he reached the old scientist, Mose tried to shake his hand but it went through the familiar man's spirit, small sparks of light flicking off his ghostly figure.

"Celia," said Jack, his eyes wide. "That's the man Mr. Urbach told us about today!"

Celia nodded in recognition.

"Max!" Dr. Moseley exclaimed. "I thought you left town." He stared in awe at Max Vidar's spirit, searching for words. "Max... I'm sorry... but what happened to you?"

"I am here to finish my work," Max Vidar began, his voice distant at first, as though echoing through a cave.

"What do you mean?" Dr. Moseley asked, bewildered.

"I have spent ages in this generating station, preparing for this very evening," Max replied, smiling.

"You mean your work on the furnace?" Dr. Moseley asked, confused.

"Blast that old furnace; it was just a ruse!" Max quipped. "I have always had a much better solution, but they insisted on keeping me from it. It all changes tonight!"

"That's right—you tried to get a fusion reactor working," Jack gushed, rushing over to Dr. Moseley's side.

"Young man, did you say I tried to get the reactor working?!" shouted Max. In the blink of an eye, he was directly in front of Jack.

"That's what it said in our science book!"

The ghost of Max Vidar smiled and laughed softly. His voice was strong and clear. "That's what they're saying, is it? Well, I can tell you now, young man, I did get it working! The science was sound, but they wouldn't help me. I just needed to sustain the reaction long enough to produce enough energy to power the whole campus. I was so close!"

"What happened?" Mose asked.

Vidar's form was glowing brightly. "At first I couldn't understand why they would not gladly accept a solution for the energy crisis ailing this town. You remember it, Dr. Moseley, I am sure. All those cold, dark winter months without electricity or heat. It affected us here at Linhurst much more than Spring Dale residents, but things were bad all around. It was only after the nuclear power plant was approved and construction nearly complete on that monstrosity that I learned of the deal that was made."

"To bring free energy to Linhurst!" Dr. Moseley guessed.

"Correct!" replied Vidar. "The people at the nuclear power plant offered free energy—but at a terrible cost. Slater, Thomson and the others took the deal—even after I begged them to let me finish my work. They agreed to create a nuclear waste storage area in the fallout shelter beneath Linhurst, completely off the books. Then they tasked these poor men here with constructing a tunnel."

"We were right, Dr. Moseley!" Jack yelped. "They're building a tunnel from the plant to the fallout shelter."

"They had you preparing to store nuclear waste beneath Linhurst?" Dr. Moseley asked Professor Vidar. "But these tunnels aren't secure—they were never built to house that kind of material. It could have devastating effects for our town!"

"It certainly could," replied Max. "They spun their tale convincingly for the public—that the process of generating energy through nuclear fission was safe and clean—but it isn't. The waste it produces is terribly dangerous and will last for many, many generations. Not to mention the potential for nuclear meltdown. It is nothing compared with the safe alternative of fusion energy. But it was people like Thomson and Slater who made me out to be crazy and why I ended up a prisoner of this place."

Max slowly made his way over to the men, and Mose and Jack followed, stepping carefully amid the rubble.

"I was the squeaky wheel, and I made too much noise for their liking," Max continued as he gathered around his fellow spirits. "Eventually Slater told me to stop working in the generating station or I would be confined to a padded room as punishment. After a little thought, I agreed to their demands—but only temporarily. I came up with a new plan, but I couldn't do it alone. I decided to show Leonard and the men my reactor project and asked for their help. I knew that given the choice, these good souls..." he gestured to the glowing spirits surrounding him "...would never have played any part in Slater and Thomson's dirty work. They were on board immediately."

"So the men dug the tunnel that brought us here?" asked Jack.

"You have it, young man!" said Max. "To get to the generating station undetected, we had to create our own secret tunnel or risk being seen on the grounds. We worked quickly to excavate the hidden passage under the guise of working on the storage construction project. It allowed us to begin in earnest on the fusion reactor. Ohm Route, as I liked to call it, became The Best Route."

"The Best Route!" Celia yelped.

"You wrote that on the map?!" Jack called out.

Max smiled conspiratorially.

"What happened next, Max?" Dr. Moseley asked. "How did you... what happened that you..."

"How did you become ghosts?!" Celia blurted out.

"They put pressure on us to speed up the dig to the fallout shelter. One day, we were making our way to the station..." Max paused "...when there was a collapse in the dig. We had no way out. No one came for us."

Celia gasped; Dr. Moseley shook his head with great sadness.

"I'm so sorry," Celia said sadly.

"Max, they are planning to demolish the buildings starting tomorrow," Dr. Moseley said.

"Yes, I am aware of their plans," said Max in an unexpectedly chipper tone. "Their workers come sneaking onto this property often enough. We've had to be careful—waiting until very late at night to continue our project."

"How do you plan to get this working?" asked Mose.

"Even in this form," Max held out his translucent arms, wisps of glowing plasma trailing away as he did, "I am still a scientist. Many said it was impossible because we would never mimic the sun's natural power to fuse two hydrogen atoms into one singular helium atom. This kind of power could release ten times the energy of the old nuclear power plant towers that are pumping out massive amounts of radiation day in and day out. With unlimited fresh water nearby, no nuclear waste, and so many other benefits, the acceleration of the particles at such high speed and a sustainable temperature will result in…"

"Is he speaking English?" Celia chirped uncontrollably. Max stopped to glare at her, then composed himself, seemingly readying for common speech as though he had to do this a thousand times in the past.

"We've discovered how to make this reactor run on energy beyond the human realm—and we are closer than ever. After tonight, I am certain we will all be free!"

Something caught Max's eye and he moved toward Jack, peering down at the amulet around his neck. He reached out a ghostly hand and touched the sun and peace symbol reverently. The amulet glowed brightly at the touch of the scientist's translucent fingertips.

"Your timing is perfect, my boy," Max said, looking Jack in the eye. "You have just what we need to complete our work this evening and move everyone on to the next world."

Jack looked curiously from Max to Celia to Dr. Moseley back to Max. *What does he mean, I have what he needs?*

Max motioned for the men to join him as he floated toward the middle of the station. Suddenly the headlights from a car illuminated the shattered windows of the generating station.

"Time to go!" Dr. Moseley turned to Jack and Celia. "My truck is just outside."

"Wait!" Jack interrupted. He pointed to Max and the men. "What are they doing?"

"Hit it, guys!" Max Vidar called to the ghosts.

They gathered around the large machine that Jack had noticed earlier in the middle of the room.

"What is that?" Celia asked.

"Max's fusion reactor, I'm guessing," Dr. Moseley replied in awe.

"It's now or never!" Max called out.

The men took up positions around the machine and began inspecting gauges, checking wires, tightening knobs and bolts. They drifted around the massive machine, adjusting and fiddling with all the parts and components.

"Jack, are you in there?" a man's voice called from outside the building.

"Oh, no! It's my dad!" Jack said, as he felt the blood draining from his face.

"Go ahead, Jack," Dr. Moseley patted him on the back. "Answer him."

Jack swallowed hard. "Dad!" he called out after a few moments of hesitation. "We're in here!"

Jack and Celia took off and sidestepped debris and rubble to reach the giant double doors of the generating station and attempted to push them open, but they were rusted shut and boarded up. Jack turned and headed to the nearest window and called for his dad to come in.

"Jack... Celia... are you okay?" Dad asked as he approached the window.

"Yes, we're okay," said Jack.

"Hi, Mr. Alexander!" said Celia.

"Call me Henry, please!"

"Sorry," Celia replied. "Mr. Henry, you have to come see this!"

"You two had me worried sick," Dad said, his eyes catching the torn flannel tied around Jack's jeans. "Jack, what happened to your leg?!"

"I'm okay. It's just a small cut," he replied. "But wait a minute, Dad, how did you know we were here?"

"I saw Nate walking around the harvest festival and—" Henry began.

"Nate! I knew we couldn't trust him!" Celia groaned.

"Hey, I heard that!" called a voice from behind Dad.

Nate appeared from the darkness, holding a ratty pillow case that looked half filled with treats. He was wearing a giant homemade pumpkin costume—plush orange fabric engulfed his entire body and a green hat that looked like a stem perched crookedly on the top of his head. Clumsily, Nate began to pull himself in through the window. Henry gave him a lift up and over. Once inside, he fell to the floor, looking for all the world like a rotten pumpkin.

"Nate, you came here, too?" Jack said in disbelief

Dad pulled himself through the window.

"Jack, we were really worried about you." Dad looked at Celia pointedly. "Nate did a really good job keeping your secret, but I pressed him until he folded and told me you were coming to Linhurst."

"I really didn't spill the beans this time, guys. Honestly!" Nate pleaded breathlessly, pulling himself off the floor and brushing off his pumpkin costume.

Jack and Celia glared at him.

"Okay, I mean, I guess I did eventually, but your dad threatened to call my parents."

Celia huffed in frustration.

"Easy, guys," Dad said, calmly. "Nate's just looking out for you two."

"You guys said you were coming here, but I totally didn't believe it at first," Nate added, looking all around the station. "You're nuts going in alone—this place is scary!"

"It's a good thing he told me you were here," Dad said sternly. "This is a dangerous place."

"We're all right, Dad," Jack replied. "Plus, we found some things."

"That's nice, Jack, but it's time to go home," Dad said firmly. "Also—I saw Danny Slater and Tommy Thomson slip into Linhurst earlier tonight. I'm sure they're up to no good."

"You saw them come after us?" Jack asked.

"Yes, and I swore I heard them say your name and Celia's, but I took it as my ears playing tricks. After I ran into Nate and he told me you were coming here, I decided I would go get the car and come looking for you. That's when I saw a blue pickup truck enter and drive down the road onto the property. There's never been so much activity here!"

"That was my truck you saw, Henry." Dr. Moseley held out a hand in greeting.

"Mose, is that you?" Dad asked, squinting over Jack's shoulder. "What are you doing here?"

"Long story, Henry," replied Dr. Moseley.

"You know each other?" Jack asked.

Dr. Moseley approached and gave Dad a hearty handshake. "Yes, we know each other," said Dr. Moseley enthusiastically. "Jack, I had a feeling you were Henry and Amanda's son!"

"You knew my mom, too?!" Jack looked at Mose, eyes wide with surprise.

"When the town began planning the construction of the nuclear power plant," Dad said, "your mom and I protested with Dr. Moseley and others. None of us believed we should have one of those facilities here in our town."

Mose leaned in to Jack and pointed to the amulet around his neck. "I recognized that necklace. I should have known it was one of a kind. I never saw your mother without it. She had such boundless energy."

Jack smiled proudly, moving his hand to the amulet.

"Jack, after I read the email from Principal Thomson—"

"Sorry, Dad!" Jack interrupted. "I... I... it's just that..."

Dad gave Jack a firm hug. "Son, it's okay. I'm just glad you're not hurt." He pulled out his cell phone and began scrolling through his contacts. "You know, I should probably give Principal Thomson a call, he'd want to know his son is in here…"

Mose stopped and put his hand on Henry's arm, interrupting him. "Henry, if what we've all learned tonight is true, Thomson and others have a lot of explaining to do about what happened here. We need to go find Captain Hadaway and bring him back here."

"How could we ever prove it?" Jack asked. "We can't tell him a ghost told us."

"What did you just say?" Dad asked, confused.

"They helped us get away," said Celia, pointing to Max and the other ghosts.

Dad's mouth fell open as his mind struggled to comprehend what he was seeing. He looked to the middle of the dark generating station, which was illuminated by the soft glow of the apparitions working around the large, strange machine.

"What are those? Are they… ghosts…" Dad stammered.

"Ghosts?" Celia said. "Yep! That's them all right. And there are more."

"Did you say ghosts?" said Nate, before promptly fainting to the floor.

Celia dashed over to Nate and attempted to shake him awake.

Dad's eyes were wide in disbelief. "Is that what I think it is?"

"Free energy!" Dr. Moseley said, nodding in affirmation.

"A small fusion reactor?" Dad asked, awestruck.

"I believe so! They're trying to get it working," said Dr. Moseley.

Max Vidar flew above the reactor and signaled down to the men working on the machine. All six ghosts stopped what they were doing and formed a ring around the reactor.

"Just like we've practiced—let's make this one count," Max called out.

"We st-still n-need m-m-more energy, Dr. Vidar," said Leonard.

"I think we'll get it tonight, my old friend," Max replied. "Once we gather everyone here, we'll be able to contain the plasma for long enough to produce the energy we need to start the reaction."

The ghosts nodded, then began to circle the reactor rapidly in a clockwise direction. The movement of the ghosts produced a suctioning effect that caused nearby dust and debris to slide toward the machine like a magnet. Suddenly, the reactor let out a thunderous roar, and the ground began to rumble beneath their feet.

"Jack!" Celia hollered. "That's the sound we've been hearing all night!"

Jack nodded at the realization.

The ground shook as the spirits flew around the reactor. Then came a deep exhale as the ghostly bodies burst into a bright green glow that lit up the entire station.

"The flash of light!" Celia yelled.

Jack nodded in wonder.

"Max Vidar spent countless hours in this building," Dr. Moseley said slowly. "Everyone, including me, assumed he was just a lonely old man who had lost his mind. The leaders were convinced he was wasting hours working on the old furnace—but perhaps he was truly a genius!"

As the group watched, mesmerized by the ghosts circling the reactor, Mose looked inspired and proud.

"And they forced him down to the tunnels to cart nuclear waste!" Celia said, shaking her head.

"Now hold on a minute," Dad interjected. "What's this about nuclear waste and tunnels?"

"John Thomson flat out told us tonight that he made a deal with the power plant executives to move nuclear waste down the tunnels under Linhurst," Dr. Moseley explained.

"That's illegal and dangerous!" Dad said, aghast. "We knew that power plant was a mistake!"

"That it was!" Dr. Moseley replied. "They died trying to make those tunnels, but thankfully those crooks haven't yet had the chance to move a single barrel."

"Look!" Celia cried out, pointing to the center of the room.

The reactor had begun to rattle and hum, and the giant inhale came on stronger and louder. Dust and bits of rust shook off the exterior of the metal machine as the ghosts raced around it in glowing orbits of green light. They circled faster and faster as sparks and smoke came from the base, shooting out into the air like sparklers and skittering across the dirt floor.

Max Vidar looked on as he floated here and there, checking gauges and knobs, looking over and under, continually inspecting the reactor as it shook to life. A small purple light began to glow from its center as it hummed louder by the second.

"This could change everything!" Dr. Moseley shouted over the low hum. "If Vidar's machine works, fusion energy could become reality!"

It struck Jack that this would be an unbelievable photo. Proof of what happened! He pulled out his phone to take a photo, but the screen was black. He hit the power button repeatedly but it wouldn't turn on.

"Out of battery!" he whispered in despair.

Just then, the door to the stairwell from the tunnels burst open and four large bodies flew into the room.

Chapter 16

True Power

"What is going on in here?!" demanded a red-faced Coach Slater.

Following closely behind him was a breathless Principal Thomson and his son Tommy—dressed for Halloween in his school blue and gold football uniform—then Slater's son Danny, wearing his Rams basketball jersey and shorts.

The foursome looked pale and queasy—Jack guessed it was from their encounter with Heather and King down in the tunnels. They were covered from head to toe in dirt and dust.

"Dad, what is that?!" Tommy hollered to Principal Thomson, pointing nervously at the reactor.

Principal Thomson walked slowly toward the machine as it sputtered and sparked and shook. The purple light grew brighter from within. The wind generated by the flying spirits was growing intense.

"They're trying to get the fusion reactor working," said Principal Thomson in awe.

"What's a fusion reactor?" Danny dumbly asked his pal.

"We learned about it in science today!" Celia scoffed across the room.

"That's Max Vidar," said Principal Thomson, pointing to the professor's ghost zipping from one place to the next as he inspected the work. "He claimed his fusion reactor would work, but we thought it was a bunch of nonsense."

"Wait a minute—you're telling me he actually built that thing?" Coach Slater bellowed. "It was here all along?!"

"What's that light going around it?" Tommy asked nervously.

"Ghosts!" Nate suddenly called out. He was sitting on the floor, costume slumped awkwardly around him. He looked completely stunned.

"More ghosts?!" Danny yelped.

"Quit being a coward!" Coach Slater hollered back at his son.

"You saw King down in the tunnels, Dad!" Danny replied. "He was scary as hell!"

"You're imagining things," Slater snapped. "That was nothing but a figment of your imagination!"

"Then how do you explain that?!" Danny called out, pointing to the vortex around the reactor.

Nate stood up next to Celia and held her arm, seeking comfort. She quickly shook him off, grimacing.

"Faster, men!" Max Vidar called. "We have to get as much energy to the core as possible!"

The ghosts sped up and their glowing green forms wove together into a solid stream of light racing around the reactor. The machine shook furiously, causing the building to rattle. Boards shook loose from the rafters up above and started to fall to the floor around them.

What little glass remained in the tall, boarded windows shattered into tiny pieces and rained down to the dirt-coated floor, shimmering in the glow of the flying spirits.

The wire from a light canister snapped and its large metal form plummeted to the ground, crashing into the wooden planks just feet away from Jack and the others.

Jack looked up and saw that the bulbs inside the remaining light fixtures hanging from the high dark ceiling were glowing orange, pulsing slowly brighter by the second.

"The lights are coming on," Jack said in amazement.

"We need to get out of here before someone gets hurt," Dad said.

"You aren't going anywhere until you explain this," Coach Slater demanded. He dashed over and pointed a finger in Dad's face. "Your kid broke in here with his girlfriend and stirred up something that should have been left alone!"

"Come on, Jack, let's get out of here before this gets worse," said Dr. Moseley, joining Dad.

"I agree," said Dad. "We've seen enough."

"You're not going anywhere!" Slater yelled. "We found your secret tunnel, Dr. Moseley!" he boomed, shaking the very paper Jack and Celia had found in the library. "What's the deal?!"

"Not my tunnel." Mose smiled mischievously. "Their tunnel!" He pointed up to Max and the spirits.

"That's ludicrous!" Slater bellowed.

"You buried those poor people in the tunnels and didn't even try to save them," Celia cried out.

"Nobody asked for your opinion!" Slater barked back.

"That's what happened down there," Thomson lamented. "We buried them alive."

"Come on, let's get out of here," said Dad, disapprovingly shaking his head at Slater and Thomson.

Jack, Celia, Dr. Moseley, Nate, and Dad started for the windows where Dad had entered.

"Are we going to let this happen, John?" Coach Slater hollered at Principal Thomson as he pointed to the reactor.

The sound from the machine grew louder and the wind was now a tempest, swirling furiously inside the old building.

The faint howl of police sirens approached from outside. The beams from car headlights raced across the walls, followed by flashing blue and red lights.

"It's over for us, Eric," Principal Thomson concluded.

"Wrong, John, it's over for them!" Slater hollered back.

An officer raced up to the windows, shining his flashlight inside. His jaw dropped at the sight of the swirling lights around the reactor.

Hilda Beck appeared at the officer's side, her hair a mess and her glasses slightly askew on her pointed face. The wind from the ghosts circling around the reactor blew her hair into her face and she brushed it away to get a closer look at Jack and Celia.

"There they are, Officer Jones!" she called out, pointing at Jack and Celia. "Arrest those children!"

"Now wait a minute," the officer demanded. "What is going on in here?"

"We messed up, Hilda—you know we never meant to hurt anyone," Principal Thomson replied. "We should have helped Professor Vidar with this, but instead we took a big risk and it cost us everything."

"We made a decision that was for the best. You keep your mouth shut, John!" Coach Slater snapped.

"I will not, Eric!" Principal Thomson bit back. "I can't take any more secrets."

"John? Eric? What's going on?" Hilda snapped, staring daggers at Principal Thomson. "We made a deal."

"A deal that will not go through!" Principal Thomson shouted back. "I was just escorted out of the tunnels by Sam King."

"King? That's just a rumor!" Slater protested.

"Can you be so sure, Eric? Look around you. We've sent so many people off to do our dirty work—and at a terrible cost. The stories are true. This place is haunted, and not just with ghosts… with the things we did."

Coach Slater raced over to Principal Thomson and grabbed hold of his jacket in a tight fist. "We agreed this would not be easy, John," Slater growled in Thomson's face. "We knew there would be great sacrifices, but this was the only way to make things work for us!"

Principal Thomson pushed the coach away with enough force to knock him back a few steps. Slater replied with a solid punch to Principal Thomson's face, causing his head to whip to the side as his glasses flew to the ground.

"Dad! What's gotten into you?!" Danny hollered. He raced over to pick up Principal Thomson's glasses and hand them to him. Thomson calmly put his glasses back on and patted his hair back down. He stared the portly coach in the eyes.

"You're done pushing me around, Eric," Thomson said in a firm voice.

"We know about the deal with the nuclear power plant," Dr. Moseley interrupted.

"How would you know about any deal?" demanded Slater. "You're just a lonely old janitor!"

"Principal Thomson admitted the whole thing," Celia answered boldly.

Slater's face burned red with rage, and he turned to look at Thomson, seething.

"Everyone out of this building now," demanded Officer Jones.

"Stay out of this!" Slater bellowed back.

"Now you hold it right there," Officer Jones shouted, reaching for his gun.

"Officer Jones… please… just a minute," Thomson replied carefully.

The officer kept his hand on his weapon but gave Thomson an affirmation to continue.

"It's true," said Thomson, turning back to Slater. "They know everything—and soon the whole town will know."

Principal Thomson turned to Dr. Moseley. "Mose, you did a remarkable job here—you were one of the good ones. I wish I had listened to you. I wish I had listened to Max."

"You could have had all this power... truly free energy," said Dr. Moseley, gesturing toward the reactor, "but you threw it all away."

"I realize that now, Mose. I'm so sorry... for everything..." Thomson replied.

"If you say another word, you will be sorry," Coach Slater hollered.

Suddenly, Danny marched right up to his father, blocking him from Principal Thomson.

"Dad, what happened here?" Danny demanded. "What are you saying?"

"The people who lived here were just a bunch of retards, Danny," said Coach Slater. "We were paid to keep them out of the public where they would be a detriment to society. That was our job."

Danny looked shocked.

"They were mentals—worthless excuses for human beings," Coach Slater continued. "Now look at them—out wandering the streets of Spring Dale. It's embarrassing!"

"Dad? You can't say that. They were people!" Danny cried out.

"Our job was to take care of them, teach them," Principal Thomson said.

"Have you ever stopped to get to know those people?" Dr. Moseley questioned. "Have you ever tried talking to Bill Williams or Aunt Edna?"

"Mam and Pap?" Celia added.

"They were deserving of our care," Dr. Moseley said softly to Coach Slater, who was squeezing his fists tightly, the veins in his neck protruding as his faced turned from red to purple.

"I've heard enough!" Slater erupted.

"Dad—this is crazy!" Danny pleaded.

"Danny, keep quiet and get out of here! You and Tommy go wait in the car while I figure out a way to shut this thing down."

"Not so fast!" Officer Jones yelled over the roaring reactor. "We're going to get to the bottom of this."

"I told you it's those two children you want!" Hilda Beck pointed to Jack and Celia. "Trespassing. Breaking and entering. These kids need to learn to mind their business."

"She's right! We're tearing this place down tomorrow, and we need this property cleared now!" Coach Slater added, then he turned to his son. "Danny, take Tommy and go wait in the car—"

"Dad…" Danny pleaded.

"Now!" Coach Slater boomed.

"Nobody move!" Officer Jones shouted over the brute as he pulled his gun out and pointed it at the reactor. The rookie policeman was trying to piece together everything happening before him, especially the awe-inspiring display of spirits zooming around the huge, metal contraption at the center of the crumbling station.

Coach Slater marched toward the machine, fists clenched, sweating profusely with rage. He got to within feet of the orbiting ghosts, looking for a way to shut it down. The wind was so strong he had to lean into it to keep upright.

Just then a blast of red light flew out of the tunnels and engulfed him, throwing him onto his back, causing him to skid in his worn tracksuit ten feet across the station floor.

He shook his head from the impact and quickly attempted to get back on his feet. The glowing body that had knocked him down rose above him and took on a human form. It was Heather, her green glow had turned to a maddening and fiery red. She pressed her ghostly face to Slater's sweating bulbous nose.

"You leave them alone!" she screamed in an echoing voice.

Slater scooched back, pushing himself to his feet. He smoothed out his sweatshirt and adjusted his cap.

"You don't scare me, little girl!" he hollered.

Then, a new body of red light blast from the tunnel door into the station, engulfing Coach Slater.

"It's the ghost!" Danny and Tommy yelled in unison.

The pair of bullies-turned-cowards ran to the window and jumped outside as more police lights appeared on the walls of the generating station.

The new energy hovering with Heather took human form, revealing a very large, strong man with hard features and deep-set eyes. He was not as easy to make out, his spirit faded in and out more than the others. He was nearly twice the size of Coach Slater and appeared to tower over him even from afar.

"King!" Slater yelled.

"He grabbed me down in the tunnels and carried me up the stairwell into the Administration Building," Principal Thomson said nervously. "He dragged me all the way to the pile of desks in the foyer and reminded me that we never made things right for him and the others." He turned to Coach Slater. "Eric, you used to torment Sam King. You used him for all your dirty work when we promised to give him a proper education and help make life better for him. He made me realize the kind of pain we left here."

"He got what he needed from us!" Slater growled.

King flew down and wrapped Slater in a tight grip, then lifted him off the ground a few inches.

"Leave now," King hollered, propelling Slater across the floor and throwing him out the window with Danny and Tommy. As his fury reached its peak, the ghost's mouth opened widely and his eyes became terrifying holes of blackness.

"Leave now!" he bellowed, a powerful howl emanating from his ghostly body.

King slowly turned to Thomson, a terrifying look on his face.

"Now, King, I didn't mean to hurt anyone," Thomson said nervously. "We didn't fix the quality of life when we could have, and we didn't go for Max Vidar's experiments. But that's all going to change tonight!"

King began to flex his aura, his color shifting to a deep reddish glow. He drifted slowly and ominously toward the principal.

Heather quickly intercepted. "King…" Heather began softly, "Let him go—he has learned."

"Heather?" Principal Thomson replied. He turned to Dr. Moseley. "Your daughter?"

"She's been keeping watch over things while we were away," said Dr. Moseley proudly.

Principal Thomson's face contorted in despair, tears pooling in his red-rimmed eyes. "It's my fault she's dead, Charles."

Dr. Moseley didn't reply but looked completely taken aback at Thomson's turn of heart.

After a few moments, the principal's face shifted, and a look of determination replaced the lines of grief and guilt. He scrubbed the sleeve of his jacket across his eyes roughly, took in a deep breath and looked at the reactor. "What do we need to do to get this working?" he asked, rolling up his sleeves.

Heather looked up at King, then King turned to Thomson.

"Leave for good," he said in a low, hollow voice, his aura spitting out red-hot sparks.

A new flashlight appeared inside the window. Captain Hadaway stared inside, mouth agape in complete shock.

"Officer Jones—what is the meaning of all this?" he demanded, yelling over the din of the machine.

"Captain Hadaway," Principal Thomson began, "the tunnels under the Administration Building will give you all the answers you need."

"John, what have you done to us?" Hilda pulled at her hair despairingly and stomped her feet like a little girl.

"Everyone outside!" demanded Captain Hadaway. "This building is not safe."

Hadaway put out a hand and helped Celia climb through the window as Dad gave her a lift up. Then Dad lifted Nate, who toppled over the window awkwardly in his bulky costume.

"I'm all right!" he hollered from the ground outside the window and Hadaway helped him to his feet.

"Let's go, John." Captain Hadaway reached a hand out for the principal and helped him up over the window.

"Come on!" Dad called to Jack, who was focused on Dr. Moseley. The old man was staring blindly at the reactor, his eyes wide. Jack turned back to his dad.

"Give me a minute," Jack replied, with a new tone of maturity in his voice.

Dad nodded anxiously, though he understood.

"Dr. Moseley—we have to go!" Jack hollered over the reactor's hum.

"I have to say goodbye first," Mose answered without turning back.

Dr. Moseley walked over to Heather, who was facing the reactor with King. They were watching in joy as the ghosts continued their route around the reactor. The ground rumbled and shook as it never had before.

"I helped them, Father," she said when he reached her side.

"I am so proud of you. This is what you were meant to do."

Heather smiled at him.

Suddenly the reactor gave out an earth-shattering roar and a blast of air. The massive machine shook intensely, sparks flying every which way. Another blast of wind came from the center of the machine, where the purple light shifted to a blinding pale green.

Jack and Dr. Moseley shielded their eyes from the light as another blast of wind struck them so powerfully it pushed them back a few feet.

"Heather... King... it is time!" Max Vidar shouted from high above.

Heather grabbed King's huge hand and raced up to Max Vidar. The professor whispered something in her ear, then King leaned down and she whispered in his.

"We are ready for you," Max called down to Jack, staring him dead in the eyes.

Jack looked to Dr. Moseley for help, but they were both completely bewildered by Max's words. They both shrugged then looked back up to see the three spirits lock arms and dive down into the twister of light, becoming one with the bright vortex.

Jack and Dr. Moseley looked toward the ceiling above the reactor. The rafters were glowing with light from the once-dead bulbs, which were now blazing in full power after years of darkness. As they stared in amazement, another light canister snapped from its wiring, plummeting toward them.

"Let's get out of here!" Dr. Moseley shouted, grabbing Jack's hand and pulling him toward the windows as the heavy canister crashed on the floor behind them.

They reached Dad at the window, who put out a hand to help them. Captain Hadaway pulled them safely to the other side. Dad hopped up over the window last, and all four ran through the thick brush and overgrowth to join the rest of the group gathered below the full moonlight at the edge of the road backed by a vast open field.

Jack noticed that the light from Celia's flashlight and headlamp were glowing brightly once again. He looked down at his own flashlight and saw that his, too, was at full power.

The bulbs in the rusted street lamps overhead were glowing and buzzing. Old security lights on the outside of the generating station fizzed and sputtered. All along the road into Linhurst, flickers of light broke through the darkness—decades-old bulbs of all shapes and sizes sparkled to life, some blowing and popping with the strain of illumination after lying dormant so many years. Through the trees, Jack could see glimmers from lights turning on all across the once-darkened campus.

Many of the boards covering the tall windows of the generating station had shaken loose in the vibrations from the reactor, and Jack could clearly see the thick line of the ghosts racing around the machine inside. The building was shaking so steadily it appeared to be rocking loose from its foundation. A low, steady hum filled the air around them as the ground beneath their feet rumbled like an earthquake. The light inside the generating station grew so powerful it was nearly blinding, and a vortex of wind howled from inside out, blowing the trees and vines off the exterior of the building.

Throughout the woods, glowing green wisps and orbs began to appear, drifting toward the generating station. As the faint bodies drew closer, they stretched and grew, taking on human form. Ghosts were emerging from every corner of the abandoned campus and flowing toward the generating station. Some of the ghosts came alone, others in pairs and groups, holding hands and helping one another. Tommy and Danny looked on in horror. Celia's face showed delight and curiosity.

Jack noticed a couple of apparitions bobbing gently down the road. They seemed to be heading right for Jack and the others. As the ghostly duo came closer to the group, Jack could see they were small children embracing one another, their arms bound by tight strips of cloth like straitjackets. And though they were uncomfortably close, they appeared to be quite happy. They passed by, completely oblivious to the humans standing at the edge of the road in front of them.

"The Henrick twins," Slater whispered in awe.

A glowing orb appeared from the woods and slowly transformed into a female figure in a loose gown. Rather than heading toward the station like other ghosts, the glowing body continued on a straight path toward the group and stopped just a foot away from a trembling Hilda Beck.

"You did this," the ghost said in an eerily calm voice.

"Karen?" Hilda shivered. "I wasn't.... I didn't mean to hurt you!"

The ghost gently drifted in midair while Hilda stood speechless, then the spirit turned and faced the station, floating just in front of the corrupt librarian for a moment. Hilda nervously reached out to touch the girl, her hand visibly shaking. Just before she could place her hand on the shoulder of the ghost, it took off quickly toward the station, blasting through the open windows and joining the vortex of light engulfing the reactor.

Every glowing apparition approached the outside of the generating station and passed right through the building's exterior, where they were sucked into the mass of ghosts already circling the reactor.

"What's happening?" Principal Thomson broke the silence.

"They're getting it working!" Dr. Moseley replied delightfully.

The last of the glowing spirits dashed inside the station and joined the swirling mass of bright light circling the reactor. The light was now ten times the size it was when the men first began circling.

Suddenly, the hum took on a lower tone, and the vortex started to slow. The light grew dim.

The wind calmed, the light inside the generating station grew faint, and all the bulbs around campus faded into blackness again.

The earth stopped rumbling abruptly and was still.

In the sudden calm and quiet, they could hear a frog croaking nearby and an owl hooting somewhere in the middle of the woods.

Another sound—a murmur of voices growing just down the road—became audible. Jack and the others looked out toward the dark winding entrance of Linhurst where glimmers of flashlights were bouncing off the tops of the trees.

"Looks like we've got company," said Captain Hadaway. "All right, folks, we are finished here."

"Wait!" Jack cried out. "We can't leave!"

"We've seen enough here, son," replied Captain Hadaway.

"What about the reactor?" Jack replied.

"It didn't work," said Dr. Moseley quietly. He looked terribly disappointed.

"I knew Vidar was a nut!" Coach Slater grumbled. He was breathing very heavily and looked extremely anxious. He turned to Captain Hadaway. "Do your job and arrest these trespassers already! Let's get on with our lives here."

"You're the one who's getting cuffed," Captain Hadaway corrected, placing handcuffs on the portly offender.

Before Slater could protest, they were interrupted by a yelp from Celia.

"Jack... look!" Celia cried out, pointing at his necklace.

Jack looked down to see that his amulet was not only glowing its signature bright green but was floating away from his chest, defying gravity. He reached up his hand and held his palm open beneath it.

"Ouch!" he cried, whipping his hand away.

"What is it?" Celia asked.

"It's hot!"

Dad approached and looked in awe at Mom's necklace floating in midair, glowing a brilliant green and sputtering tiny sparks of white light.

"Amanda?" he said in shock.

Jack looked up at his dad then back to the necklace. "Mom?" he whispered.

As the amulet glowed and floated, it started to stretch out taut around his neck. It was pulling him in the direction of the generating station.

Jack and the others stared at the glowing amulet, completely perplexed.

"What do I do?"

"Take it off, Jack," Celia whispered.

"I can't!" Jack implored. He couldn't bear the thought of letting go of his mother's necklace.

"It's okay, Jack," Dad said. "She wants to help."

Jack paused. Mom wants to help?

He looked down at the amulet pulling hard against the back of his neck, then back to his dad, who was nodding approval to pull the necklace off. He looked at Dr. Moseley, who just smiled and nodded encouragingly, as if to say, "You can do this."

He turned to Celia, who reached a hand out to him. She gently took his hand in hers and squeezed it caringly, then rubbed the back of his hand with her thumb.

His mind raced back to the story his mother had told him about Linhurst. It was their last night together. Then he recalled the dream he had when his mother came to him and she said: *Come with me... we'll uncover the truth together!*

Suddenly it seemed like she was closer to him than he could ever remember.

Without warning, a brilliant explosion of light burst forth from the face of the amulet and flooded the area around Jack with what appeared to be pure daylight. A glowing white orb drifted up from the middle of the sun and peace symbol and settled gently in front of Jack.

The orb slowly transformed into a new spirit body—a long gown and flowing hair became visible almost instantly. Then he saw it—the face of the spirit.

"Mom?!" Jack whispered. His voice echoed around him as though he was standing inside a giant cathedral.

Am I dreaming? Jack wondered, turning to look around in awe. He could see, just outside the circle of bright white light, his father, Celia, and the others, standing in their places, moving in slow motion as if they were frozen in time.

He turned back to the spirit in front of him, studying her carefully.

"Mom… it is you," he said, his voice overflowing with sadness and joy at once.

"Jackie," she replied, her voice emanating softly. "It's me." She smiled grandly at him.

"Where did you come from?" Jack said.

"I was with you all this time," she replied.

"I don't understand," he said.

"I told you the night I gave you the necklace how I wished I could be with you always… and there I was," she said.

She was in the necklace? But how?

"We did it, Jack," she said proudly. "We uncovered the truth."

"The truth? What do you mean, Mom?"

"The secrets of Linhurst are yours now… you freed them," she said.

Jack smiled. He could tell she really was proud of him.

"Are you ready?" she asked calmly.

"Ready? Ready for what?"

"It's time to finish the work," she replied.

"What work?"

She didn't reply, only smiled at him very calmly.

Jack sighed. "Mom…" he began pleadingly, "I've missed you… Dad misses you… I am so lost," Jack's voice cracked, failing him as emotions began to overwhelm him.

"But you are not," she said, moving in closer to him. Her figure was so much clearer than any of the other spirits they had encountered that night. He could almost make out every line on her face and every strand of hair.

"I don't know what to do now," Jack said, his eyes welling with tears.

"I think you do, Jackie," she said, smiling widely.

"I don't know that I can," he pleaded.

"Yes, you can. I was with you all this time. I gave you strength… but now, Professor Vidar cannot finish his work without me. My life energy is much stronger than the others who have been trapped here."

"But, Mom… what will happen to you? Can't you come back?"

She smiled wonderfully and tipped her head toward him with great affection. "I think you know the answer to that," she said softly. "The time is right for me to move on to a new place, for now."

She placed her spirit hand on his chest, her open palm over his heart. He felt a warm sensation inside—it felt like never-ending love.

"I will be here for you always," she said. "Tell Dad I love him, and I'm proud of you. My boys have great work ahead of them."

She pulled away and her figure began to fade slowly.

"Mom!" Jack pleaded, reaching out for her fading figure. "Mom… please… wait!"

"Goodbye, Jackie... I love you," she said, her voice going farther away as her light faded slowly and grew smaller.

"Mom!" Jack screamed.

"It's time, Jack... set us free!" her voice echoed from far away.

"Jack?" a new voice called.

"Jack?" said another voice.

"Jack! Are you okay?!" Celia cried.

Everything was dark suddenly, and Jack could no longer see his mother. It sounded like hundreds of voices were filling the air around him. He rubbed his eyes and saw the darkened generating station sitting a hundred feet away.

Jack looked up to see Dad, Celia, and Dr. Moseley hovering over him. He had fallen to the ground. Dad pulled him to his feet—the necklace was still hanging in midair, pulling on his neck.

He looked to Celia and saw the compassion in her face. He nodded to Celia—Jack knew he could do this with her by his side.

Jack reached up behind his head and unhooked the necklace from the back of his neck. As he held it out in front of him, the silver medallion with the sun and peace symbol glowed brighter than before. A line of white light appeared around the edges of the embossing.

"You did it, Jack," said Celia.

Jack released the necklace. It floated in front of him as though it was being held in an invisible gravitational field. He felt a small breath of air come from the amulet, then the round metal piece with the sun and peace symbol circled in front of him, then brushed his hands gently.

Then, the amulet shot off like a rocket toward the generating station and disappeared through the shattered windows inside the darkened building.

Suddenly a great explosion of light and wind came from inside the reactor's core. The group instinctively hit the ground as a circular corona of light exploded above their heads.

Green light shot from the smoke stack into the sky overhead.

Jack could see the reactor shaking and rocking furiously inside the station. A light around the reactor contracted before blasting into the sky and disappearing into the atmosphere.

The reactor suddenly stopped moving. Every light inside the generating station was glowing.

Then all was calm.

There was no more wind or rumbling coming from within the generating station. The group looked all around to see the buildings and street lights on the campus glowing brightly. Every flashlight among those now gathered was giving off brilliant white light.

"They're free," said Celia.

"Free," Jack repeated softly. He looked down at the strong beam of light emanating from his flashlight. The spot on his chest where his mother's necklace once rested was illuminated in the glow from Celia's headlamp. He reached his hand up instinctively, gripping the fabric of his shirt. It would take time to get used to living without it. His eyes followed the path the amulet had taken through the window into the generating station. *Energy may change form*, he thought, as a mixture of joy and sadness settled in his heart, *but it cannot be created or destroyed*.

As the group at the generating station gathered themselves, they could hear the murmur of voices traveling up the road growing closer. A large group of Spring Dale residents was coming around the bend in the road leading up to the generating station. Some were dressed for Halloween, some in plain clothes and even others in pajamas. Most were holding flashlights or using cell phones to light up the path.

"The events that happened here must have been seen for miles," said Captain Hadaway.

The people of Spring Dale had all come to find out what the commotion was about. It was probably the first time since the grand opening of Linhurst in 1908 that so many people had entered the property at once.

Captain Hadaway shook his head in amazement at all they had just witnessed, then pulled himself together. With determination, he pulled Principal Thomson to his feet and placed handcuffs on him.

"I need to take you in for questioning, John," Captain Hadaway said to the principal, who nodded solemnly. Captain Hadaway walked Principal Thomson over to the patrol car and placed him inside. Officer Jones pulled Coach Slater to his feet and walked him to his patrol car, parked just in front of Slater's cherry-red antique Corvette.

Up the road, two women broke away from the crowd and ran forward. One raced over to Captain Hadaway as he closed the door of his police cruiser. "Where are you taking my husband?" she questioned nervously.

"Ma'am, your husband is going downtown this evening," replied Captain Hadaway. "You can report there."

"Mom!" Tommy ran over to his mother.

The woman turned and embraced her son. "Tommy! What is happening here?"

"Long story," said Tommy and he began to walk her back up the road.

"Danny! Eric!" cried the other woman as Coach Slater was being placed in the back of Officer Jones' cruiser. Her face turned red as she locked eyes with her husband, looking up at her from the backseat. "What did you do?!" she screamed, her bulbous figure rolling with her flying arm movements.

Officer Jones gently placed a hand on her shoulder. "Downtown, ma'am."

She fell into Danny's arms, sobbing and shaking. Danny walked her away from the scene.

"Not so fast!" Captain Hadaway shouted as he spied Hilda Beck attempting to slip away into the crowd. "You're coming, too."

"But I'm innocent!" Hilda protested. "They planned the whole thing. I only worked here!"

"We'll see about that." Captain Hadaway cuffed Hilda's hands, firmly reading her Miranda rights as he took her to the other side of his car then placed her in.

Captain Hadaway returned to Jack and the group. "You all have been through a lot tonight. Are you folks okay?"

"We'll be fine from here," Dr. Moseley replied.

"You understand you can't be on this property," said the captain. "I will have to ask you to head home. In the morning, I plan to stop by to ask a few questions about what happened here tonight... though it sounds like this is a fairly open and shut case."

Dr. Moseley and Dad both nodded.

"But please," Captain Hadaway began again with more care in his voice, "take your time." He took one last look at the generating station and shook his head in disbelief. "Take as much time as you need," he repeated, then walked over to control the crowd coming into the property. The townspeople stared in awe and wonder at Linhurst State Hospital alight and alive once more.

Jack felt a vibration in his pocket. He reached inside and pulled out his phone. It was lit up with a message reading: *Hi, Jack, it's Lisa Lexington. Nate gave me your number. Is it true you went to Linhurst?*

At first, he couldn't believe Lisa Lexington knew about him going to Linhurst. Then he couldn't believe she'd actually texted him after how he responded to her invitation earlier that night.

As it dawned on him, he realized the most shocking thing was that his phone was no longer dead. The battery was fully charged.

He opened the camera app on his phone and took some photos of the generating station, then slid through the others he had taken.

"Celia, you've got to see this!" he exclaimed.

She looked over his shoulder to see that every photo Jack had taken that night had one or several spirits lingering in the corners.

"There were so many of them, and they didn't even bother with us!" Celia said, delighted.

"Celia!" a woman called from the crowd. They saw Celia's mom, dressed in floral pajamas, break from the crowd and run toward them with her dad in tow. They reached Celia and embraced her tightly.

"Are you okay, sweetheart?" her dad asked.

Celia pushed away and gave them a reassuring look. "Mom, Dad, everything is okay."

"What happened here?" her mom asked. Celia turned to Jack and gave him an awkward smile, then turned back to her parents.

"I'll tell you about it on the way home," she replied and turned to give Jack a small punch in the arm. "Good work tonight, Jack." He smiled, and she turned and made her way home with her parents.

"Let's go home, son," Dad said. "It's over now."

Jack nodded. He paused for a moment then turned to look for Dr. Moseley—but he was nowhere to be found.

As they made their way to the car, Jack saw that a group of people had gathered together near the fork in the road by the generating station. They were pointing at the building, the street lamps, and inside the generating station, talking, laughing and gesturing in amazement. A group of former residents—including Bill Williams, Mam and Pap, Lawrence, Aunt Edna, and many more—stood side by side with the other townspeople, mingling and chatting. Jack's heart swelled as he realized that they were sharing their stories about Linhurst, and the people of Spring Dale were listening.

As Jack and his dad continued past the crowd, Dad slung his arm over his shoulders, which were nearly parallel with his own. "I'm proud of you, Jack. And I know your mom is, too."

Jack smiled broadly, feeling tears form at the corners of his eyes.

"You know," Dad continued, pulling his son into a big hug, "you have a lot of your mom in you."

Chapter 17

A New Life

One year later…

Jack awoke full of energy. He looked up at his ninth-grade writing assignment—titled Adventures in Spring Dale—framed and hanging on the wall by his bed. There was a big "A++" written in red marker above a note that read *What a story, Jack! So exciting and imaginative… ghosts and everything!*

As he stretched, he heard something flop onto the floor. He looked over the side of the bed and saw a newspaper lying by his glow-in-the-dark constellation slippers. He reached down and picked it up. There was a sticky note attached that read:

Eggs and bacon at nine then we're off to the grand opening at ten!

Love,
Dad

Jack peeled the note off, revealing the newspaper headline:

Linhurst Revealed: The Final Chapter in Our 12-Part Series

By Aurora Lux
(In Memory of Amanda Alexander)

Grand Opening of Linhurst Gardens

After a year of major renovations and cleanup, the brand new Linhurst Gardens will open on November 1st. It is the first time the property once known as Linhurst State School and Hospital will be publicly used since the operation closed due to patient abuse, inadequate funding, and energy problems. The former state hospital—a dark chapter in the history of Spring Dale—had remained vacant and derelict since its closure decades ago.

Now, after countless hours of work by volunteers and paid contractors working side by side, the beautifully renovated buildings once slated for demolition will now be a mixed-income community shared by all residents of Spring

Dale—from the wealthiest to the former residents of the state hospital who were once pushed to the streets upon its closure.

Still under investigation are the accusations by former Spring Dale High School Principal John Thomson claiming that high-ranking officials at Spring Dale Nuclear Generating Station conspired with Linhurst leadership to store nuclear waste at the hospital while it was still in operation. Thomson has suggested that he and other leaders at the time were bribed to transport and store nuclear waste generated by the station in exchange for free energy from the power plant. The mysterious disappearance and now known deaths of seven former residents have been linked to this illicit arrangement.

In an ironic twist of fate, the buildings were scheduled for demolition the very morning after the arrest of Principal John Thomson, Coach Eric Slater, and Spring Dale Head Librarian Hilda Beck. Demolition was immediately halted for an investigation into the still unexplained events that occurred on the grounds of Linhurst that Halloween night a year ago, which uncovered the ongoing construction of a new tunnel system linking Linhurst to the nuclear power plant. Thomson confessed the deal was set in motion to use the underground system as a storage route for nuclear waste, and the demolition of the buildings was planned as a containment measure for the project.

Power plant officials declined to comment on the allegations at this point, saying their focus is to find a new plan for the canceled deal to build new towers at the Linhurst property in Spring Dale after they lost their contract in a legal dispute.

One of the amenities of the sold out Linhurst Gardens is free electricity, which the new owners won't discuss until the approval of a pending patent.

The property has raised nearly $1 million to support the continuing care of former residents of Linhurst State School and Hospital by providing ghost tours of the tunnels. Some say the underground passages are actually haunted, but Linhurst spokesman Charles Moseley insists these are "just fun rumors" and he encourages all to consider a visit.

"Jack!" his dad called up the stairs. "It's 9:15—are you getting up?"

"Yeah, Dad!" Jack replied. "I'll be down in a minute."

Jack hopped up from his bed and walked to the window. He pulled the curtains open to let in the warm light from the last days of summer and pushed up the window to let the air in through the screen. As he looked out from his new bedroom onto the second floor of Building C, he could see his friend Celia reading a book by the new fountain in the center of the courtyard between

Buildings A and D. Nate was sitting right next to her, sorting through baseball cards and talking her ear off.

Mam and Pap Saunders walked around the outside of the courtyard, picking up stray pieces of trash. Bill Williams was greeting some of the residents carrying in boxes and furniture. Aunt Edna sat peacefully by the pond, working her way through another cigar.

As he surveyed his new front yard, Jack caught sight of Marcy Higgins walking toward the fountain with Lisa Lexington. Lisa looked up, catching sight of Jack in his window. She smiled and waved.

"I'll be right down!" he called to her.

On the far side of the courtyard, Jack could see Dr. Moseley standing in the cemetery of newly laid memorials. He knelt and placed a bouquet of flowers by a small white cross. He paused for just a moment then placed his gray cap on his head and turned to view the scene all around him. He took in a deep breath and looked up to see Jack at his window. Dr. Mosely gave a huge smile and a wave and Jack reciprocated. Mayor Helowski approached Dr. Moseley and shook his hand firmly, then the two turned and headed up the steps to the stage and podium.

"Good morning, people of Spring Dale!" Mayor Helowski called into the microphone. "It is with great pleasure I welcome you today to this grand reopening."

The people in the courtyard gathered together in a large group. Mam and Pap Saunders paced around the fountain mumbling obscenities at the birds.

Jack grabbed his jacket from the end of his bed, quickly pulled on a pair of jeans, then raced down the stairs and out of their apartment into the halls of Building C.

He made his way through the great room—where he and Celia had met Heather only a year ago. The space was brightly lit from the warm sunshine outside. The walls were freshly painted, there was new carpeting on the floor, fresh flowers were set out on tables and shelves decorating the space that was now a lounge and game room for the building's residents.

He dashed down the hall, past more apartments—stepped around the spot that once featured a gaping hole responsible for the long scar on his leg—it was a habit now for him to hop over the spot even though it was sound and sturdy—and out the front door onto a beautiful front porch.

He joined the large crowd that had gathered and found his dad.

Mayor Helowski continued by thanking everyone who had helped with renovation and construction and announced plans to improve more buildings on the old campus of Linhurst, including bringing back some of the old buildings like the general store, laundry, and even the dairy barn. He predicted that one day, Linhurst would be like a town within the town of Spring Dale.

"I assure you that Spring Dale will continue exploring newer, safer ways to power our homes, our cars, and our businesses," the mayor proclaimed with great pride. "As we retire the aging nuclear power plant and prepare for a brighter tomorrow, Spring Dale will be a beacon for the world—a town of the future, harnessing the power of renewable, clean resources to fuel our lives."

The crowd cheered loudly. Mayor Helowski smiled confidently at his new promise.

"To honor the people who were once imprisoned in this place and who are now able to call Linhurst a home without walls or bars, I welcome Dr. Charles Moseley as our new director of the Linhurst Care Center. The care center will continue a tradition of excellent health care—mental and physical—with all people accepted equally."

Another uproar of applause came from the crowd. Jack could see Mam and Pap Saunders standing with Bill Williams. All three looked just like anyone else in the crowd as they stood side by side with fellow Spring Dalers. They wiped tears from their eyes at the mayor's proclamation of equal attention to their concerns.

"While we remember the past with heavy hearts, and promise never to forget, it is with great pride and enthusiasm that we bring new life to this place. As Mayor of Spring Dale, I officially declare Linhurst Gardens open for the people of Spring Dale!"

A great wave of applause and cheers erupted. He handed Dr. Moseley a large pair of scissors, and the doctor turned and cut an oversized red ribbon hanging across a ceremonial gateway on the stage. Another round of applause followed.

Jack turned and looked at the new Linhurst Gardens sign being placed over the gateway by two workers. Above the bold lettering of the sign was a beautifully carved sun and peace symbol painted a brilliant platinum.

With a grand smile on his face and great warmth in his heart, Jack said proudly, "We did it, Mom."

WITH THANKS

*The most thanks for Freeing Linhurst go to Rachel Elizabeth
Miner, who hopped on three titles ago and helped take this story to
the next level through clever editing and helpful plot ideas.*

*I would also like to thank to Tracy Seybold
for taking the editing process through the final steps.*

*A huge debt of gratitude to all my friends and family
who supported me through this process,
especially Grady and Wyatt,
whose child-like curiosity throughout the writing and illustration
of this book energized me and made me realize there was at least
one good reason to complete it.*

*And finally to the many daring, curious, adventurous, and
downright mischievous teens
who braved the abandoned campus at Pennhurst
and so many other places the great United States of America
left to wither and die without retribution or proper replacement.
It is one thing to remember the past but another to ignore that
it happened while pretending to be doing something
to rectify the wrongs that took place. Thank you all for bucking the
system and remembering to care about those who suffered.*

Here's hoping those many places are free one day!

About the Author

After focusing on arts in high school and graduating from The Art Institute of Philadelphia, Al Cassidy dove into the working world, merging his skills as an artist with communication in business. He quickly learned the ropes of branding, marketing and advertising, working with agencies whose clients included nationally recognized brands, small businesses, musicians, individuals and everyone in between. After 15 years primarily serving for-profit clients, Al chose to redirect his focus to non-profit organizations.

Like the characters in his childhood comics, Al believes each of us as human beings has a certain something that sets us apart. Whether someone is wealthy or poor, black or white, genius or mentally challenged, he believes we all have something valuable to contribute to society. He became impassioned to write the story of Freeing Linhurst, and wanted to tell a tale from a side of mental institutions as seen—not from the perspective of those who created them, those who are afraid of them, or those who over-glorify the horrors that may have existed—from the viewpoint of innocent and curious kids growing up in the presence of the secrecy and mystery that surrounds such vacant properties.